Bathing
the Lion

Bathing the Lion

JONATHAN CARROLL

St. Martin's Press ✖ New York

BATHING THE LION. Copyright © 2013 by Jonathan Carroll. All rights reserved. Printed in the United States of America. For information, address St. Martin's Press, 175 Fifth Avenue, New York, N.Y. 10010.

www.stmartins.com

Designed by Molly Rose Murphy

Library of Congress Cataloging-in-Publication Data

Carroll, Jonathan, 1949–
    Bathing the Lion / Jonathan Carroll.
        p. cm.
    ISBN 978-1-250-04826-4 (hardcover)
    ISBN 978-1-4668-4891-7 (e-book)
    1. Dreams—Fiction.   I. Title.
    PS3553.A7646B57 1991
    813'.54—dc23
                                    2014021408

St. Martin's Press books may be purchased for educational, business, or promotional use. For information on bulk purchases, please contact Macmillan Corporate and Premium Sales Department at 1-800-221-7945, extension 5442, or write specialmarkets@macmillan.com.

First published in Poland by Rebis

First U.S. Edition: October 2014

10 9 8 7 6 5 4 3 2 1

For Izabela Kedziora

ACKNOWLEDGMENTS

Heartfelt thanks to Ellen Datlow and Jeffrey Capshew
for helping to bring this lion to life.

THE HOUSE INSIDE THE HORSE

O N E

Most men think they are good drivers. Most women think they are good in bed. They aren't.

She'd said that an hour earlier, apropos of nothing, as he was walking out the door with the new sled under his arm. Sitting at the kitchen table with a mug of fragrant coffee in her hands, she spoke while staring out the window at the snow.

"Am I . . . Am I supposed to respond?"

"No. I was only making an observation." She did not look at him while speaking, but that was nothing new. Sometimes she spouted these non sequiturs while staring into the distance, as if she were addressing an invisible audience out there in the ethers.

Impatient to get going, he was nevertheless tempted to ask if she would like him to write down her remark for posterity. She had high opinions of both herself and her insights. Part of their recent trouble was he did not.

These days the couple coexisted uneasily in an edgy state where both knew a separation was inevitable and imminent but neither was brave enough to say so. They were in the almost-terminal stage where trivial things the partner does are keenly noticed and continuously resented: how they wipe the kitchen counters after a meal, the messy state of the bathroom after their shower, the toilet seat up, the toilet seat down. Things routinely ignored before, much less cared about, now glimmered like they were Day-Glo purple, or stunk like milk gone bad.

It was why he liked the sled. Months before on first seeing the ad for the Alurunner Sports Sled in a magazine, he whistled in admiration at its incredibly sleek all-aluminum body. It looked like a toboggan on steroids and had an overall allure that somehow touched both the boy and man in him. It said, "You wanna go fast? Get on and I'll show you what fast is." One extremely cool object. But who would pay so much money for a *sled*? Later he made the mistake of telling her about it. She looked at her husband as if he'd said he was buying a nuclear submarine. "A *sled*? Why would you want a sled?"

"To go sledding. That's what you usually do with them."

She smiled wanly at him. "At least you don't want a Porsche."

"What do you mean?"

"Most men want to buy Porsches when they're going through midlife crisis. But you only want a sled. Peculiar, but at least you're not a cliché."

"Do you think I'm going through a midlife crisis?"

She smirked. "A textbook case. You shouldn't worry though. Women have menopause, men midlife crisis and Porsche envy. The joys of middle age, partner."

Turning slowly now, he leaned his new silver sled against a wall. Then he squatted down with his hands resting on bent knees and looked at her. "This isn't working between us anymore. Both of us know that and it's time we talked about it."

She pressed the cup hard against her lower lip and continued staring out the window. They had been together twelve years, married nine. Sometimes he tried to pinpoint exactly when their love had turned from solid to liquid to steam to thin air. Sometimes he wondered when she had stopped loving him. At this stage he didn't care.

"What do you want to do about it?" She looked at him. Her eyes were gray-green, beautiful and expressionless.

"I don't think we like each other anymore. It's that simple. Why live with someone you don't like?"

"You don't like me?" Her voice came out somewhere between a statement and a question.

"No, not often. Do you like me?"

She blinked several times and then silently mouthed no.

He nodded, unaffected.

She tried to swallow; her mouth had suddenly gone dry. "Wow. I guess *that* cat's out of the bag now." She was deeply impressed he had finally said it.

"Yes, it is. And now we must talk about it."

Leaning forward she put the cup down. "Wow." Placing both hands flat on the table, she lowered her head between them until her right cheek touched the cool wood. Her heart was pounding. She could feel it pulse up through her outstretched arms. "This sounds dumb, but I don't know what to say now. I'm an absolute blank."

He remained silent. She *always* had something to say. It was just a matter of time before it came.

His cell phone rang. The shrill sound was a reminder that a normal world existed nearby where people not teetering on the edge of their lives did things like make telephone calls and wait for them to be answered.

They were glad his phone rang a long time. It gave them both a chance to breathe a little and think about what next. But the ringing eventually stopped. Looking at each other, they waited to see who would speak first.

Even in the few minutes that had elapsed since he spoke, important things had already begun to shift between them. A completely new and different light now lit this person who had slept peacefully beside them last night.

"It's so bizarre—I think I should cry or shout or something, but I only feel empty. You want us to separate? To divorce?"

He nodded. "I think we need to talk about our options."

"Like when? Very soon?"

Gesturing over his shoulder he said, "Do you see my sled? I thought I bought it because it looked so great and just the idea of sledding again, do something I loved so much as a kid, after all these years, was really appealing. But you know what I like most about it now? I do it alone. It's just me out there with nature and speed and those great pungent winter smells we always talk about. . . . But you have never even asked where I go when I do it. Not once."

She lifted her head a few inches off the table. "You go to the park. The big hill there—"

"Wrong. I never go to the park, never. See? We don't *interest* each other anymore."

She stiffened and venom seeped into her voice now. "How do you know? Because I don't ask where you go *sledding*?"

"Cut the crap; don't be facile. You know exactly what I'm saying."

"No, not really. I guess I'm just too stupid. Maybe you need to spell it out for me. Maybe after twelve years together I at least deserve clarity."

"You can spell fine." He rose slowly. Looking directly at her, his face gave away nothing. She was so used to his face, so used to the familiar expressions and wrinkles there. They usually showed her what he was thinking. Now his face said nothing except pay attention to what I'm saying. He had gone from being her husband of a decade to a stranger in less than ten sentences.

"I'm going sledding now. Then I'm going to stay away from here for the rest of the day. It's better I do. It'll let us both think this over alone. When I get back here tonight we can talk about it if you want."

She was dismayed. "You're going *out* now? How can you, for God's sake? You said it yourself—we have to talk about this."

He took his sled from the wall. "And we will. But first we should think about it alone. Then we can talk. I'm sorry if you don't like it, but it's what I want to do." He stretched out his left arm and looked at his wristwatch. "It's 8:30 now. I'll come back tonight around 8:30 and we can talk more then."

"I cannot believe you're doing this, Dean. I can't believe you're walking out of here after saying those things." Her voice was as sharp and mean as a paper cut. She used the tone whenever she felt wronged or morally superior.

"Believe it." He shifted the sled in his arms to balance its weight better. "What did I say you didn't already know, something new? Did I suddenly break new ground in our relationship? I don't think so.

"Stop playing the wounded victim here, Vanessa, because you're not, not by a long shot. *Both* of us have to deal with this; you're not the only one.

"I don't believe we like each other anymore—plural. The ground has shifted and we've got to deal with it now. We've both avoided it because it's ugly and scary. But it's true and it's here: *We don't like each other anymore.*" He waited for her to reply: to say something typically snide, cutting, or self-pitying.

"Okay." She put her hands in her lap, swallowed, and straightened up. She looked at the clock on the kitchen wall. "Twelve hours. Okay."

Surprised at her reaction, he didn't move. He was curious to see what came next.

She waved a hand toward the door. "Go. What are you waiting for?"

"Five minutes ago you said—"

"That was five minutes ago." She stood, walked over to the stove, and poured herself more coffee from the pot.

"Okay." He started for the door, passing near her, heartened she appeared to be all right with this.

"But what if I'm not here when you come back, Dean? What if I decide to leave in those twelve hours?"

He closed his eyes and scowled. He knew it was too easy. "Why would you want to? Don't you think we need to talk this whole thing over when we're both calmer and clearer in our heads? Let's have a day apart to put our thoughts in order and then come back and talk it through."

Without warning, she abruptly flicked her hand out at him—as if throwing a Frisbee. A long ribbon of hot black coffee flew through the air and splashed against his chest, the silver sled, and his bare hands. Burning drops hit his face. The sled clattered to the floor when he threw up both hands to his stinging cheeks. Luckily he was wearing a thick ski jacket so the coffee that hit his body did not burn him.

Aghast and thrilled by what she had just done, Vanessa didn't want him to see her face because she had no idea what expression was there. It might have been delight, because it was definitely part of what she felt. Hurrying from the room, she put her head down so her chin almost touched her chest. Fleeing, she brushed him and he jerked away from the contact.

His fingers on his face trembled. Bringing both hands down quickly, he was someway ashamed to be shaking then. He didn't know what to do. Her action had been so unexpected and shocking. Did she really hate him so much? What had he said she didn't already know and feel? Did the truth out loud set her free, or simply free her inner bitch?

When the electric air of alarm and disbelief had lessened, he wanted to know only one thing: Had she done it to hurt him? Or was it only an unplanned emotional act, a lightning bolt of sudden madness or fury she'd take back now if she could? An *oh shit* moment in life where you wish you could rewind time back ten seconds and do it again differently or not at all. Did she wish it now or was she happy to have flung scalding coffee at him? Was she somewhere in this house grinning and thinking, yes, I'm glad I did it?

It was all he wanted to know because it was the only thing he cared about now. He did not care if she was angry or hurt by what he'd said. Her act put them way past that. He had a temper too. Sometimes he flared up and acted rashly without thinking. But he would never do what she had just done. When he read accounts of domestic violence, he questioned himself and invariably came to the same conclusion—no, I couldn't do those things even if I were furious. If a situation ever got *so* bad, I'd leave. Get out of the relationship while you both still had your sanity and dignity. You did not act like that toward another person, especially not your partner, no matter how angry you were.

His instincts now said go find her and ask what the hell she was thinking. But it might have been exactly what she wanted, her way of making him stay at home now. He wasn't going to give her anything. Looking at his watch again, he was surprised to see only four minutes had passed since he last looked at it and told her he would return in twelve hours. Standing there with coffee still dripping down his coat, he reviewed the last few minutes. Perhaps there was something he had missed or forgotten about their confrontation, a word or significant sentence gone unnoticed before or after the violence of her gesture.

No, he was not going to try to find a logical, acceptable reason for her act. What she'd done was wrong—out of limits, way over the line wrong. He hated how people always searched for reasons to justify others' bad behavior. Because sometimes it *isn't* justifiable—it's only bad: period, end of discussion. Sometimes people are just shits and their acts prove it.

He went to the sink, wet a sponge, and brushed it briskly across the front of his jacket. Then he tore off a paper towel and patted the jacket dry. He was wiping her act off his body now, not the coffee.

An incident from a few nights ago came to mind. After working late at the store, he stopped at the town diner on the way home for something to eat. The place was almost empty so he noticed the other customers. In a booth directly across the room a couple were eating hamburgers and horsing around. Probably twenty years old, they were obviously crazy for each other and their happiness was as thick as the smell of spring lilacs. They ate and talked with the liveliness and intensity of children. You forget what it is like to be new in love. You forget how you want to tell your flame everything and hear everything they have to say. It does not matter what it is, so long as they keep talking.

His food came and he ate while sneaking glances at them whenever possible. He didn't want to be too obvious so as not to embarrass the couple or make them feel self-conscious. What he liked most was, neither of them was trying to be cool or aloof. Even from this distance he saw the flurry of goofy loving expressions on their faces, the constant touching, the giggling and talk talk talk. They weren't trying to impress or play superior. They were wholly comfortable showing each other their joy. It was lovely to see. After his meal he ordered a cup of tea he didn't want just so he could stay a while longer and watch them some more.

Eventually the young man stood up and walked to the toilet. Almost as soon as he disappeared behind the restroom door, the girl began crying. Sitting there alone, her face tightened and then the tears came. She cried silently but made no attempt to hide it.

Dean couldn't believe it. Why was she crying? Moments before she'd been laughing and flirting, touching her boyfriend's arm and slapping a hand over her mouth in giggly delight. Now her face was tight as a fist and red in anguish. Why? Had something been said? Or had she waited till her boyfriend was gone before showing her real feelings?

Fascinated by this disturbing change, he could not stop staring at the distraught girl. In the end she noticed Dean and looked over at him with hatred in her eyes—as if *he* were to blame for her tears and sadness, whatever the cause. He was so flustered and distressed by her glare that he threw some money down to pay for his meal and left.

Standing now at the kitchen sink, he looked at the damp white, brown-stained paper towel in his hand. Had the same thing happened to his wife? Had she thrown the coffee at him because he mentioned separation, or because of other things in their past building up over time to this boiling point?

He would love to have known why the girl in the diner suddenly started crying. He could find out right now why his wife had tried to hurt him.

"Vanessa?" He waited for an answer but none came. Dropping the towel in the garbage beneath the sink, he went to find her. A few steps out of the kitchen, he heard a car start and knew by its signature sound it was hers. He stood in the hallway while a picture of him racing out the front door and trying to stop her glided across his mind like a news ticker at the bottom of a television screen. But the image evaporated because it was wrong. Why should he run after her when she had hurt him? Come back come back—I'm sorry for making you burn me. She wanted to leave? Fine. He'd return in twelve hours and if she was here, they would talk. If not, he would deal with it then.

What kept him standing there was the sudden realization he felt no curiosity about where she was going now, absolutely none. He had not been curious about her life for a long time. What she did with her days, what she thought about things, what mattered or distressed his wife . . . he was indifferent to all of it now. It was ambient sound to him. Granted, some of it was louder and some softer. Generally though it was all just background noise, or the soft tune playing in an elevator as you ascended to your floor. Familiar and trivial, the most effect it had was to stay in your mind a few seconds after you'd left the elevator. Perhaps you whistled a few notes of it before moving on to what mattered, but no more. For years she had been one of the most important parts of his life. But in recent times what she did, what she thought, where she went, or what left her lips was like hearing the song "Raindrops Keep Fallin' on My Head" for the 2,000th time.

He walked to a window with a view onto the street and saw her red car moving away down the block. It stood out vividly against the background of white snow everywhere. He was certain she would have music playing. Classic rock and roll or dance music, most likely Jagger singing "Gimme Shelter," or something up-tempo from The Brothers Johnson. She played fast, fist-pumping-in-the-air music when she was upset. Whenever he'd walk into their house or get into the car and she was driving, if there was dance music on loud he would not know what to expect. It generally meant something bad had happened and she was playing it to lift her spirits.

Some people want you to share their moods, feel their pain, hate or rejoice or get drunk along with them. Others want your sympathy, a foot rub, their hand held, or a cup of hot tea. His wife, Vanessa, wanted none of those things. Give her space and silence and be sure to leave her alone. If you happened to be around when she was unhappy, the best thing to do was retreat to the other side of the house and ignore her until she showed she was ready to communicate again.

Locking his hands over his head, he stared out at the snow and wondered if telling her how he felt had been wrong. But what was the alternative? Going on for more months or even years in a house full of barbed wire conversations and too many instances when it was very plain neither of you wanted to be in the same room together? He assumed she felt the same way, especially judging by how she had acted toward him the last six months. Someone once told him most people would rather die than change. At the time he thought that was generally accurate, but now? Sometimes death came if you *didn't* change. Not the stopped heart/no pulse/flatline kind, but the death of curiosity, optimism, and desire.

On impulse, he put out a hand and touched the window. Feeling the cold beneath his fingertips, he slid them around and around on the glass as if they were skating. "I have a question. Can I ask you a question?" He did not think it odd to speak out loud now, although his wife was not there. He had a question he wanted her to answer. He knew she was gone. He watched her car move away down the street. "I have a question for you."

TWO

The steering wheel was icy cold. Vanessa kept lifting her hands off it one at a time, making fists and blowing on them to bring back some heat. Everything was quiet except for the car heater and the muted sound of the tires crunching snow. When she entered the car minutes before, her first impulse had been to turn on loud music. But her heart wasn't in it and she let the quiet stay where it was.

In such a rush to escape the house, she drove three blocks before pulling the car over to the curb to check and see if she'd brought everything she needed. The last thing she wanted right now was to have to go back home and sheepishly retrieve her cell phone or wallet while he watched.

Thank God she'd brought it all. But what was she going to do now? Where was she going to go for the rest of the day? Out of the blue, her life had capsized and suddenly she was hanging on to a piece of shipwreck in the middle of a vast and dangerous morning.

Picking up the phone, she pressed #9 and held it down to speed-dial Kaspar. While waiting, she prayed he would answer. He was the only one she could talk to about this.

"Hi. This is Kaspar. Leave a message."

Grimacing, she said to *please* call her back as soon as he got this message. It was an emergency and she was desperate for his help. Vanessa was certain her message would grab his attention because in all the time they had spent together she'd never used a phrase like "desperate for his help" or any other like it. With Kaspar she was the Queen of Cool and Independence. Even in bed, where they devoured each other, she held certain things back. This was the first time she had ever said she *needed* him. It was going to be interesting to see how he responded.

Still holding the telephone in her hand, she wondered who else she could call now for help. Her sister was a horror and a judgmental twit. Her parents lived a thousand miles away and loved her husband much more than her. She didn't blame them though because Dean *was* a much nicer person than she. Vanessa loved that about him and had often used his kindness either against him or to her advantage.

If she had been someone else, Vanessa probably would have been upset or disheartened to realize there was no person other than her lover who she could call at this paradigm moment. But this was Vanessa Corbin, who placed "friends" down around number twelve on her list of the most important things in her life.

She dropped the phone into her lap and picked up the wallet. Inside it were fifty-seven dollars and three credit cards, two of them on Dean's account. Lifting her head and looking through the windshield, she began to smile. One T-shirt she owned said, "When the going gets tough, the tough go shopping," and that's exactly what Vanessa would do now. Go to the mall and spend a lovely long morning shopping and charging things on her husband's credit cards. No, even better—she'd shop as if she were going on a long trip. Since she didn't know where the trip would take her, she'd have to buy both winter and summer things to cover all possibilities. Afterward she'd have a gorgeous lunch at her favorite restaurant near the mall and then perhaps see a movie. . . .

She had a plan now. Whether or not Kaspar called, there was plenty to keep her busy for the next few hours. Reaching forward, she pushed a CD into the machine. An old woman shoveling snow ten feet away looked up quickly when James Brown's voice exploded from inside the little red car as it pulled away from the curb.

A quarter of an hour later, Dean Corbin's telephone rang again. This time he answered it. Pulling the phone out of a pocket, he momentarily wondered if it was Vanessa. But it wasn't her style. When his wife was wrong about something she did not like to admit it. Prove her wrong and she turned stony. She was an Aries. People born under the sign evidently think they're never wrong about anything. Dean didn't much believe in astrology, but this detail was correct about her. Over their years together he had learned the best way to keep things peaceful between them was to back off when confrontations arose about who was right. Generally he was an easygoing man and letting his wife have her way didn't bother him. Besides, he had always enjoyed Vanessa's passion. It was one of the first things to attract him years ago. Her passion and her talent lassoed his heart and bound it tight to her. A person cannot be passionate without a strong ego, because "I" plays the main role in any kind of passion: I love. I want. I need.

Before they met, Dean's life had been relatively pleasant, quiet, and uneventful. Then one night after work he walked into a bar in Greenwich Village for a drink with some friends and there she was at the piano singing The Beatles' haunting song "For No One." Dean loved that tune, but the way this woman sang it was like nothing he had ever heard before. He was absolutely spellbound. Somehow she managed to imbue her voice and phrasing with grief, longing, passion, and even contrarily hope—all at the same time. After ten minutes of listening to the singer, Dean had forgotten his friends and his drink and was thinking, "I have got to talk to her. I've got to tell her . . . I don't know *what* I've got to tell her, but I have *got* to talk to this woman."

At the end of the set, she went and sat alone at the bar. After several deep breaths to rouse his courage, Dean Corbin got up and walked over. Because he could not think of anything else to say, he shyly asked if she'd recorded a CD he could buy.

Without hesitating she patted the red leather barstool next to her and said, "Sit down. You are wearing a very beautiful tie; the most beautiful tie I have seen in I don't know how long. Any man who likes my singing and has such great taste in ties, him I want to talk to. Sit."

On top of the sledding hill now Dean took off his gloves and looked at the telephone screen to see who was calling. On recognizing the name, he visibly relaxed. "Hello?"

"We've got a problem." The voice was deep, warm, and soothing—like the sound of a cello. It said the word "problem" as if it were something fun and interesting.

Dean moved the phone from one ear to the other. "No, *you've* got a problem. I've got the day off, remember?" Sitting on his sled at the top of Donut Hill, he still hadn't ridden down yet because he was enjoying the moment too much. Being up there with those dazzling views of the town and the valley, the snow-covered Vermont mountains in the background, and winter's crisp cold embrace, it was more than enough for him to just sit there, take it all in, and be grateful.

"The shipment of Borrelli shirts didn't come in and we're screwed. We're not going to have them by Christmas."

"I'm not listening to you, Kaspar. It's my day off, remember?" Smiling, he continued looking at the spectacular view from the top of the hill.

"Why do you sound so happy, Dean? It's too early in the day to be happy. Did something happen?"

"Yes, I guess you could say it did."

"What?"

"I told Vanessa I think maybe we should separate."

There was a long low whistle on the other end of the line and then Kaspar asked, "No kidding?"

"Nope. We had a fight this morning because I said we don't like each other anymore so what's the point of staying together?"

"And you're not in the house now?"

"No. I'm up on Donut Hill with my sled. The snow is perfect, the view is beautiful, and I am ready to fly. I'm telling you, Kaspar—sledding makes me feel ten years old again and after what happened this morning, I need some speed to clear my head."

"Where's Vanessa?"

"I do not know, my friend. She threw a cup of coffee at me after I told her; boiling hot coffee, can you imagine? Then she stormed out of the house and drove away. It was all very dramatic."

Kaspar had ignored Vanessa's phone call earlier because he was not in the mood to talk. After listening to her message, he really wanted to avoid her. Vanessa was a drama queen of epic proportions. When he heard her message saying she was desperate, he took it as his cue to disappear from her radar screen for a while. "Aren't you worried about where she went?"

"No. My wife is not Anna Karenina. She won't throw herself under a train, especially not for me."

"You sound way too upbeat about this whole thing, Dean. Aren't you upset at all?"

"No, I'm relieved. It's been building up between us for way too long. Something had to give."

Kaspar half-listened to what his partner said while trying to figure out how to avoid Dean's wife for the next few days. At least until some of the dust had settled from this unexpected bomb.

Being around Vanessa Corbin any time was like eating a piece of double rich chocolate cake: You were hungry for the first few bites and they were absolutely scrumptious, but halfway through you'd had enough. If you ate more, you usually felt ill.

Kaspar Benn was one of those people to whom nice things happen all the time. Partly because they're genuinely nice but mostly because they just seem to be blessed, as if life watches out for them and often serves them the nicest slice of meat. Although he was heavy and plain looking (like an East German metal worker, as he often described himself), women were attracted to him because he knew how to make them laugh and more important, feel cherished. He had almost no morals but did his best not to hurt others if it was possible. However, he didn't think twice about sleeping with his partner's wife when the opportunity arose years before. The way he saw it, what went on between Vanessa and him was their concern and no one else's. He ate at their house at least twice a month and the three of them hung around together frequently. Dean never suspected anything because they never gave him reason to suspect. When the three were together, Kaspar was smart, charming, and witty as hell. He treated Vanessa with fond respect and kept his distance from her except for hello and good-bye kisses on the cheek.

She was dull in bed but a great cook, and Kaspar liked food more than anything. He was an accomplished lover but couldn't boil an egg. One of his dreams in life was to make enough money to hire a really first-class full-time cook. Vanessa suggested he marry someone who was good in the kitchen, but marriage was not for him. He believed people should marry only in their twenties or late fifties. No other time. When you're twenty you can build a life together; after fifty, you marry for companionship. Who wants to be alone when they're old?

". . . is it all right with you?"

Thinking about Vanessa, Kaspar had tuned Dean out completely. "Excuse me; I'm still in shock from what you told me. What did you say?"

"I asked if we could hang up now so I can go back to my day off?"

"Yes, of course. Sure. Listen, if there's anything I can do for you or Vanessa . . ."

"Thanks buddy, but this is only round one with her. You can be sure there's going to be a lot more to come. Bye-bye." Dean broke the connection and slipped the phone back into his pocket. Sighing, he let his mind wander. He could take off right now and begin a whole new life somewhere else. Take a wad of money out of the bank; leave her a note saying, "I want to live the rest of my life wonderfully," and then head for . . . Fiji. Or the Florida Keys. Margaritaville, ahoy! Maybe someplace grim and original, like Bucharest. Or Estonia. He had recently read a magazine article that said Estonian women were uncommonly beautiful, so why not go there? Dear Vanessa, I am living in Estonia with a six-foot-tall blond mathematician named Triin Ploomipuu.

He looked up in the sky and saw an airplane miles overhead moving south in front of a long white softening contrail it was drawing across the cornflower blue sky. When was the last time Vanessa and he had flown anywhere together? Last May to Italy on the buying trip for the store. A nice two weeks, but so what? What difference did it make now? "The cat is out of the bag," as she had rightly said, so those nice trips, nice meals, and nice years when they had been genuinely happy together were like Confederate Army money now: they looked pretty but were worthless. He thought, in just sixty minutes what once *was*, meant next to nothing. An hour after the confrontation in their kitchen, the life they had created together for a decade was completely in limbo. Everything stable and sure had the foundation knocked out from under it and gone wobbly.

Shaking his head, Dean Corbin looked once again at the town and the mountains. He closed his eyes and kept them closed. He could only hear and smell the familiar world. He wondered what it smelled like in Estonia.

The first person Vanessa ran into at the mall was her boss. By then she was feeling more balanced, considering what had just happened to her at home. She'd bought a new cinnamon-colored bra at La Perla. It looked pretty damned nice on her. Now she was thinking about going back and buying a cute purse she had seen a few minutes before.

Vanessa was standing there thinking about what direction to take when a smoky voice behind her asked, "Whatcha got in the bag?"

Without turning around Vanessa asked, "Do lesbians go out and buy underwear the minute their partner says the relationship is over? Or is that a strictly heterosexual reaction?"

The other woman said, "I don't *need* an excuse to buy new underpants. I have this self-timer thing inside me—like an egg timer, you know? Whenever it goes ping, it's time for me to go to a lingerie shop.

"Why, are you and Dean calling it quits? That's surprising." Although the voice showed no surprise at all.

Jane Claudius was the most poised, elegant woman Vanessa had ever known. She would have been a wonderful diplomat because in whatever she did she acted with a combination of intelligence, natural grace, and great humor that was very winning. People liked her but were also slightly hesitant because she kept her distance. Kaspar described Jane as "nice but magisterial," and he was right. She was very black and quite tall, which added to her stature. She was open and casual about being lesbian but in no way aggressive about it. Vanessa once admitted to Jane that she couldn't picture her all down and dirty, sweaty and groaning.

Jane had grinned and said, "Butter wouldn't melt in my bed, huh?"

"Maybe butter, but not you. I can't imagine you breaking a sweat over anything, boss."

Now Jane asked if Vanessa would like to go for a cup of coffee and talk. Vanessa thought about it but said no. "I'm not really ready to yet. Right now I have the feeling you get in your stomach after eating something bad and your body is deciding how to react. You don't know if you're going to puke or not. . . ."

Jane patted her arm. "I know the feeling; it'll pass. Today's your day off, right? Are you coming in tomorrow or do you want some time off?"

"Oh no, I'll be in. It's the best way to take my mind off this."

"I agree. So I'll see you tomorrow."

Vanessa nodded and watched the tall woman walk away. Catching a whiff of Jane's woody perfume, she wondered for the hundredth time what it would be like to touch her. She called out, "Hey Jane, were you ever here? I mean, did this ever happen to you? Someone you loved said it's finished— I want out."

Smiling, Jane walked back. "Of course, everybody's been there. Nobody gets out of love alive, Vanessa. That's half the deal and we all know it by the time we're fifteen years old. You gamble and lose about 90 percent of the time. It's like buying a lottery ticket. The chances of winning anything are a million to one. We know it but it doesn't stop us from trying again and again." She held up her index finger. "Which I think is *good* because it shows people are optimistic about the most important thing in life.

"But are you sure it's finished? Or are you two just going through an intermission?"

Vanessa said quietly, "Dean told me he wanted to separate."

Jane put a hand behind her neck and leaned back on one leg. By day she dressed like a hip kid. Now she was wearing a black ski jacket as shiny as licorice, army pants with lots of pockets, and scuffed hiking boots. In great contrast, at night in the bar she always wore the same all-black out-fit—a silk shirt beneath a sleekly tailored jacket and matching slacks. It made her look like a silky ninja. "If things really do go bad between the two of you, you can always come and stay with us, Vanessa. Remember that. I hope you don't need it, but when the same thing happened to me a few years ago I had nowhere to go, which made it a world worse. Just know the offer's there."

"*Wow!* Well, thank you. I mean, I wasn't expecting you to—" Surprised and overcome by the kindness of the offer, Vanessa was at a loss for what to say.

"You're welcome. See you tomorrow."

Jane did not like Vanessa Corbin but was indebted to her. Two years before, her bar was failing. She'd invested every cent of her money and time into it. But like so many bars and restaurants, Jane's did not possess the mysterious ineffable magic always needed to bring customers in to a new place. She had studied interior design in college so from the first day the builders started work on the space she knew exactly what kind of feeling and look she wanted them to create. She hired a good piano player from the music department at the local college, a skilled cook, and a bartender who had worked for fifteen years at the Locke-Ober restaurant in Boston before retiring to this idyllic Vermont town. What more could she have done? Jane had planned every detail and saved up for years to do this. The bar had been her life's dream, but as the dream evaporated, she didn't know how to save it.

One night a pretty, overweight woman sat down at the piano and began playing the song "I Wish I Were in Love Again." After she sang the first verse, most of the people in the room had gone quiet and were listening. By the time she finished the song, almost everyone applauded enthusiastically.

She was *that* good. She looked at Jane and asked if it was all right to continue. Jane steepled her fingers as if praying and said, "Please!"

The singer was exceptional. Not only did she play the piano beautifully, but her voice covered three octaves. After she'd sung five songs ranging from standards to pop to country and western, she asked the audience if they had any requests. She was obviously used to doing this. Her demeanor was funny, intimate, and completely relaxed in front of listeners. Someone called for Steve Winwood's "Back in the High Life Again" and she knocked the song out of the park.

For an hour this big stranger did what Jane Claudius had been unable to do in all the time she had run her bar: she made it magical. When the woman finished with a slow, dreamy rendition of the '50s classic rock song "He's So Fine," the whole room was hers; they loved her.

She walked back to a table and sat down next to a thin bald man dressed in an elegant pinstripe suit and open-necked white shirt with silver cufflinks. He kissed her on the cheek. Smiling, she put her forehead on his arm. Jane went over to them and signed to the bartender to bring drinks. She asked if she could join the couple. Both seemed happy for her company.

They were the Corbins, Vanessa and Dean. Along with a business partner, Dean owned the stylish men's store on the town's main street. Like Jane, the Corbins were ex–New Yorkers who had gotten fed up with city life after having been robbed twice. They moved here to Vermont because Dean had attended college here years before and both of them loved the intimate yet urbane feel of this town.

Despite its size, it was a wealthy community. The college was small but exclusive and cost a fortune to attend. Most of the students had a lot of pocket money, and in winter the skiing in the area was so good that expensive sports cars and SUVs with Connecticut, Massachusetts, and

New York license plates lined the streets. A bar like Jane's or an upscale clothing store fit well into the demographic.

They chatted for a long time. Vanessa didn't say much about herself, but she did most of the talking. Only late in the conversation did it come out she had been a successful club singer in New York and had even released a CD. After another round of drinks and some more talk, Jane asked if Vanessa would consider performing here a few nights each week. The pay wouldn't be as good as in New York but Jane would improve it if business picked up.

Vanessa looked at Dean. Smiling, he touched her hand and said, "It's your decision, sweetheart."

She continued looking at him, her questioning eyes examining his whole face as if she were looking for any telltale traces there that betrayed what he'd just said to her. When she was convinced he really meant it, she turned to Jane. "I get scared. It's one of the reasons why I stopped singing and we moved here."

Dean began to speak but Vanessa shook her head to stop him. She wanted to talk; she wanted to tell Jane this information. "It started a couple of years ago for no reason and then got a lot worse. I never even knew what a panic attack was but suddenly I began having them regularly, but only when I'd perform. I'd be singing along fine when BAM—everything inside me froze and my hands started shaking so badly I couldn't play. Why? I don't know. It was terrifying."

Jane looked away in embarrassment, but she also admired this stranger for being so frank. Looking again, she saw Vanessa was staring at her drink, trying to keep control.

"I love to sing; I love it more than anything in the world. You know why, Jane? Because there is all of this incredible music out there which to me is like the most delicious variety of ingredients imaginable for a recipe—and *I get to cook it*. My suppliers are The Beatles and Gershwin and Noël Coward and a hundred other geniuses. They give me all their best . . . and I get to prepare it my way and then serve it to the world." Vanessa paused, took a sip of her drink, and squeezed her husband's hand. "So when this fear started happening every time I performed, I went to an analyst; two, in fact. They gave me pills . . . I took them and had things pretty much under control physically. But whenever I sang there was always a very good chance I'd freeze up again and that ruined it for me. I used to love to perform but now I was afraid."

Jane was confused. "But you sounded great out there just now—so strong and confident."

"Sure, because it was a onetime spontaneous thing. There was no pressure. On the spur of the moment I sat down at a piano and played. It felt wonderful—like old times. I loved it—I *love* to sing! It used to be my life."

"It still is!" Dean protested.

Vanessa smiled ruefully at him. "I hope so. I hope this is just a phase; my scaredy-cat phase." She stood up and walked toward the toilet. Jane and Dean watched her go. Halfway there, a woman stopped her to congratulate Vanessa on her performance.

When she was gone, Jane said, "Jeez, what a rotten thing to happen: your own ghosts scare away the thing you love."

Dean played with a cufflink and nodded. "She was on her way to the top. Everyone who heard her perform said she was going to make it big and I believe it. She kept getting better and better. Audiences love her because she's so friendly and at ease with them. You saw it."

"I did. What does she do in the meantime, since you moved here?"

"Fixed up our house after we bought it. She's an excellent cook, although it doesn't interest her; it's just another one of her natural talents. She reads, plays the piano for herself . . ." His voice trailed off, defeated.

"To make things worse, after she started having those panic attacks we were robbed a second time. It was brutal and really traumatized her; three junkies with a hunting knife held us up on the street near our apartment in Brooklyn. It just broke her. It was a bad time for both of us and we definitely needed a big change. I suggested we try living up here in Vermont because we always came for the skiing and she loved the town as much as I did."

"*What* do I love?" Vanessa returned to the table and sat down.

"This town. I was telling Jane how we ended up here."

"Did you tell her about the guys with the big knife?"

Dean nodded.

"An idea just came to me in the bathroom, Jane: what if I sing here without working for you, without a formal job? What if I come in when I feel I just want to sing, like today?"

Jane and Dean exchanged puzzled looks. "How do you mean?"

Vanessa pointed across the room at the piano. "It felt really good playing tonight. Normal, happy—the way I want things to be. No pressure, no strings—just sit down and play because I felt like it. Maybe if I do it regularly here, I'll get back in the groove. And if *that* happens, then I can work for you on a more formal basis."

"Are you sure you want to?"

Vanessa put both hands in her black hair and pushed it back and forth. "No, I'm not sure of *anything* anymore, but it's worth a try."

It was one of the best and worst things to happen to Jane Claudius. In the following months, Vanessa regularly performed at Jane's a couple of nights a week, usually at either end—Monday and Friday or Saturday. Jane never knew how long she would play—sometimes only half an hour, other times she'd perform for two hours straight. Word got around fast—more and more people came to listen to the charismatic new singer. In retrospect it was very good at the beginning that no one ever knew when Vanessa would show up at the bar because the elusiveness added to her mystique and allure.

There was never any fanfare when she showed up. Usually Jane didn't even know Vanessa had arrived except if the regular pianist were performing, he would immediately stop playing. A short silence followed and then Vanessa would begin. The feeling in the room changed right away. It became more intense and unified, as if the audience simultaneously turned their full attention to the same single thing and focused only on it. The singer didn't appear to notice. Typically she began her set with something fanciful or funny, like her rendition of "Yellow Submarine." Perhaps an obscure Frank Loesser, Arthur Siegel, or Rodgers and Hart song no one knew but immediately liked when she sang it. If the crowd was restless or particularly boisterous she often started out very sexy and sassy with songs like "Urgent" or The Pretenders' great '80s standard "Brass in Pocket." Inevitably the few people who hadn't been listening to her suddenly were.

Vanessa had the important ability to quickly sense the mood or personality of a crowd and play right to the heart of it. If there were lots of college kids in the bar, customarily she would do more songs they'd likely know, but always with her inventive spin on them, her signature arrangements that made the music sound new and compelling to everyone. However, if she sensed the room was sad or withdrawn no matter who was there, she performed mostly piano music like excerpts from Keith Jarrett's *Köln Concerts* or George Winston and then slowly segue into tunes that definitely belonged there too. She never tried to lift or change a mood; only embellished it with her smart and thoughtful choices.

One late night in the middle of a song called "Dancing with Ghosts," a woman sitting by herself suddenly stood up, said very loudly "Yes, you're exactly right!" and hurried out of the bar crying. Dramatic as it was, few people seemed to notice, caught up as they were in their own thoughts and blues, enhanced by this empathetic singer.

At the beginning, Dean always accompanied Vanessa to the bar, sat through the performances, and then took her home afterward. But after a while she started coming in alone. When Jane asked about it, Vanessa beamed and said, "I told him I don't think he needs to babysit me anymore."

The crowds grew and so did her confidence. She played longer sets and began performing one more night a week. Jane was careful and solicitous. She watched Vanessa closely and entered Dean's telephone number on her phone's speed dials just in case she needed to reach him quickly.

At the same time, Jane was working twice as hard to keep up with the large increase in customers. She had always firmly believed if people would only visit her bar a couple of times and get a feel for its ambience, they would want to return regularly. Her new singer was the catalyst. What heartened Jane most was after Vanessa had been there a while and established a fixed schedule, the place was still almost full on the nights she didn't perform.

Of course there was a "but" in all this. There's always a "but" in any triumph. The nasty little bone in the delicious piece of fish, the dangerous slick spot on the just-waxed gleaming floor, the "no" hiding under "yes's" bed, waiting for the right moment to spring out and bite you. The worm in Jane's beautiful new apple was paradoxically Vanessa's success. As time passed and her confidence grew, the talented singer became demanding, difficult, and in due course the most exasperating kind of diva.

At first it was small understandable things—adjust the lighting on her three different times, buy expensive new microphones, tune the piano, and then have someone else tune it again because Vanessa was still dissatisfied with the sound.

Then one day she "suggested" Jane fire the nice, very capable pianist who filled in for Vanessa on her days off. This man was also a big fan of

Vanessa, which made it even harder for Jane to understand why she wanted him out. When asked, the singer tsked like a petulant child and muttered, "It's difficult to explain."

Jane said no. Vanessa's face tightened but she said nothing.

When she came into the bar two nights later, she played for exactly twenty-nine minutes and then stopped. By then she usually played for at least an hour. Passing Jane who was sitting at the bar, the two women exchanged stony glances. The next two times she performed that evening, Vanessa repeated this abbreviated twenty-nine-minute set. The audience didn't appear to notice because luckily it was a raucous crowd content with its own company.

Coincidentally it happened to be payday. After the third twenty-nine-minute set, Jane went back to her office and rewrote the singer's salary check for the week. At the end of the evening she handed it over as always in a blank envelope. As if expecting something, Vanessa opened the envelope immediately and saw her employer had reduced her salary accordingly.

"I waited my whole life to have this place, Vanessa. You've only been here three months but you're already trying to tell me how to run it. I won't let you; it's neither right nor fair. I love having you here and we both know how much you've helped my business, but you cannot do this." Then Jane smiled. It was cordial and warm, with not the slightest bit of challenge or scold in it. A smile that said, let's drop this right now and move forward, on to more important things we both want.

The smile more than anything else disarmed Vanessa. She backed off and things were all right for a while afterward. But as she grew more self-assured as a performer, her selfishness manifested itself in other unpleasant ways.

In contrast, the longer Jane knew him, the more she liked Dean Corbin. He was kind, intelligent, and very good company. But when she spoke to him about Vanessa's bad behavior, he only made excuses for his wife's conduct and downplayed every example of bad behavior she brought to his attention. He believed you must treat artists differently and make allowances for their shortcomings, because in the end their work brings so much joy to others. Jane delicately argued talent is no excuse for meanness. But she couldn't convince him to talk to his wife about this matter. Luckily at a certain point Vanessa's divatude leveled off at borderline bearable, but the two women never stopped sparring and challenging each other.

Whenever it got to be too much, Jane went skating. She kept a pair of inline skates under the desk in her office. A few nights a week, as soon as the bar closed at 2 A.M., she would change clothes, put on her skates, and roll out the back door. One of her favorite things was to skate late at night down the town streets when they were empty and still. She had grown up in Brooklyn and as a girl went with her father almost every weekend to the legendary roller-skating rink on Empire Boulevard. All her life she had skated and as she grew older, it became as much therapy as a hobby for her. Sometimes she skated to think through problems in her life. Other times she willed her mind to empty so she could simply enjoy the feel of her body slicing through the air, wheels whizzing across the ground beneath her feet. It was why she was at the shopping mall when she met Vanessa after her confrontation with Dean. Jane had been on her way to buy a protective helmet. She had recently begun learning how to speed ice-skate at the college and her instructor was adamant she wear the proper protection.

Walking now toward the sporting goods store, she wondered what had caused Dean Corbin to tell Vanessa he'd had enough of her.

Jane's partner, Felice, believed it is almost always something small or unexpected that ends a relationship. In general the hammer blow does not come from things like finding out your partner has been unfaithful, or they become unbearable behind closed doors. Those revelations may knock you to your knees, but it is actually seeing the secret snapshot of them with the other person, both looking so happy, so completely stoned on love or sex, that finishes it. Or the slight wicked smile on their face after they have been intentionally cruel to you. The end, like God, is in the details.

In this instance, Jane would have been truly surprised to learn something *she'd* said was the tipping point for Dean. The night before, while chatting at the bar with Vanessa about relationships and sex, Jane had said offhandedly, "Most men think they are good drivers. Most women think they're good in bed. They aren't." The line made Vanessa laugh, but it sure didn't tickle Dean when it was repeated to him earlier that morning.

"Were you talking to Vanessa Corbin?"

Jane turned around and there was Felice. As always, she was delighted to see her love. "I was. How'd you know I was here?"

Felice handed her a brown bag containing a fresh blueberry muffin the size of a shot put and a small cup of black coffee—Jane's favorite breakfast. "I was getting something to eat in the food court and saw you two talking. Then I remembered you were coming here this morning."

Felice managed the bookstore on the next floor up in the mall. It's how they had originally met—luckily for both women, Jane was an avid reader. She happened to visit the store a month after Felice took over as manager there. The very first time she saw Jane, standing in front of the fiction section with her arms already full of novels, Felice said to herself, "If there *is* a God, that woman is gay."

"What did Mrs. Diva have to say? Didn't you just see her last night?" Felice disliked Vanessa because Jane disliked her.

"Her husband wants to split up."

Felice grabbed and squeezed Jane's arm. "No *way*! You always said he adored her."

"Apparently not anymore. Wanna go sit down someplace for five minutes so I can eat this? I know you've got to get back to work. I'll eat fast."

They walked to a wooden bench near a fountain and sat with their four knees touching. They had been together a year but were still jubilant to have found each other. Neither woman had ever been successful at love. Certainly over the years it had flirted with both of them; sometimes it had even given them short intense embraces. But each time love pulled away much too soon and fled or turned into a lumpy pumpkin at some unexpected or undeserved midnight. So as both women grew older, Jane and Felice became more resigned and self-sufficient. They welcomed romance whenever it appeared at their doors, but in the long stretches without it they worked hard to fill their days with engaging people and activities that made them feel pretty good most of the time.

In the beginning of their relationship, both women proceeded as if they had entered a very dark room and were sliding their hands hesitantly up and down all the walls, feeling for a light switch while at the same time afraid they might touch something sharp or dangerous. But from the minute they met there was absolutely no game playing between them. Both had had more than enough of it in their lives. They were eager to get to the heart of this matter. They wanted to reach the point as soon as possible where sharing silence was just as good as sharing their life stories.

They were both neat. They both wanted to laugh often. One of them liked sex more than the other but they worked it out. All in all, the ease with which they fit into each other's lives made them both skeptical. It doesn't happen this way; it's never this *easy*. Where were the difficulties? One night soon after they had moved in together while eating large bowls of ramen soup Jane had microwaved for them, she put down her spoon and said out of the blue, "Maybe it just *is* and I'm not going to worry about it anymore, you know? Maybe we're just lucky this time. Maybe there really *is* such a thing as luck. I never believed it before, but maybe there is."

"What are you talking about, dear?"

"*Us.* You know exactly what I'm talking about."

Felice grinned and whizzed her spoon around in her soup.

Months later sitting together in the shopping mall, Jane said incomprehensibly through a mouthful of blueberry muffin, "Maybe it was the secret and the monster."

Felice reached over and breaking off a piece of the muffin popped it into her mouth. "*What* did you say?"

Jane felt like a kid stuffing her mouth and then trying to talk through it. She swallowed, sipped some coffee, and repeated, "Maybe it was the secret and the monster that broke them up."

"It's possible; or else just one or the other. Usually one of them is ugly enough to do it for most couples." Felice believed you could never really know a person until you'd learned at least one of their deepest secrets, and seen the monster we keep hidden within and only allow to surface when we're truly out of control, or trust someone enough to feel we can let our guard down around them and allow our honest emotion to show.

"You've never told me any of your secrets, do you realize that?"

Jane stopped chewing. . . . Looking at Felice, she pointed to her mouth as if to say, let me finish this first and then I'll respond.

Felice continued. "It's true though, Jane. I told you about me and the guy at the gas station when I was fourteen, but you've never told me even one of your secrets."

Jane swallowed and brushed crumbs off her hands. "I know who we were."

Felice waited for her to say more, then shook her head. "I have no idea what you're talking about."

"I know who we both were in our last lives."

Whatever Felice had been expecting to hear, it certainly wasn't *this.* "What do you mean?"

"Don't you have to get back to work? We can talk about it later."

Felice shook her head. "Harry Potter can wait five more minutes. Explain please."

Jane turned the cardboard coffee cup around and around in her hands. "I told you; I know who we were in our last lives. Whenever I meet somebody, I can see it immediately. It's always been like that, ever since I was a little girl."

"All right then, who were you? Who was I?" Despite being skeptical about the subject, Felice couldn't resist asking.

Jane answered matter-of-factly, "Your name was Stina Salmi. You lived in Helsinki, Finland, where you were an industrial designer and worked for an associate of Alvar Aalto. You died of a cerebral hemorrhage during little vappu in 1971."

Felice looked at her lover's black hands holding the blue coffee cup on her lap now. When she looked at Jane's face again, she was smiling. "You're joking, right?"

Jane shook her head. "I'm totally serious."

"Helsinki?"

"Helsinki."

"What's 'little vappu'?"

"A Finnish summer festival. Everyone drinks a lot."

"This is mega-bizarre. How do you know these things?"

Jane shrugged. "You asked for one of my secrets so I told you."

"Who were *you*?"

"My name was Milton Rice. I was born in Barbados in 1946, lived three days, and then died in the hospital—bad heart and lungs."

"A boy? You were a *boy*?"

Jane stood up. "Not for long. Only three days."

Felice pushed her hair back behind one ear. "And what were you before that? Do you remember?"

"No. I can only see one life ago for anyone, including me. Come on, I'll walk you back to the store."

Felice stood up and shook all over, like a dog shaking water off its body. "What an interesting way to start the morning"—she looked at her partner and raised one eyebrow—"*Milton.*"

THREE

A child was running across rooftops. No one saw her this time because no one happened to look up at just the right moment to see a little girl in a yellow dress and green sneakers running in such a crazy, dangerous place. Why on earth was she up there? If she were someone's daughter her parents would be screaming, "Get down! Get down from there this instant! What are you *doing?* Come down right now before you fall and break your neck." But the little girl wouldn't. She would not come down. She had been doing this for months, day and night.

Jane Claudius saw her one morning at three o'clock. Rollerblading home after work, she looked up and saw something, some*one* small move surefooted across the roof of the town bakery. But Jane was tired and distracted. She'd just had another upsetting confrontation with Vanessa Corbin and wasn't interested in what she was seeing. Her eyes said look—something's up there! It's a child, did you see? Yes I saw, but I don't care. Right now I can only think about that horrible woman.

Vanessa Corbin saw the girl a week later. The kid stood unmoving on top of the flat roof of the high school, looking down at the world below. Driving by the building, Vanessa caught a glimpse of her but only thought the girl was up there for school or something related. Maybe her whole class was on the roof working together on a science project. Vanessa didn't think twice about it and drove on.

Dean Corbin and Kaspar Benn saw the child one afternoon standing on the roof of the railroad station being photographed by a man with a very professional-looking camera. They thought the picture was for a magazine advertisement or an article about their beautiful town. Of course they didn't know the photographer was a hedge fund manager whose hobby was photography and who just happened to look up at the right moment and saw this little girl standing on the roof of the lovingly restored 1920s station.

This man was set in his ways. A traditionalist, he didn't like digital cameras, no matter how many millions of pixels they were capable of producing today. To him, half the pleasure of taking pictures was working in a darkroom bringing photos manually to life. He disliked the immediacy of digital cameras—how you could see a picture seconds after taking it. He thought photography should have mystery in it, something indefinable and elusive. This was why he liked working in a darkroom developing pictures. It was a hands-on process you could never measure or replicate exactly. A photographic image slowly emerging in a chemical bath was like a woman undressing in front of you—slowly, slowly, you got to see everything.

Except for this little girl. As soon as he saw her up on that roof, the man snapped off seven pictures of her in quick succession. On the last one she looked down at him and smiled. Then she turned around and walked back toward the middle of the building and disappeared. He assumed a door was there for her to use to get back into the station again.

He spent the rest of the morning taking pictures of the town. It was his first visit there. He was delighted with the combination of hip but at the same time pastoral feel of the place. He shot three rolls of film over the weekend. When he got home to Hartford Sunday afternoon, he went straight to his darkroom and developed half of them. In that batch were the seven pictures he'd taken of the girl on the roof. But he could not find them. In their place were photographs of seven different vegetables: beautiful, stunning pictures—of vegetables. Butternut squash, lima beans, bell peppers . . . none of a little girl standing on a roof. He had never in his life taken a single photograph of a vegetable, but there they were in his developing tray—spectacular images that looked like the still lifes of Georgia O'Keeffe or Robert Mapplethorpe. They were the best photographs he had ever taken. Only *he* hadn't taken them. All seven were in black-and-white. The striking combination of dramatic shadows and tones made those banal objects transcendently beautiful.

But he never used black-and-white film in any of his cameras.

This morning the child looked down from a roof and saw Kaspar Benn standing and smoking a cigarette in the doorway of his store across the street. His mind was still galloping in panicked circles around the news of the Corbins' breakup. Staring straight ahead, he wondered what to do next. He was worried at any minute impulsive Vanessa would show up in tears or even hysterics demanding his help, his advice, his home to hide in, or something else to cause his comfortable status quo to drop dead on the spot. How *would* he handle her if she asked him for something really extreme?

And how would he handle his business partner and friend when Dean inevitably learned Kaspar had been diddling his wife? He knew Dean and Vanessa had been having problems recently, but all married couples did at one point or another. You could not live intimately with someone day in and day out for years without knocking heads occasionally. But his affair with Vanessa had nothing to do with the Corbins' problems. It had to do with the fact that when both Kaspar and Vanessa wanted something, they took it.

"My name is Josephine."

Kaspar was so caught up in his concerns he did not hear the child's voice until she repeated the sentence a second time.

"My name is Josephine."

He looked down. The girl from the roof was standing by his side and staring up at him. He flicked his cigarette away and gave her a thin false smile. "Hello, Josephine. You have a lovely name." Kaspar didn't like children but was always civil to them. He spoke to them as little as possible but always in the voice of an equal; if a kid didn't like it, too bad.

Josephine said, "Today is my last day."

"Your last day for what?"

"After today I go away forever. I don't know how or when, but today for sure. It's the last day I can help you."

Kaspar scratched his cheek and looked at a silver Porsche Cayman driving slowly down the street. "How do you know? You're pretty young to go away forever."

The girl cupped her hands and blew on them. "And you, Muba? How do you feel today?"

He reran the ridiculous name in his mind and closed one eye. "*Muba?* Or did you say 'mover'? What do you mean?" Kaspar now had a sinking feeling this was about to turn into one of those loony conversations you have with children after they've eaten too much sugar.

The girl touched her stomach. "Do you have owls in your bowels? I do. I know I'm not supposed to, but I do." She smiled and shrugged.

"*Owls?* Listen, Josephine, I have to go now. It's been nice talking to you." Kaspar Benn walked back into his store. At the counter he turned around and the little girl was standing right behind him. It was very strange because he had no sense of her following him in, but there she was, inches away.

The phone in his pocket rang. He let it ring once more before taking it out because he was trying to process what the girl had said. Between "Muba" and "owls in the bowels," he was so distracted it never crossed his mind not to answer the phone because it might be—"Hello?"

"Kaspar! Finally! Thank God. It's Vanessa. Look, we've got to talk. I think Dean left me this morning."

The little girl next to him began shaking her head. "Don't listen to her."

Frowning, Kaspar lowered the phone and asked exasperatedly, "Why not?"

"You've got other things to do."

He made a sour face while lifting the phone back up to his ear. "Why don't you come to the store, Vanessa? Dean's sledding up on the hill all morning and I'm here alone. I talked to him before and he told me about you two."

Vanessa gave a surprised *oh!* and then asked, "You talked to him? What did he say?"

"He said you two fought and things were dicey."

"Anything more? Did he say anything else?"

"No, not really. Just he was sledding and wanted to think things over up there before he made any decisions. He always says sledding is his therapy."

Josephine stared at Kaspar while he spoke. Her expression was disconcerting. He averted his eyes.

"I didn't see this coming, Kaspar, not at all. We've been having some arguments, sure, but I had no idea he felt like this. Really, it's the truth."

Before he could stop himself, the normally tactful Kaspar blurted out, "You *can* be a handful at times, Vanessa."

"I know, but still, he wants to *leave*?" She paused to breathe a few times. "Out of the blue he throws this bomb at me? We're supposed to talk about it first. You're supposed to talk things like this out before you make such big decisions. Right?"

"I don't know, Vanessa. I've never been married. It obviously depends on the people involved. Dean's a quiet guy. You never know what's going on with some quiet people . . ."

She expected him to continue but he didn't. She waited for him to say something more but he didn't. His silence held. "Kaspar?"

Nothing.

"Kaspar, are you still there? Did you get cut off?" Hearing nothing, she grimaced, ended the call, and tried his number again. But it just rang and rang unanswered on the other end.

Sitting in her car in the mall parking lot, Vanessa put the useless phone on the seat next to her and closed her eyes. "*Now what?*" she asked the empty space around her. She decided to do as he had suggested—go to the store and meet him there. Even a short conversation with her lover might help her regain some perspective, some balance now that all the gravity had suddenly evaporated from her life.

At his feet, Kaspar's cell phone burned brightly on a green throw rug under him. Speechless, he watched it crackle and hiss as the molten plastic bubbled and melted into a blob. Its parts twisted and fused together in the intense heat. One moment he'd been talking on that phone to Vanessa. The next, he was yelping against the fiery pain across his palm where he was holding it.

The little girl stood with a hand extended over the small blaze on the floor. He didn't realize until later that it did not burn the rug. When he eventually lifted the charred melted mess off the floor to throw it away, there was no mark—no blackened spot, no heat-scorched carpet pile.

"You can't be stupid today, Muba, not today. If you're not going to be smart on your own, then I have to help you because you've got to be very clever and think straight. You can't make any mistakes today."

Kaspar put his hand on top of his head as if to keep it from blowing off. "What the hell are you talking about? Who is 'Muba'? What do you *want* from me?" He was angry and beginning to be afraid.

He was forty-eight years old, thirty-one pounds overweight. Seven cashmere sports jackets hung in his closet at home. There were five different kinds of mustard in his refrigerator. He'd had two serious relationships in his life. Both women (smart and accomplished—real catches) had grown terminally frustrated with him and left in similar heartbroken huffs. He succeeded in small matters with almost no effort at all because of his great natural charm and the not-so-common ability to give something his full attention when it interested him.

But the few times in his life when the stakes had been high and he was put to the test, he'd always either chickened out or failed. It didn't bother him though because more often than not, Kaspar Benn was genuinely satisfied with things easy for him to obtain—good food, women who said yes more than they said no, elegant clothes that made him look and feel both more prosperous and attractive than he was.

Somewhere in our life's cast of characters most of us know a person like Kaspar. These people are fun to be around but not essential. If we don't encounter them for months or even years it doesn't matter. When they show up at a party, we think, oh good, I haven't seen them for ages. Often it's difficult to pinpoint when you last *did* see them or what you talked about. They are effusive in their greetings, entertaining; their many stories make you laugh and gasp—lots of flash and good fun. They're sort of like Italian variety shows on TV. But just like those shows, you forget about them quickly. Accused by one of his girlfriends of being facile, Kaspar said, "I make no pretense." She shot back, "No, you make no *effort*."

The little girl Josephine now said to him, "You have to go see Edmonds. You have to find him right now."

Kaspar didn't know what she was talking about. "Edmonds? Who's Edmonds?"

"William Edmonds. Find him and talk to him. He'll help you. He sent me to get you." She lifted her arm and looked at her yellow wristwatch. "You don't have any time to waste. Everything happens today. Find him."

Edmonds knew she would be there when he turned around but felt in no hurry to see her. Eating from a plastic cup filled with bland butterscotch pudding, he stared out the small window at his snow-covered backyard. He was hoping to see some birds but today there were none.

"Did you tell him?" he asked, with his back still turned to the girl.

"Yes."

"What did he say?"

"He was confused."

Edmonds sniffed the pudding. "I'll bet."

Josephine pulled her hair. "I did what you told me to do with his phone—I set it on fire."

"Good—it always gets people's attention."

"But why make me do it? Why couldn't I just tell him to come and talk to you?"

The gray-haired man put down the pudding. "People are like pigs lying in mud—nothing gets them to move except food or danger. I heard Kaspar Benn is a lazy guy. He needs encouragement."

"But you could have just asked him to come." Her voice was defiant, offended.

"True." Edmonds turned now and looked at the girl. Her face was solemn and set—she was prepared to argue with him about this. "Thanks for your opinion. Now go away."

She vanished.

Edmonds could not stop blaming himself for the death of his wife, although she'd died of liver cancer and there was nothing he could do about it but hold her hand while she wasted away. Eventually, when his remorse got so bad, he underwent analysis. His doctor said guilt was like a traffic light: A pedestrian comes to a red light. After looking both ways and seeing the coast is clear, he decides to ignore the warning and cross the street anyway.

Guilt is that traffic light. Stop—don't do this because it's dangerous/ bad/selfish . . . Don't smoke a cigarette. Don't have an affair. You think you're to blame for your wife's death. Seeing the red light, you recognize its warning. Then you must decide whether you want to go anyway. If you cross the street and ignore the warning, you don't think, oh no, what am I doing? Did I make the wrong decision by crossing? Should I go back and wait? Of course not—you move to the other side and keep walking. The analyst told Edmonds holding on to guilt is like carrying the red traffic light around with you, which is ridiculous.

So William Edmonds gradually learned to listen to his inner voices, consider what they said, and then make his decision. Now once he made up his mind on something he rarely looked back.

Today he'd needed the girl to convince Kaspar Benn to contact him. Mission accomplished. The fact the child didn't approve of his method was unimportant.

———————

"He's no filet mignon; he's not even *steak*. He's chuck roast, maybe. London broil at best."

This is how it began for Edmonds. It was the first thing he'd heard that morning after he sat down in the blue chair and looking out the window, asked himself, what the hell am I doing here? But he knew it was either get on the bus, or go home and kill himself. The choice was that stark and simple.

The big black and white bus sat parked at the curb with its motor running and gray exhaust fumes puffing out its pipes. The driver leaned against the side of the bus by the open door, smoking a cigarette and incuriously watching the crowd. A large group of old people stood on the sidewalk nearby, clearly waiting to board.

Earlier while walking down the street toward them, Edmonds smiled for the first time that morning when he noticed how dressed up all those oldies were. The women had high frozen hairdos that clearly indicated they'd just been to the hairdresser. Most of the men wore brand-new shoes with no creases or scuffs on them, and dark suits or perfectly pressed jackets. All of them appeared to be wearing neckties, despite the fact it was only six o'clock in the morning and their days of going to an office were long past.

Someone from the neighborhood had told Edmonds that once a month a bus parked at this spot, loaded up, and then rumbled off for a day's outing arranged by the town or a local senior citizens' club. It took pensioners to neighboring towns with museums or historical sites worth visiting. Sometimes they motored into the nearby national park, had a hike around, lunch, and then returned to this drop-off spot with some sun on their cheeks, tired legs, and the good feeling of knowing their cameras were full of new pictures and the day had meant something.

Approaching this crowd now, Edmonds was hit by thick waves of warring perfumes. He could imagine every single woman there spritzing on her favorite fragrance as she prepared to leave her house earlier this morning. Did the single women put on more perfume, hoping to catch the attention of the available bachelors who would be on the bus? Or was it the married gals who drenched themselves with scents so strong they almost physically stopped Edmonds when he was ten feet away? Were there many single people in this group? If so, were there more men or women? When you are sixty-five, seventy, seventy-five . . . are you still looking for a life partner or only a nice companion for the day?

The sight of all those dapper old people eager to be off on their day's jaunt wearing their wide neckties and thick-as-lead perfumes, together with the thought of actually *having* a partner on a trip when you were seventy-five years old, almost cut Edmonds in half with grief and longing for his lost beloved wife. The impulse to go home and finish it, end his life, was very powerful. End this unrelenting suffering and just go to sleep forever.

He had a friend who was a cop. This guy said if done correctly, hanging yourself was the best and most painless way to die. After many beers, he even demonstrated how to do it, not noticing his pal Bill was paying very close attention.

Edmonds would be alone when he was seventy-five, he was certain of it; if he even lived *that* long. There was always the good chance he'd contract some monstrous disease like his poor wife had, which would brutally devour his insides *before* killing him.

Passing the door of the bus, he spontaneously veered hard left and climbed on. The driver saw this but said nothing. Why did Edmonds do it? Who knows? Self-preservation, or just *why the hell not?* Maybe even a blissful, utterly unexpected moment of sheer lunacy?

He was the first passenger to enter the vehicle. Walking down the narrow aisle he chose an empty seat in the middle of the bus, plopped down into it, and turned to look out the window. The cold stale air in there smelled of cigarette smoke and some kind of chemical industrial something—cleaner or the synthetic cloth on the seats?

People began appearing at the front of the aisle. Some of them glanced at him as they passed; others eased themselves slowly and carefully into seats. Many grunted and puffed while doing it, their hands and arms shaking as they performed the twists and turns their stiff old bodies needed to make so they could land in the proper place. Edmonds too had reached an age where he found it harder getting into and out of chairs, cars, bathtubs, and other places where his body had to bend at unfamiliar angles in order to fit. He often groaned unconsciously now when sitting down—either from gratitude or weariness. Yet one more real sign he was aging and the wear and tear of time was beginning to gnaw in earnest on his body.

"He's no filet mignon; he's not even *steak*. He's chuck roast, maybe. London broil at best."

A very thin woman in a pink dress was walking down the aisle, her man right behind, talking loudly to her back. When she reached the two empty seats directly in front of Edmonds she glanced at him, moved sideways into the row, and sat down by the window. Her husband followed and took the aisle seat. You could tell by the fluid way both of them moved that they were very used to this seating arrangement.

"I don't know why you think so highly of him."

"Ssh, not so loud; the whole bus can hear you."

Her husband half-turned, glared at Edmonds as if he were to blame for something, and then turned back. "Okay, all right," he lowered his voice a tad. "But really, tell me what it is about him you like so much?"

The woman took her time answering. "I like how dignified he is. I admire the way he hides his pain. It's very . . . noble. Many people who lose their partners want you to know how hard it is for them being alone and what they're going through every day. They want your pity. But not him. . . . You know how bad he's hurting and what a loss it was for him. You can't be so close to someone all those years and *not* suffer when they die. But he never shows it, never burdens you with his pain."

Edmonds frowned. Who were they talking about? *It all sounded pretty damned familiar.*

The husband started to mumble something but she cut it off with a rushed "Ssh—he's coming. He just got on."

Edmonds looked up and saw an ordinary old man moving slowly toward them. On reaching the couple, he stopped and smiled. "Good morning, you two; ready for a little walking?"

"Good morning, Ken. Yeah, we're ready to go."

Ken smiled and moved on.

A few minutes later Edmonds turned and looked for the old man. He was sitting alone reading a newspaper on the long bench seat at the very back of the bus. Edmonds stood up, walked to the end of the aisle, and sat down next to him.

"Do you mind?"

"Not at all; it'll be nice having some company on this ride. I'm Ken Alford." He put out his right hand.

"William Edmonds."

Both men gave good strong shakes.

"Is it Bill or William?"

"Either—it doesn't matter."

"Okay, Bill. Would you like to share some breakfast?" Out of his coat pockets Ken pulled a cheese Danish wrapped in glistening plastic and a small red and white carton of chocolate milk. Edmonds gestured thanks but no thanks. Alford nodded, opened the milk, and took a swig. Carefully capping it again, he put it down on the seat between his legs. With his teeth he tore open the plastic around the pastry and took a big bite. It was clear he really liked what he was eating because he kept closing his eyes and making mmh-*mmh!* sounds deep in his throat.

Edmonds smiled. Ken looked and sounded like one of those actors on a television commercial loving some new breakfast food or chocolate bar that was being promoted.

"This is the first time I've seen you on here, Bill."

"Yes, it's my first trip."

"Well, some of them are good and some are boring, but there's always one or two worthwhile things to see."

A few moments later the front door hissed shut and the bus pulled slowly away from the curb. A few people here and there clapped.

"I lost my wife last year and that's when I started going on them. She didn't like to travel much, not even day trips, so we stayed pretty close to home. Then when she got sick . . ." Ken's voice remained steady and unemotional.

In contrast, Edmonds couldn't talk about his dead wife without tearing up or his voice catching in his throat every single time.

"Are you married, Bill?"

Edmonds looked at his hands. "My wife died too. Recently."

"Ahh, it's tough. I'm sorry for you." But Ken didn't sound sorry at all—if anything he sounded sort of . . . buoyant. "Hold on—I want to show you something." Stuffing the rest of the pastry into his mouth, he brushed the crumbs off his hands and reached into another pocket. This time he brought out a very sleek, quite beautiful folding knife. "Look at this—it's my Vedran Ćorluka." He held the knife out for Edmonds to take, but the other man only stared at him.

"Why do you call it that? Vedran Ćorluka is a professional soccer player."

Ken grinned and snapped his fingers. "Right! You're a soccer fan too.

Excellent. Yes, Ćorluka plays for the Croatian national team. But I call it that for a specific reason. This was the last Christmas present my wife gave me. I like pocketknives; I have a collection. But this one—well, you can see how especially nice it is. Nancy had it custom-made by a master craftsman in Montana. I liked it a lot when she gave it to me, but only after she died did I really start paying attention to it."

"Paying attention? What do you mean?"

"I went a little crazy after my wife died, Bill. We were married thirty-seven years and most of them were damned good. Did you have a good marriage?"

Edmonds nodded.

"Then you know what I'm talking about. Vedran Ćorluka was Nancy's favorite player. She didn't know beans about soccer, but just liked his name; she liked to say it. Whenever I was watching a game on TV, she always came in at some point and asked if *Vedran Ćorluka* was playing today.

"So that's why I named my knife after him. It was her last present and he was her favorite player: a perfect match. I always carry it now, no matter where I'm going or what I'm doing. When I get really depressed I just grip it tight in my pocket. It usually makes me feel a little better. It's my ground stone and makes some of the sadness go away."

"A really nice story, Ken. Can I see it again?" Edmonds took the knife and examined it closely. It was a fine-looking object. But he was distracted by what Alford was saying now.

"We don't pay enough attention to things in our lives, Bill. We know that, but we still don't do it. Only after something's over, or someone's dead, or we've lost them, or it's just too damned late do we realize we've been speed-reading life or people and missing all the great details.

"After my Nancy died, I decided to go back over everything we shared—the things we owned, the memories I had of her, the memories other people had of her. . . . But this time I gave it every bit of my attention. You know, I *re-viewed* it a hundred percent, like never before. It made such a difference, Bill!

"I can't be with my wife any longer because she's gone. But I can *know* her better than ever before—better than when she was alive. Whenever I pay really close attention to the details, I learn more about her all the time. I discover things I never knew or even thought about. It puts Nancy in a whole new light—like somehow I'm just meeting her for the first time.

"Sure it's a substitute for the real thing, but it's all I've got left of her. It's the best I can do." Ken took Vedran out of Edmonds's hands and said, "A couple of months ago I wrote the knife maker and asked if he had kept Nancy's letter ordering this. He returned it to me and I have it framed above my desk at home.

"See how beautifully the blade is carved? It's got perfect balance too. This kind of precision work has to be done by hand. All the best things in life are handmade, Bill: knife blades, bread, clocks, loving someone . . ."

When Edmonds got home later he sat down on the couch in the living room while still in his coat and looked around at the place for a long time. Where was his Vedran? What could he carry in his pocket that would always make him feel his wife's presence?

What was the last present she had given *him* before she died? And what was the last one he had given her? Ashamed, he could not remember either gift. But was it really important? If you live together with someone for six thousand days, so much is shared. Does it matter if you can't remember every little thing?

With this in mind, Edmonds walked around their house. When he saw something unfamiliar—a book or a porcelain figure, a knickknack— he picked it up and tried not to put it down again until he could recall where the object came from, who had bought or given it, the circum-stances, and how it came to become part of their lives.

There were many things—the blue and white porcelain music box from Amsterdam, the ball made of hematite her sister had given them, and the elephant carved out of amber he'd brought his wife from Poland. Had she liked it? Frustrated, he couldn't remember. It was kind of a kitschy object, but nice in its way. He stared at the small tawny animal while trying to remember the details, *any* details about the day he'd given it to her or what she'd said about it. But he could not remember even one thing.

There were so many blanks; his memory of their life was full of black holes. He reviled himself for having forgotten so much about his wife and their years together. How could it be? How could he have been so care-less? How could he have let so many precious particulars slip through the cracks? Memories of a genuinely happy life shared were the only real trea-sure Time permitted you to keep.

And what a deep personal insult to her memory to have forgotten so much! He lived in a house furnished with belongings that had decorated and enhanced their life. But now he could not remember where too many of them came from or why they were even there.

Humbled and dismayed, over the next days William Edmonds moved around his house like a tourist visiting a famous museum for the first time, only his guidebook was his flawed memories. Whenever he drew a blank looking at something, he studied the various objects until either their significance emerged or he realized his recollection of them was gone forever. He put all of those "dead" items in one corner of the living room and tried to avoid looking at them because every time he did, he despaired. He planned to move them all into a closet and not think about them until he had sorted through what he *did* know.

When a week had passed, a whole week, he called Ken Alford and asked one question. The two men had had a fine day on the bus hanging around together and talking about their lives. At the end of it they'd exchanged telephone numbers. Now after Alford answered the phone, Edmonds identified himself and got right to the point. "Ken, what if I can't find my Vedran? What if there's not a single thing I can hold on to and feel better because I know she's still in it, like your knife?"

"Oh, it's there, Bill; somewhere in your house, your life, or your memory, the Vedran is there. You just haven't found it yet. Sometimes it takes a while." The old man's voice sounded confident.

Edmonds lowered his head to his chest and pressed the receiver tightly to his ear. "But just the opposite's been happening, Ken: the more I look for it, the more I discover I don't remember. I don't remember *so much* . . . it's terrible. It feels like whole chunks of my brain have been cut out. In my own home I'm surrounded by things I neither recognize nor remember! But all of them were obviously part of our life together." Edmonds heard his voice at the end of the sentence and it sounded scared. He *was* scared.

Alford was silent a while but eventually said, "Maybe the first half of our life is meant for living, and the second half is for remembering—or trying to. When you consider it that way, both of us were wrong to waste time missing our wives so much after they died. Because mourning does no good: it only makes you feel helpless and lost.

"What we *should* do instead is try to remember and then savor whatever details we're able to dredge up from our past. This is possible and each time you do it you feel good because it brings something more of them back to you; like you're rebuilding them from scratch." Ken suddenly laughed. "It's a little bit like making your own Frankenstein version of your wife out of what you still remember about her." He chuckled again. "I'm being facetious, Bill, but you know what I mean. It's one of the reasons why I always keep the knife in my pocket: touching it reminds me to stop regretting and keep trying to remember."

While listening to Ken speak, Edmonds held the ocher-colored elephant and turned it over and over in his hand. He wanted it to speak too. He wanted it to recount exactly what happened the day he gave it to his wife. What *had* she said? What was she wearing? As Ken Alford talked, Edmonds closed his fingers around the elephant and silently mouthed the words, "Tell me."

Josephine appeared for the first time after his bus ride with Ken Alford. Edmonds had followed Alford's advice and tried finding his lost wife and their life together in everything he did. It was like an Easter egg hunt. In the most unlikely places he rediscovered memories or things about Lola he'd forgotten or knew that he knew. One afternoon while retrieving a jar of mango chutney off a shelf in the refrigerator, the sight of the thick brown condiment unloosed memories of the way she'd spread chutney on the bologna and Laughing Cow cheese sandwiches she often made them for lunch. While eating, she would wiggle one leg under the table like a fidgety child. She often did that—it was her unconscious way of showing she liked whatever it was she was eating. The leg wiggling—how could he have forgotten it?

Or once around Christmastime while walking down the street early in the morning, he'd looked up and seen a long white airplane contrail across the dawning sky. He suddenly remembered Lola loved contrails, and seeing this one brought her immediately to mind. Then Edmonds shifted his eyes a little to the left and on the balcony of an apartment was a small squat Christmas tree full of blinking white lights. It was exactly the same kind of tree and lights she would set up in their living room year after year. Edmonds was indifferent to the holidays but his sentimental Italian wife loved everything about them. A contrail and a Christmas tree in the sky at the same time? Suddenly he felt like she was very close and talking loudly to him, saying hello there, Pulcino—remember these things?

The little girl appeared an hour after he'd seen the Christmas tree on the balcony. Edmonds was having breakfast at the diner five doors down from Kaspar Benn's store. He ate breakfast there every day and always ordered the same thing: fried eggs, bacon, a plain donut, and hash brown potatoes. Two cups of coffee and the check, please.

While chewing a piece of bacon, he saw the girl enter the place holding a small plastic Christmas tree in her left hand. She walked to his booth and without asking permission sat down across from him. She put the tree on the red Formica table.

Neither of them spoke. Edmonds's eyes drifted between the shabby little tree, the room, and the girl while waiting for her to say something. She was nothing special to look at. She was pie-faced, and her expressionless eyes appeared to be green. Her lips were thin and pale. Was she smiling? He couldn't really tell. Her ears stuck out from her head a bit. She looked seven or eight years old. She wore a brown parka half opened and a red sweater beneath it that matched the color of the table.

"This is for you." She slid the little tree toward him. The branches and tiny ornaments shivered as it moved.

"Thanks. Who are you?"

"You can call me Vedran if you want."

Edmonds put down the piece of bacon he was about to eat and wiped his lips with a paper napkin he pulled from a silver dispenser on the table. "Did Ken send you?"

"Nope."

"I don't believe you. I think he did." Lifting his gaze he scanned the diner again, sure he'd see Ken Alford somewhere nearby just waiting to catch his eye. But Ken wasn't there. "Where is he?"

"Who?"

"Ken Alford."

"I don't know. Can I have a piece of your bacon?"

Edmonds slid his plate across the table to her. Right away she began gobbling up what was left.

"How do you know about Vedran?"

Having just swallowed, the girl said, "Lola told me."

"*Lola* told you?"

"Yes." She bit off another piece of bacon while looking him straight in the eye.

"When did she tell you this?"

"Today. Before I came here."

"*Today?*" Edmonds slid both hands up and down his thighs and took a long deep breath. "That's not funny. Whoever told you to say *that*, it's not funny at all."

"I don't think it's funny either. But you asked the question and I answered it."

"You talked to *Lola* today? My wife, Lola?"

"Yes."

"Lola's dead."

"Yes, she is."

This child with her plastic Christmas tree, eating his breakfast, saying she'd spoken to his dead wife.

"Who are you? What are you doing here? What do you want?" He spoke harshly, really irritated now, despite the fact he was talking to a child.

"Do you want to know about the amber elephant? The story you keep trying to remember?"

How could she know?

"You went to Krakow to meet up with old Marine friends who were stationed with you at the embassy in Warsaw. After you visited the Wawel

Castle, you were walking back to your hotel on Kanonicza Street and saw the store that sold nice amber things. You went in and couldn't decide between a necklace and the elephant. But you didn't want to spend much money so you bought her the elephant."

"My name's not really Vedran—it's Josephine. I only said Vedran to make you pay attention to me."

Josephine was the name Edmonds and his wife had chosen if they ever had a girl: Josephine for a girl, Nevan for a boy. Lola found the name "Nevan." Edmonds had never heard it before. It meant "little holy one" in Gaelic. It was the sort of thing Lola loved—strange, beautiful, and obscure. More important, they had never told anyone the names they chose for their children. Both thought if they did it would jinx their chances of it happening.

But they never were able to have children, although they tried for years. It had made Lola's death even more difficult for Edmonds to bear because when she was gone there was no physical trace left of her. A child; how wonderful it would have been to have had their child to hold his hand during those days of black grief after his wife's death.

"I'm here to stay with you now a while."

"What do you mean, *stay?*"

Josephine finished eating from his plate and licked her fingers one by one. "Lola was wearing her faded rose robe when you gave her the elephant. While she opened the package she kept looking at you and then the box. She was excited because she thought it was going to be something really good. She kept asking what was inside but you wouldn't say. When she saw what it was, you could tell how disappointed she was. Because the box was small, she was *hoping* you'd brought her a piece of jewelry, which she loved, like a nice ring or earrings. But there was only the dumb yellow elephant instead. She tried to pretend she liked it, but you knew she didn't. Lola wasn't very good at pretending, remember?"

Edmonds said nothing. Lola was terrible at pretending.

The girl stared at him, her expression saying nothing. "Do you want me to tell you other things?"

He didn't know what to say.

Afterward they left the diner together. The fifteen-minute walk back to his house was done in silence. Josephine didn't seem to mind. She skipped most of the way there, sometimes lagging behind, sometimes running way up ahead of him. Edmonds didn't notice. He looked at his boots mostly. Thick comfortable Red Wing boots he'd bought at a store in Seattle while visiting another Marine friend out there after he'd retired. That was what, six years ago? Seven? Time doesn't fly, it *steals*. Like some skilled pickpocket or magician, it gets you to look the other way and when you do, it ruthlessly steals your essential things—memories, great moments that end much too soon, the lives of those you love. It knows how to trick you and then steal you blind. What had he done on that Seattle trip? He couldn't really remember anymore except for a few silly details. Why hadn't Lola gone with him? He couldn't remember. He'd bought these boots. He'd bought these boots and eaten lots of fried oysters. And now here was this mysterious child telling him things about his own life he should have remembered but didn't.

While skipping along in front of him, the girl asked over her shoulder, "Do you remember anything?"

"What do you mean?"

"Tenbrink. Do you remember what that is?"

"Ten *what*? No."

"What about Pipetoe?"

Pipetoe?

When Edmonds didn't respond, Josephine craned her head forward and nodded slowly in an exaggerated way, as if he were very dumb and she was trying to encourage him to give the correct answer.

"What are you *talking* about?"

"Grassmugg or red slap? *The House Inside the Horse?* Come on, you've got to remember some of those things! No? Really? Wow. All right, forget it. Where were you born?"

Edmonds stopped walking. "New York."

"Where?"

"Doctors Hospital."

"When?"

"In 1949."

Josephine slapped her cheek in obvious exasperation. Turning away, she skipped off down the street. He could only follow her.

She was waiting on the porch of his house by the front door when he walked up the path.

He reached into his pocket for the keys. "Where's your Christmas tree? Did you leave it back at the diner?"

"No, it's inside on your kitchen table. I thought you would like it there."

Edmonds scowled but said nothing. Pushing her gently aside, he unlocked the front door with the key Lola had once used and walked into his house.

"There, look." Before he had a chance to turn around and see what she was talking about, Josephine had crossed the hall to the living room and walked over to a potbellied stove, an original Railway King he'd found years ago at a junk store and lovingly restored to its original condition. She took something off the top of the stove and turning to him, extended her hand.

She held a small aluminum coffeepot. An Italian Bialetti Brikka Lola bought on a visit to her home in Gallarate many years ago. It was one of his few truly treasured possessions because stained, streaked, and scratched as it was, it held the memories of thousands of breakfasts together, snow out in the yard, or the kitchen windows wide open to let the redolent summer breezes blow through, Lola's dark red lipstick on a white mug, her scratchy cigarette voice saying to him, "This morning I am *arrapata* for you. Come on, enough coffee, let's go back to bed."

Edmonds looked at the coffeepot and then at Josephine. Taking it out of her hand he placed it back on top of the stove. She snatched it off and jumped away from him when he reached for it.

"Give it to me. Come on, kid, don't fool around."

"Nope. You have to start thinking now. You really have to get going."

Edmonds's first impulse was to just grab the girl and get his damned coffeepot back. But her voice was so solemn and adult that it made him hesitate. "What do you *want* from me? What are you doing here?"

Ignoring his questions, she walked around the living room instead, stopping here and there to examine specific objects. All the while she held the silver Brikka to her chest with two hands as if it were a doll.

"This whole room is full of signs and reminders, Edmonds. Don't you recognize *any* of them? How can you not see?"

What she said made him feel both stupid and cross. It was not a good mix for this choleric man, especially coming from the mouth of a sassy eight-year-old child. "And you're totally annoying. How can you not see *that?*" he spat out.

"You were supposed to have a daughter named Josephine with Lola, but they decided against it. I'm sorry. It would have been nice for her to live here with you. I really like your house."

He heard what she said but could find no words to respond. His daughter, Josephine? *They?*

She put his coffeepot on a side table and sat down on the sofa. Her legs were so short they didn't touch the floor. "Do you want to know why not?

Because sometimes children touch a universal core. When it happens, you start remembering things. They didn't want you to remember anything . . . until now.

"All right, let's try this." Josephine went to the other side of the room and took an object off a shelf there. It was a small netsuke figure of a sumo wrestler. Holding it out on her open palm, she extended it in front of her toward Edmonds.

He looked at the little sumo and said, "Keebler."

The girl shook her head: she didn't understand what he was talking about.

"Lola called him Keebler. I don't know why. When she bought it she said that's what his name was. When I asked why, she said it's just Keebler."

Josephine put the brown figure down next to the silver coffeepot. "Do you see anything? Seeing the Keebler and your coffeepot sitting there next to each other like that?"

Edmonds studied the tableau a long time. "No."

Frustrated, Josephine rubbed both cheeks very fast with open hands. "This is going to take *forever*. Okay. We've got to get started."

Several months later Edmonds stood in his living room, thinking about what Josephine had just said about her visit to Kaspar Benn. Stretching his thick arms over his head, he alternately reached left/right/left/right for the ceiling. Then joining his hands together, he slowly stretched up till he heard a satisfying crack in either his neck or back—he could never be sure which one it was when he did this. He rolled his shoulders forward a few times, a few times back. He twisted his head hard left, then hard right, again and again until the tension in his neck muscles gave way a little.

Music came on from somewhere in the back of the house: Gershwin's *Cuban Overture*. Josephine loved music. Whenever she was up and about she had the radio or CD player on, often humming along loudly to whatever was playing.

The first few times the girl did this it jarred Edmonds because since his wife's death he was accustomed to a silent house. At the time it seemed right, a fitting tribute. Their home *should* remain quiet because Lola was the one who'd always filled it and their days together with both sound and life. Lola with her music and her singing, her banging around in the kitchen as she prepared their meals, or watching soap operas and game shows on the different TVs around the house. Sometimes she would have all three televisions on at the same time tuned to different channels.

Not only do you lose a person to death, but you lose their *noise* too—their noise and smells, gestures and facial expressions. You lose the way they talk and phrase things and laugh, the way they fill in your blanks without ever thinking about it or having to try. You lose things you love about them they don't even know they possess.

But eventually, sooner than he would have thought possible, William Edmonds grew to enjoy the sound of music again playing in the rooms of his house.

He remembered very vividly what was playing the afternoon he found out the truth about Lola. Again Gershwin, only that time it was "An American in Paris." Edmonds was drinking soup when it happened: thick, pulpy pumpkin soup with a squiggle of green pumpkin oil across the surface. He had cooked up a big batch of the soup and he, Josephine, and Keebler were all sitting at the table eating it for lunch.

Keebler still had not grown accustomed to his new large body. He moved very awkwardly and to the others' annoyance, *squeaked* all the time. Whenever he moved he sounded like lots of footsteps walking on old warped wooden floors. Edmonds oiled him daily but it did little good.

Keebler also couldn't get used to eating. Before he grew to human size, he had never eaten anything. He had never even opened his mouth, much less put anything inside of it. Why would he? Until recently he had been a two-inch-high netsuke figure sitting on a shelf. Then from one moment to the next he was transformed into a six-foot-tall, two-hundred-pound semi-human being with a fat guy's appetite. Josephine said this would change as he gradually transformed into a complete person. But at the time he was only a very large semi-man who wanted to eat constantly.

"This is good," Josephine said with a nod and a smile.

"Thanks. Lola liked it a lot too."

Keebler held his bowl in both hands and drank the soup in big loud gluggy gulps, despite the fact the stuff was just off the stove and piping hot.

"Doesn't it burn your throat when you drink it like that?"

"Why would soup burn my throat? It's not made of skin."

"Good point."

"She *didn't* like it though, you're wrong," Keebler said as he raised the bowl again to his mouth.

"What are you talking about?"

"Your wife, Lola; she *didn't* like this soup. She made a face every time you served it. She just didn't want you to know."

Josephine frowned at Keebler. She was beginning to think he enjoyed being cruel. She had seen example after example of his gratuitous meanness and she'd had enough. "Why do you say those things? What's the point? Why are you always so nasty?"

"I'm only telling the truth."

"Well, *eat* your truth. Nobody wants to hear it."

"She really didn't like my soup?" Edmonds was crestfallen. Lola taught him how to make *zuppa di zucca* based on her family's recipe. He'd always been very proud of it. "What didn't she like?"

"She didn't like anything you cooked."

"*Keebler!*"

The netsuke man looked at the girl. "Why don't you tell him, Josephine? Save us all time and just say it. Why are you coddling him? How much longer do we have to wait for him to get it? He's got to learn." Keebler walked over to the kitchen sink, bent down, and drank from the hissing faucet for a long time. When he was done he stood up and wiped his mouth with his fingers. "Because if you don't tell him, I will."

"Tell me what?"

"*Don't*, Keebler!"

"Your life was an illusion, Edmonds. The whole thing was a setup—Lola, this life, everything. You were manipulated."

"What do you mean, 'Lola was a setup'?" Edmonds's voice was a threat. "Explain that, Keebler. Tell me what you're talking about."

Josephine started to protest but Edmonds gave her a "shut up" look, and she did.

"Come on—tell me."

"There are these things called mechanics—"

"Talk about Lola."

"I *will*, but let me tell it my way." Keebler stepped away from the sink. "There are mechanics. They run things. They do their job for a while, some centuries usually, and then retire. Or rather they *have* to retire—it's the rule."

Edmonds glanced at Josephine as if expecting her to clarify what he'd just heard. She held up a finger for him to wait.

"When they're finished, when they're retired, some are transformed into humans. As soon as it happens they forget everything about their past existence. They're given new lives as human beings of all ages—some are made young, others are middle aged like you, it varies tremendously. They try to place you where they think you'll be most content. This new life was created specifically for you and it was complete down to the last microscopic detail. Even the real human beings who interact with you believe you've always been here. One day you blinked and when you opened your eyes again you were Bill Edmonds, retired tree surgeon.

"All retired mechanics spend the rest of their days in these second lives until they die natural deaths. Lola was part of the new life made for you."

"*What?*" Incredulous, Edmonds looked again at the little girl. She wouldn't make eye contact.

"She was another piece of your second life."

"Bullshit! Prove it." Edmonds had his back to the hallway. Rather than answer, Keebler lifted his chin to indicate the other turn and look behind him. Edmonds hesitated but turned.

Lola stood four feet away, wearing his black-and-green wool mackinaw coat. But this Lola was twenty-seven years old, her age when they'd first met. The year she dyed her red hair white and cut it very short, like it was now. The coat she was wearing he had bought for himself two years before she died. She'd loved it the moment she saw it and with his permission, made it her own. So here in front of Bill Edmonds was young Lola wearing a coat her older self had on the week before she died in the hospital at forty-six years old. She had even asked to be buried in it.

Edmonds did not move toward his wife. He did not reach out and try to touch her. He did not know what to do. She was dead. Only in the last months had he finally begun to accept the fact Lola *was* gone forever. Even his mulishly stubborn heart had now admitted it was true—*she was dead.* But in an instant here she was again, only looking like she did when they'd first met decades ago. The time when he fell so hard in love with Lola Dippolito that it felt like he was a character in a cartoon with little hearts and chirping birds floating drunkenly around his head.

Lola said in a low, tremulous voice, "I'm sorry, Pulcino, but it's true. Everything Keebler said is true. You *are* a mechanic. Or you were, before you got retired. But they need you again, Bill. They need you to do something for them. It's why all of us are here—Josephine, Keebler, and me—we're all here to help. It's why he's telling you these things, even though it's a bad way to find out. I know, Bill—it *is* terrible to have to learn the truth about these things after all you have gone through. You don't deserve such a shock."

William Edmonds looked at his young dead wife, the netsuke man, then at Josephine. "These things really do exist? These mechanics?"

All three of them nodded at different speeds. Edmonds looked at his beloved Lola. A week after she died he was so staggered, so deranged by her loss, that he had walked into the closet where her clothes still hung and masturbated while weeping for her. How could any of this be true?

Lola stepped forward and gently touched his arm. He looked at her hand and saw the tattoo of the blue accordion there she had gotten while on their honeymoon trip to San Francisco. "This is the life you wanted, Bill. It was what you asked for when they retired you."

"What did I ask for?"

"Love. You wanted to be loved fully and deeply until you died."

"But *you* died and I was all alone, Lola!"

She answered gently, soothingly—as if speaking to a hysterical child. "It was their first step toward bringing you to this moment. They knew you would never leave here as long as I was around." Her hand tightened on his arm. "They understood how much you loved me."

Edmonds pulled away from his wife. He snatched his arm back as if she had no right touching him. "And did you love me, Lola? Was it real? What am I supposed to believe now?" He spread both arms as if to take in the entire world around them.

"It's the life you asked for," Josephine said from over in a corner of the room. "You told them what you wanted—"

"Down to the last detail," Keebler added.

Josephine continued. "And they created it just for you. This is it. But can I ask one thing? Didn't it bother you at all when I came to live here? And Keebler—remember the first time you saw him alive and how big he had grown? You weren't surprised, not a bit. You just accepted it all.

"Any other person would have freaked out but not you, Edmonds. Haven't you *ever* thought about it? Haven't you wondered about your calm reaction to so many crazy impossible things happening in your life?

"It's because you're *used* to them, or were when you were a mechanic. There was a time things like this were a normal part of your everyday life. So when you see them now you don't care. Me moving into your house, Keebler . . . one minute he was a four-centimeter-tall figure on a shelf. The next he's sitting at the table eating your soup. Normal people would go crazy if any of this happened to them, but you didn't. Don't you get what it *means*, Edmonds?"

FOUR

"Bill Edmonds? Sure I know him. Nice old guy, but nutty as a can of cashews. I mean *really* crazy. His wife died a few years ago and he's never been the same since. It sent him into a total tailspin; it's very sad. I've known him a long time and he always was a good guy. He still is, but now you've got to take everything he says with a pound of salt."

Kaspar Benn sat at the counter of the same diner where Edmonds had first encountered Josephine. Kaspar was talking to Nathan Ballard, the owner of Out of Order, the town bookstore. Ballard's shop was three doors down from Kaspar's so the two men often bumped into each other here in the morning, when they both ate breakfast.

"Where does he live?"

"Bill? He's got a house out at the end of Salt Pond Road. You can't miss it because it's bright red and white. I think he repaints the place every year. It looks like the kind of perfect toy house you'd see on an electric train layout."

"And what about the little girl? Is she his daughter?"

"What girl?" Nathan looked at Kaspar quizzically and shook his head as if to say he didn't know what he was talking about.

"The little girl who . . ." Kaspar pictured the mysterious child who'd burned his cell phone and insisted he contact Edmonds.

"Bill lives alone. As far as I know he has no children and I've known him twenty years."

"What does he do for a living?"

"He used to be a tree surgeon up until a few years ago. Then he fell out of a tree during an ice storm and cracked his skull pretty badly. That was the end of it for him. A few months later his wife died of cancer. Poor guy; it was like a one-two knockout punch." Ballard shook his head and sipped his coffee. "People who know Bill can't agree if it was the accident or Lola's death that sent him around the bend."

"What kind of crazy do you mean, Nathan?"

"Well for one, Bill carries a little carved figure in his pocket he calls Keebler. Don't ask me why. I think it's Japanese or something. Sometimes he puts it on the counter here and talks to it while he's eating."

"Yikes!"

"Yeah, exactly—yikes. Ava—tell Kaspar about Bill Edmonds."

Ava Mount, the owner of the diner, had come by to refill their coffee cups. "Bill? He's a nice guy. A little bit bonkers, but hey, aren't we all? He always orders exactly the same breakfast every morning. Know why? Because it's what his wife cooked him when she was alive. I think it's very sad and sweet."

"But is he crazy?"

Ava glanced at Nathan, and after hesitating a moment they both nodded.

"Well, I've got to go see him today about something. I've never heard of the guy before. I guess from your description I'd better call before to let him know I'm coming."

Ava put down the coffeepot. "Wait a minute. I just remembered—I'll show you something." She walked back into the kitchen and returned shortly with a large photograph in her hand. She put it on the counter between the two men. Pointing to someone in the picture she said, "That's him. That's Bill last Christmas here at the diner with Lola. She was his wife. We were having our Christmas party and the place was packed."

Glancing at the picture, Kaspar did a dramatic double take when he noticed a woman sitting in the booth along with Edmonds and his wife. Sweeping the photo up in his right hand he brought it closer to his face and gaped, incredulous. "*No WAY!*" He looked at Ava and then at Nathan. His eyes were enormous. "*Jezik?* It's not possible!" Before the others could say anything, Kaspar Benn rushed out of the diner without paying for his coffee.

Vanessa Corbin arrived at her husband's store a few minutes after Kaspar had run out of the diner on his way to William Edmonds's house. When she found the door to the store was locked and a CLOSED sign hung in the front window, she nearly lost it.

Generally speaking, spoiled people have an almost psychic knack for finding others who will indulge them. Vanessa was a prime example of this. For years her husband, Dean, had spoiled her rotten because he loved her. Jane Claudius grudgingly spoiled her because she needed Vanessa to continue singing in her bar. And Kaspar Benn spoiled her because her way of making drama out of everything tickled him most of the time, plus he loved her cooking.

But today no one had spoiled her—just the opposite. Dean announced he wanted to break up. On hearing this news, Jane Claudius stared at Vanessa like she was no more than a pathetic loser. And Kaspar hadn't even cared enough to meet her here although he'd said he would, while knowing full well she was in the middle of a ferocious red zone meltdown crisis.

"What are *you* doing here?" A very familiar but unwelcome voice behind her made Vanessa stiffen and grimace. How perfect! Exactly what she did *not* need now.

Steeling herself, she managed to say, "Is there a new law today saying I'm not allowed to be here?" she asked before turning slowly around with as much hauteur and dignity as she could muster. It wasn't very much though because hearing her husband's voice so unexpectedly made her tremble.

Dean stood nearby with hands on hips, mouth tight, his face one big neon sign of irritation. "Did you come here to see me? You heard what I said about not meeting up again till tonight."

"No, I didn't come here to see *you*; I came to see Kaspar. I just wanted to talk to him."

"About *what?*" He took a step toward her. Was it some kind of challenge? She remembered the cup of very hot coffee she'd thrown at him.

"He's my friend too, Dean. You don't *own* Kaspar just because he's your partner." At that molten lava emotional moment, she wanted to blab everything; she wanted to spit the truth about her affair with Kaspar Benn right in her husband's face.

"*Talk about what, Vanessa?*"

"Oh okay, let me think. Hmm. Well, we could start with my husband *leaving* me. What do you think, Kaspar? You know Dean pretty well. Why do you think he wants to do it just, like, out of the blue?"

Dean didn't respond. He didn't say a thing. He stared over his wife's shoulder into the store. He must have seen something interesting in there. Pushing her brusquely aside, he turned the handle and strode in without another word.

"I'm still talking to you!" Vanessa wasn't about to let him just walk away. She followed him right into the store.

A few steps across the threshold, both Dean and Vanessa Corbin stopped, paralyzed by what they saw. It was so impossible and completely wrong that Vanessa instinctively moved closer to her husband for protection, although against *what* exactly she didn't know.

The name of Dean's business was "Benn Corbin." Before it became a luxury men's store, it was one of the town's two magazine and candy shops. People bought their daily newspapers there, cigarettes and pipe tobacco, chewing gum and chocolate bars. Kids were always loitering around the store looking at the car, sports, music, or movie magazines while waiting for something more interesting to happen in their lives. The previous owner decided to retire about the time Dean and Kaspar began looking for a commercial space in the middle of town. The sale was arranged quickly and to everyone's satisfaction.

But the partners felt real sadness when they gutted the place to turn it into "Benn Corbin." Both men prized the funky vintage 1950s feel of the store. The uneven, deeply scratched and scuffed pumpkin pine floors; fifty-year-old cast-iron wood-burning stove; the cheap magazine racks and metal shelves the color of oyster shell carrying an array of disparate objects no one wanted but which nonetheless had never been moved or taken down because the owner was too lazy or he wasn't even aware those things were still on display. Things like six-year-old comic books and dull Hallmark greeting cards, yellowed and bent paperback novels by the likes of Fletcher Knebel, Calder Willingham, and Roderick Thorp. The small faded red-and-white cardboard display that still held two cheap yellowing Timex watches on it. And a slightly sinister-looking toy kangaroo that, when wound up, banged furiously on a tiny drum. There were Wiffle balls and bats, and a large plastic Revell model of the aircraft carrier USS *Forrestal*. Dean got a kick out of the fact old Ayres, the previous owner, had painted the brick walls white to brighten up the place rather than spend a few dollars more to install good lighting.

After buying the store, the men had the wooden floors sanded and sealed until they glistened and glowed a deep rich honey brown. The white was stripped off the walls, returning the bricks to their original terra-cotta color. Finally, the new owners paid thousands of dollars to install state-of-the-art lighting so everything in there, especially the clothes on display, looked exceptional.

Ayres was invited to the grand opening of Benn Corbin, but shortly after walking in and seeing what they had done to his store, it was plain the previous owner was at first dismayed and then genuinely upset at the transformation.

"Everything's gone, even the smell. You took away the *smell* of my store!" The old man didn't have to say anything more. Dean and Kaspar knew exactly what he was talking about.

Ayres's news store had had a distinct aroma all its own. Whether it was nice or not was debatable. A combination of fresh printer's ink on newspaper, mildewed cloth, decades of tracked-in mud and dirt (depending on the season), candy, summer dust, winter slush, body odor, cigar and cigarette smoke, hot sulfur from just-lit matches, and an array of other unidentifiable but strong ingredients. All of them had accumulated, accreted, and emulsified in the store for decades, creating a distinctive odor instantly familiar to anyone who frequented the place. For better or worse it was a smell you knew in an instant.

When Dean and Vanessa walked in that morning, the aroma of Ayres's store was the first thing to meet them. The delicately delectable smells of the various Diptyque scented candles used in the swank Benn Corbin were no longer there. They had been blotted out completely by the signature stench of the old news store.

More surprises were waiting for the Corbins, many more, but the fusty odor was the first clue. It was as strong and pervasive as it had once been; it hogged all the air in the room. Of course such a singular smell did not belong in the home of handmade suits from Naples and Scottish cashmere scarves costing as much as a small car.

After the seconds it took their brains to identify the tang, the couple was faced with the next impossible fact: Benn Corbin no longer existed. The store had somehow transformed back to old Ayres's newspaper shop.

Dean had glimpsed it through the front window over Vanessa's shoulder when they'd stood outside on the sidewalk arguing. Naturally he couldn't believe what he saw, so he pushed his wife aside and opened the door to investigate.

Everything was gone—the luxurious clothes, the custom-made mannequins from Antwerp, the antique walnut display cases, the Mission furniture, the overall *lightness* of the store they had so carefully planned and created. Instead, the Corbins were now surrounded by a dark, dank, dumpy dated shop that sold stale Hershey bars and three copies of *Road & Track* magazine a month.

"What *is* this?"

"I don't know."

"What *happened* here?"

"I don't know, Vanessa. I don't . . . know."

"Where are all the clothes? Where is your *store?*"

He didn't answer because he had no answer. Instead, Dean walked into his store and began looking around, looking at various objects in there, looking for answers and clues, possible reasons for why and how this had happened.

Vanessa was too afraid to move. She stayed right where she was, a few feet into the shop, close enough to the exit so if something worse happened she could flee fast.

Dean kept moving, touching things and sniffing the air like a curious animal on a scent. As always he seemed unruffled. Watching from a distance, Vanessa loved his ability to stay calm and resolute when all she wanted to do was scream and run.

Out of nowhere she remembered a note Dean had written to her years ago after they'd first begun sleeping together. "There is the morning and there is you. On the good days, the best days, I have both." She didn't know if she loved her husband anymore, but *parts* of her still loved parts of him, and isn't this love too? Does it have to be everything to qualify for that holiest of words? In this particular situation there was no one on earth she'd rather have been with than calm, clear Dean Corbin, life's premier problem solver.

"We're leaving. I don't even begin to understand this. Let's find Kaspar. Maybe he'll . . ." Dean took out his phone and gestured for Vanessa to wait while he dialed. He stared at a white wall while waiting for the call to connect, but it didn't. Looking at the telephone screen, he saw there was no signal. He tried again but the screen still said no. "Okay, let's just go. I'll call from outside."

Vanessa was close enough to the door so all she had to do was turn, take three steps, and her hand was on the knob. Turning it, she opened the door and stepped outside. But Dean didn't follow. Looking over her shoulder, she saw he was looking across the room. A man came into view from the back of the store, wiping his hands on a cloth.

"Hello. Can I help you folks?"

At first she didn't know him. Then she did: it was Whit Ayres, the former owner of her husband's store. She hadn't recognized him because this man was thirty years younger than the old grouch she used to buy her newspapers and fashion magazines from when they first moved to town. But this Whit Ayres had a full head of spicy red-brown hair sprouting willfully out in all directions. He was sort of handsome in a 1960s hippy, *Whole Earth Catalog* way. To fit the part he even wore a plaid flannel shirt and brown Carhartt work pants. In contrast, the old Ayres she knew always wore the same outfit—a threadbare tweed jacket, chambray shirt, and black jeans faded almost to gray.

The Ayres she knew also had a face as wrinkled as an unironed handkerchief and a mouth that said no without ever having to say it. A grumpy fussbudget, a peek-sneaker at your breasts when he thought you weren't looking; the old guy never deigned to say hello or thank you for anything.

"Sir, were you looking for anything in particular?"

"Are you Whit Ayres?"

The man's face changed. It softened when he heard his name spoken. "Yes, I am. Do we know each other?"

Dean ignored the question. "Can I ask how long you've been here? How long you've had this store?"

Ayres looked toward the ceiling a few seconds as if calculating and then said, "Twelve years."

"*Twelve* years? Only twelve?"

"Correct. Why do you ask? And how do you know my name?"

Dean stared at him in silence. Ayres smiled but said nothing either. The silence went on until it became uncomfortable. Vanessa tugged on her husband's sleeve. "Come on, honey, we've got to go." She'd never called him "honey" in their entire married life.

At last Dean started to move but stopped again to pick up a copy of *Esquire* magazine on display nearby. He looked at the cover, looked some more, and then held it out for Vanessa to see while he pointed to the date. It was thirty years old. Putting it down, he picked up a copy of a *Field & Stream* magazine and again pointed to the date on its cover—thirty years ago.

Vanessa shook her head. How was it possible? What did it mean?

"Could you tell me the date today, please?"

Ayres looked at a *New York Times* beneath his hand and said, "February 3."

"And the year?"

"The *year*? It's 1979."

"Right. Well, thank you. We have to go now, but we'll be back."

"You didn't say how you know my name."

"The sign over your front door: 'Newsland—proprietor W. Ayres,' right?"

"Riiiiight, but how did you know the 'W' meant Whit?"

Dean waved at him and took Vanessa by the arm. "A lucky guess. Thanks again." He hurried them both out of the store and onto the sidewalk. As soon as they were there Vanessa freed her arm from her husband's tight grasp.

"How did you know about the sign?"

His back to the store, Dean pointed over his shoulder and up with his thumb. Above the front door was a long white rectangular sign with forest green lettering: NEWSLAND—PROPRIETOR W. AYRES. "We almost kept his sign on a wall in the store after we renovated. But Ayres wanted it back."

Vanessa glanced at the sign, then at her husband. "But how did you know it was there?"

"It was up when we bought the place. If the old store is back the way it was, I assumed his sign would be too."

"What are you going to do now, Dean?"

"Find Kaspar and hope maybe *he* knows what the hell is going on here." Dean took out the phone and called his partner's number again. Nothing. "Maybe he's having breakfast. He usually is around this time of morning, which means he'll be at the diner. Let's go there first." Without another word Dean walked away. Vanessa hurried after, not given time to think if his abrupt departure was an insult or just that he was preoccupied.

A few minutes later they left the diner after having learned Kaspar had been there earlier and was probably at Bill Edmonds's house now. They walked back toward Dean's car.

"Do you know this Edmonds? I think I know him from the bar." Vanessa was two steps behind her husband as they moved down the sidewalk. Keeping up with his quick pace was always difficult.

"I've heard the name before, but I've never met him, no. This is about to change."

They passed Dean's store on the way to the car. He stopped and stared in the window. It looked the same as it had minutes before. Ayres was out of sight but inside it was still dark, full of dusty jumble and junk and magazines dated 1979.

"You see what's in there don't you, Vanessa?" Dean pointed at the store window. "You saw what it was like in there before, right? I'm not nuts? What I saw was real and I'm not just hallucinating?"

Vanessa nearly didn't recognize her husband's voice. It was needy and perplexed at the same time. It asked but also demanded to know—you saw the same things I saw, *right?* His tone of voice clearly indicated Dean was afraid she might say no, I don't know what you're talking about. You're the only crazy person around here, husband.

"Yes, Dean, I saw it too. Your store is gone. Ayres *was* young. I don't understand any of it either."

He nodded, clearly relieved. "I passed here this morning on my way to sledding. I drove by and looked at the place as I always do—my little visual hello. Everything was all right then. Everything was as usual."

"Let's go find Kaspar, Dean. Maybe he does know something that'll help. Come on." She spoke gently while tugging on his sleeve.

"Yeah, okay."

This time Vanessa led the way. She kept hold of Dean's jacket as he followed behind, sometimes looking back over his shoulder to make sure his store was still there.

Jane Claudius loved this part of her run. The long glide down Stadion-kade Road, 'round a wide soft corner at the bottom, then hit the straight-away, usually not worrying about traffic because few cars came out here at this time of morning.

The frigid invigorating air was full of an array of winter's best smells—woodsmoke, wet earth and stone, a moment's heavenly whiff of something baking nearby. She pictured the baker hot and sweaty from her work, throwing open a window to let in a rush of icy air to cool the kitchen. Jane inhaled it all in grateful gulps and gasps.

She had found her right rhythm now. Her breathing and footfalls were in synch, her arms sawing easily back and forth as she jogged home from the mall with the new skating helmet in her backpack. Of course she would have preferred to be on Rollerblades, but the roads were still cov-ered with snow and wicked patches of ice hid everywhere, so she jogged in her winter boots, which always made Felice smile and call her G.I. Jane.

As was often the case when she exercised, Jane felt bulletproof. Even if a car were to come out of nowhere now and hit her square on, she had the feeling she would fly unhurt through the air like a trapeze artist, land gracefully on her feet again, and keep running: yet another reason why she loved to exercise. It was really the only time of day when she stopped thinking altogether and just *felt*. If she was feeling right, if her body was loose and frisky, she was wholly content. Felice joked it was the only satori a middle-class woman in a pair of sneakers could ever achieve. As soon as Jane stopped moving (skating, jogging, speed walking) her brain began chattering again and immediately took over full operations.

So it took some time for her to register and then distinguish the smell of a different kind of smoke in the air. The first smell of something burning had been winter-friendly—woodsmoke from a chimney, a nice blaze going in a fireplace, sitting in a comfy chair while chatting, reading, or staring peacefully deep into cozy tame flames.

But this new smoke smell was brutal, repellent. It was not fragrant wood burning, although wood might have been part of the mix. Mostly it was chemicals on fire—rayon curtains, carbon fiber; the bitter odor of fake things melting—plastic, linoleum, Fortrel carpet; an acrid nasty stink punched your nose. The face recoils in disgust even before the brain registers what's going on. When you get it, when you understand what the smells probably mean, it scares the hell out of you. Because you realize something big and wrong is on fire—like a house or a car—something you know should never be burning.

Alarmed, Jane slowed and stopped. Looking around, she didn't see anything suspicious at first. Then farther off down the road to the right there it was—the smoke—and it wasn't far away.

She started jogging toward it, patting a side pocket to make sure her phone was there in case she needed it.

Sometimes Jane Claudius was good in emergencies, sometimes not. She was *very* good at faking things, at putting on the right composed face and attitude in a crisis so people *thought* she was in control, but frequently she wasn't. What about now? What would she do when she got to the fire?

Call the fire department? The police? What if people were hurt? She felt for the phone again. At least she had it to help her.

Down the road, she ran diagonally across someone's front yard and then onto another smaller road that went in the direction of the smoke. Maybe she should call the fire department right now. But what if they'd already been called and trucks were on the way?

It didn't matter. You can never be too careful about emergencies— Jane realized she was only looking for an excuse to stop moving and not go any farther, even if it meant only for a minute or two. She did not *want* to reach the fire and have to act.

Enough of this: Get going. Get *moving*. Hating herself for hesitating, for being a coward when someone near might need her help, she started running again.

She could really smell burning things now—the caustic odor owned the air, pushing away all others. Her heavy boots on the snow-covered ground made almost no noise, yet everything sounded loud—her footfalls, birdsong, the sound of her breath pumping out, a plane flying by overhead (she wondered for a second if looking down from up there in the sky the passengers could see the smoke). A motorcycle growled along on the road behind her. Could the rider smell the smoke too? How great it would be if the biker caught up and accompanied her. But to her dismay she heard the machine move off into the distance. The sound of its motor grew fainter and fainter until it was gone.

She saw this now: a small bright red house set back from the road a ways. The roof was smoking and then flames shot out from the side of the building. Two men stood in front of the house with their backs to the road. Neither of them was moving, which struck her as very strange. Why weren't they doing anything? Why weren't they trying to put out the fire?

At least no one was hurt. She ran toward them. If they were both just standing she assumed they were the only ones who'd been inside the burn-ing building. She called out, "Is everyone all right?" The larger of the two men turned around. She stopped abruptly when she recognized him. "Kaspar?"

"Jane! What are you doing here?"

"Jogging. What's going on? Have you called the fire department?" The only thing she could think to do next was point to the fire.

The other man turned around and she knew him too. He often drank at her bar. "Bill! Is this your house?"

"Hi Jane. Yes, but it's okay. We got out safely. Everything else is okay."

Confused and frightened she managed to ask, "You were the only ones inside?"

"Yes."

And then without warning their world disappeared. Although Jane and the two men remained, everything else around them vanished: the landscape, sky, all smells and sounds . . . everything except them.

It was as if they stood now on an empty stage or in the middle of a dimly lit tunnel. There was light but nothing else around them, absolutely nothing. All three looked around in that weak light, trying to find some clue, sign, or indication of what had just happened. Where were they? Seeing nothing anywhere, they looked at each other.

"What is this? What happened?" Jane asked the men.

Bill Edmonds shook his head but said nothing.

"Kaspar?"

"I don't know. Where'd everything go?"

"There's no sounds either, just us. Did you notice?"

"Or smells—the air doesn't smell of anything, nothing."

Without a word Kaspar walked away into the shadows. The other two exchanged glances. Jane nodded—maybe it was a good idea. Maybe something out there in the gloom would explain this: something that would clear up this impossible mystery. They took off in opposite directions.

But nothing was out there. More "stage," more emptiness and faint sad light illuminating only this bare new world so unexpectedly thrust on them.

In time Jane and Edmonds returned to where they'd been. But Kaspar stayed away. They first thought maybe he'd found something. Then they thought, what if he doesn't come back?

"Bill, what did you mean when you said, 'Everything is okay'? Back there when your *house* was burning? Right before this—" Jane put out a hand to indicate the emptiness around them.

Bill squinted at her. She could see he was deliberating whether to speak or not.

"*What?* What do you know?"

Instead of answering he asked quietly, "Is this yours, Jane? Is it your dream?"

The questions were so odd and out of context. She could only shake her head, not knowing what he was talking about, waiting for him to say something else to clarify things. Seconds passed before she demanded, "What do you mean? What are you asking?"

He stared at her, adding things up in his head. "It makes sense. Just as it started burning, just after we got out of the house, *you* appeared out of nowhere. Why? It's a hell of a coincidence, wouldn't you say?"

Jane shook her head again. "What are you *talking* about?"

Bill stared at her, his face giving no indication of what he was thinking.

Kaspar reappeared out of the shadows and said, "My guess is they woke up. It's why we're here; it's why everything disappeared. Whoever's dreaming all this woke up and left us here. We're still somewhere in their head, but just the basics—just us and nothing else.

"You know how when you wake up at night to go pee after having had a strong dream? You carry it with you to the toilet. Not all of it, but enough. Look around us—maybe this is all that's left of someone's dream." Kaspar grunted. "Let's hope they're only taking a piss and haven't woken up for good. And let's also hope if they *do* go back to sleep afterwards they don't start dreaming about something else. Because then kids, we're cooked; we might all just be about to disappear for good."

"How do you know this, Kaspar? How can you tell?" Bill sounded like a worried child asking his father if the thunder outside would pass.

"I don't know if I'm right. It's all a guess, but it makes sense if it *is* a dream. Think about it—where do dreams go after we wake up? They've gotta go somewhere in our head. Some great big dream storage locker we all have."

Jane stepped forward. "You're saying everything—all this and everything before—is a *dream*? That's what you believe—it's all a dream?"

Kaspar nodded, looking straight at her. Yes, he was sure.

"How do you know?"

"I'll tell you more about it if we get out of here. If we don't, there's no point explaining it because we're finished anyway."

"But whose dream *is* it?"

Kaspar smiled and shrugged. "I don't know. You've asked the big question. It could be mine, yours, Bill's . . . or even someone else who knows all three of us. If we knew who, it might make understanding things simpler—or not."

As quickly as it came, it was gone. Which only made matters worse. Moments before, the Corbins had been held fast in some gray-lit twilight zone mysterious nowhere/what-the-hell-*is*-this land.

How did they get there? Not a clue.

An instant later they were standing in the middle of wide open spaces on an unfamiliar country road with a large black leather desk chair between them.

How did they get *there*? Not a clue. The air smelled heavily of newly laid asphalt, dung, and ripe plowed earth.

They had started out driving to Bill Edmonds's house to find Kaspar through a gorgeous snow-covered winter morning. Now they were surrounded by vast flat green fields and a high-summer afternoon. They were clueless, trying to make sense of anything and everything.

Both of them wore goose down parkas and winter boots. Vanessa also had on a Russian sable fur hat with long earflaps, which made her look particularly ridiculous on such a hot sunny day.

"I don't know," Dean said.

"You don't know *what?*"

"How we got here. So don't ask."

"Thank you, husband; thanks for being so sympathetic today."

Dean's voice rose. "I don't know what else to say, Vanessa. You were going to ask if I knew what this is, right? But I don't. I just said it because I know you were going to ask."

"You're wrong." She pulled off the large hat, shook her hair, and began to wiggle-waggle out of her coat. "I was going to ask what's with this chair." Her voice was snooty and dismissive.

They looked at the big black chair as if it were a third person waiting alongside them for someone to explain what was going on.

A horn honked nearby. Hurrying off the road, Dean pulled the chair behind him like a parent pulling his child to safety. Luckily it was on wheels, although the back two were squirrelly. It wobbled like a wonky supermarket cart all the way. Seconds later a shiny blue Chevrolet pickup truck rushed past, the driver not even glancing at them as he powered off down the road.

"Thank you."

"For what?" Dean asked warily. He was sure Vanessa was going to whip another nasty zinger at him.

"The chair said that, not me. I was just telling you what it said—thanks for pulling it off the road."

Dean semi-smiled. Maybe this was his wife's way of apologizing for being bitchy. Say the chair thanks you for saving it from being hit by a truck. It was a weird but cute enough way to reboot their conversation in a different direction. He decided to say nothing and just move on.

Taking off his coat, he dropped it on the seat of the chair. "I don't understand any of this, Vanessa. Maybe if we find some people from around here they can tell us something. I think we should just keep walking on this road and either flag down the next car, or hope we meet up with someone along the way. What do you think?"

"Don't you remember?"

"Remember what?"

"The talking chair—Blackwelder."

Dean's eyes panned from his wife to the chair and back to Vanessa again. "No."

"*Blackwelder*—from *The House Inside the Horse*, the kids' book? It's the *talking chair*. Come on, Dean, of course you remember."

He shrugged.

"You know—"

"No, I really don't." But then he did. Like lightning skittering across his brain, in an instant Dean remembered everything about *The House Inside the Horse*. He even saw the cover of the book—a realistic painting of five adults sitting next to each other with their legs dangling over the edge of a gigantic black leather chair that dwarfed all of them. The chair in the book looked exactly like the one he was touching now.

"Jane gave us a copy; she has a whole bunch of them in her office. She even keeps one on the bar because she likes it so much. You see customers reading the book all the time when they're sitting by themselves. It's like the bar's mascot."

"Yes, now I remember."

"And the talking chair in the story is named Blackwelder."

"Yes, Vanessa, I *remember*."

"Well good, because it just said thank-you."

"Nice," he said sarcastically, and looked down the road to see if more cars were coming.

"No, Dean, it *really* did say thank you."

Against his better instincts, he slowly turned and stared at his wife. "This chair spoke to you?"

"Yes. It thanked you for pulling it off the road."

Dean looked at his big brown boots. The weather was sweltering August hot. Cicadas scritch-screeched all around them. Once upon a very short time ago, he and his wife were driving in the middle of a New England winter. Now it was summer and Vanessa said furniture spoke to her. "Is this hell? Did we die when I wasn't looking and this is hell?"

She didn't appear fazed by the question. "I don't think so. Anyway, someone's coming—look."

Far down the road, people were walking toward them. It looked like three but Dean couldn't be sure. "Wait here." He started away.

Vanessa watched him. Then she sat down in Blackwelder and almost pitched over backward. The chair was perched precariously on the sloping shoulder of the road. She was a large woman. Whenever she sat down fast there was a lot of weight in the drop.

"Watch it!" the chair scolded.

She staggered back to her feet. Trying to regain some dignity, Vanessa straightened her shoulders and wouldn't deign to look at the talking chair.

In the meantime, her husband walked down the road toward the people coming his way. He wasn't sure whether he was glad or alarmed when he recognized two of them. He was certainly surprised.

"Jane? *Kaspar?*"

They didn't seem surprised to see Dean Corbin out there in the middle of wherever-they-were.

The third guy was a stranger. Short white hair like a military man, he appeared to be in his sixties but very fit and sturdy looking. If you arm-wrestled with him you'd probably lose. It took Dean a few moments to register these three were also dressed in winter clothing.

"What *is* this? Do you know what's going on? Or where we are?"

"Were you in an empty place before this, Dean? Did you just come from there?"

"Yes, exactly! Vanessa and I were driving through town. The next moment we were out of the car and standing in a *place* that was empty and completely barren; nothing was there. It was like—"

"We know."

Dean said, "And just as suddenly we were *here*."

Jane and the men exchanged looks but didn't say anything.

"Do *you* know where we are?"

The white-haired man spoke. "Yes—we believe it's someone's dream, but we don't know whose yet. Maybe one of us is having it but we don't know. It could just as easily be somebody else's. Probably not you or me though because we don't know each other. I don't usually dream about people I've never met. I'm Bill Edmonds."

Dean pointed at him. "Ah! We were driving to your house when all this happened. We were looking for Kaspar."

Despite the weirdness of the situation, Kaspar Benn stiffened on hearing this. He was afraid Vanessa had told Dean about their affair and his friend had come for revenge.

"You, um, wanted me, Dean? How come?"

"Did you see our store today? Did you see what's happened to it?"

Kaspar relaxed slightly. "Yes, well no—I mean, I was there this morning. Everything was fine. I called you from there, remember—about the shirts? What about the store? What's wrong with it?"

"It's not *there* anymore, Kaspar. Benn Corbin has somehow turned back into Newsland, and the owner is Whit Ayres. A thirty-years-younger Whit Ayres, if you can believe it. He was in the store behind the counter when we went in. The whole inside of the place is Newsland as it must have been in 1979. Our store is gone."

Bill Edmonds said right away, "No it's not."

All of them looked at him.

"In real life I bet it's still there, all of our lives are exactly like they were. But here in *this* place it's gone. Whoever's dreaming all this"—he gestured toward the surroundings—"is muddling and moving our lives and the facts of our lives together so it's all just a big jumble. Some of it's true, some isn't. Mixing them all together like a tossed salad.

"I've seen things here that are completely true about experiences I've had. But other stuff has been crazily distorted and bent—like looking at my life reflected in a funhouse mirror. I'll bet you five dollars I'm right: this is a dream and someone we all know is dreaming it—with us right in the middle."

Hearing that small sum made both Jane and Dean smile despite the circumstances. I'll bet you five whole dollars this madness we're trapped in now is only someone's dream.

Bill continued, "I'm not worried about *that* though; I'm worried about who's actually having the dream and what we're supposed to do here while it's happening."

"How are you so sure about these things?" Dean asked suspiciously.

"Because I've had the dream before," Jane said.

"So did I," said Bill.

"Me too. Well, parts of it—a lot of parts of it, more and more recently. They're different than Jane's and Bill's, but when you put all our parts together, all our dreams combined—," Kaspar added, but was cut off from saying more when Vanessa boomed: "Hello, everyone! Looks like the gang's all here, plus Bill Edmonds too. Hi Bill." Dean had forgotten about Vanessa. Hearing her voice now, he turned and saw his wife walking their way. Five feet behind her, the black chair was rolling toward them on its own.

Dean did not see Jane Claudius's face as she watched the clumsily moving chair. He did not see her smile grow and grow until it couldn't stretch any farther. Jane put a hand over her mouth to contain her joy. In this chaotic, anything-goes dreamworld they'd all been dropped into, it was hard to trust what she was seeing. But the closer the chair came, the more she believed. Finally she gave in and accepted the miraculous: it *was* Blackwelder. Blackwelder was moving toward them and soon there was not a single doubt in her mind it was here—the talking chair from one of her favorite books in the world, *The House Inside the Horse*.

Jane had met the book for the first time on one of the worst days of her adult life. Hours before, she had been dumped for good by the woman she once thought she'd happily grow old with, Black Nell.

Her real name was Nell Ferrow but in the weeks before their relationship died, Jane had taken to referring to her girlfriend as either White Nell or Black Nell. The names had nothing to do with the color of her skin, but rather the color of her ever-changing moods and whims from day to day and frequently from hour to hour. Nell thought both nicknames were funny and right except when she didn't and flew into one of her extensive variety of rages, snits, silences, or full-blown tantrums. At the end of their time together there weren't many White Nell days.

As is so often the case when one is on the receiving end of a bad relationship, Jane felt bewildered and untethered from her life too much of the time, despite trying as hard as she could to keep herself balanced and whole. Like an angry monkey, Black Nell shook everything in their life together like the bars of a cage holding her in.

The crowning insult was, she left without saying a word. Jane came home from work one Thursday to discover her lover and all of her possessions had disappeared, right down to her green toothbrush and full quart of Ben & Jerry's Cookie Dough ice cream Jane had brought home the night before because she knew it was her partner's favorite. When Jane saw *that* was gone she knew Nell must already have a place to live since she needed to put the ice cream in a freezer before it melted.

Creeped out by the thought of staying in the apartment they had shared after her wrenching discovery, Jane walked right back outside and went to an expensive restaurant for dinner. She had a superb meal, which she didn't taste, and three glasses of Barolo wine, which she did.

Afterward, still not ready to go back to the scene of Nell's crime, Jane wandered into a bookstore. Stopping at a display table, she picked up the first book she saw because the cover illustration caught her eye—five people sitting side by side on an enormous black chair.

Then she opened the book and gasped. Because she was drunk, when she first saw the word "Blackwelder" she thought she saw "Black Nell" and was agog at the impossible coincidence. Then she looked again and laughed at her mistake. The perfidious Nell Ferrow was everywhere—even in a children's story.

Jane had never heard of it but she took the book over to a corner of the room where a cozy-looking chestnut-colored easy chair was waiting for her. Whether it was due to the sadness of the night, the wine she had drunk, the excellence of the story or something else, Jane read *The House Inside the Horse* three times straight through. Then she bought the book, brought it home to her empty apartment, and sitting on the floor in the middle of the living room, read it again.

We're often wrong at predicting who or what will transform us. Encountering certain people, books, music, places, or ideas . . . at just the right time can immediately make our lives happier, richer, more beautiful, resonant, or meaningful. When it happens, we feel a kind of instant love for them, both deep and abiding. Now and then it can be something as trifling as a children's book, a returned telephone call, or a night at a seaside bar in Mykonos.

Jane felt love and gratitude for *The House Inside the Horse* because it kept her company throughout a very bad, dark time. For some unexplainable reason, whenever she felt on the verge of bottoming out again because of Nell's leaving, she would reread the story. It invariably calmed or kept her busy. It tided her over till the sadness, the anger, or the panic attacks passed and she was pretty much all right again. People—family, lovers, friends—are supposed to do that: keep us sane or balanced at difficult times. But sometimes *things* really are better at pulling us back from the edge.

Years later when she saw the beloved Blackwelder rumbling down the road toward her in this mysterious place, Jane didn't think it was impossible. She saw it and was overjoyed. The only thing going through her head was, there it *is*!

Running over to the black chair, she swept Dean and Vanessa's coats off the seat and sat down on it, something she had wanted to do ever since the first time she read the book.

As anyone who ever read *The House Inside the Horse* knew, Blackwelder only spoke to women.

"Excuse me, but do I know you?" the chair asked in a stern male voice after she sat down. It was the voice of a railroad conductor asking, "Tickets, please."

"My name is Jane Claudius and I know you're Blackwelder."

"I am. But you know this *is* a dream, of course."

Jane tightly gripped the arms of the chair. "Yes, but I'm so happy you're in it. You're actually here."

"Tell me who these other people are, please."

Those other people watched Jane have a conversation with herself, or so it appeared.

"Who's she talking to?" Kaspar asked as quietly as he could.

Dean didn't care who Jane was talking to. He wanted to know what the hell was going on around them. "Tell me about this dream stuff you were talking about before."

"I will, as soon as *this* thing passes; if it doesn't plan on stomping us first. Anyone here have elephants in their dreams?" Edmonds's voice was calm and collected, considering what he was looking at.

Lumbering toward them now from the same direction that Vanessa and Blackwelder had come was an enormous red elephant. It was not sort of red like an old faded sweatshirt or a slapped cheek. This elephant was the by-God brassy red of a candy apple or a clown's nose. It was red with a capital "R" and easily weighed twelve thousand pounds. It moved quickly in a very determined manner—so determined that at first glance it was easy to think, the elephant is very *pissed off*. I'd better run.

Jane leapt out of the chair and began pulling it as hard as she could out of the path of the pachyderm. Edmonds and Kaspar Benn started jogging down the road together, both of them looking back over their shoulders often at the approaching red beast.

But Dean and Vanessa Corbin stayed right where they were. The expressions on their faces showed no fear or shock.

"It's Muba," Dean said.

"You think so?" his wife asked, both hands in fists at her mouth.

"Absolutely, there's no question. Muba, stop."

Thirty feet away, the giant red animal slowed and came to a stop in the middle of the road. Swinging its head from side to side, it blew off a trumpeting call. It straightened everyone up wherever they were. The elephant was wearing a gigantic wristwatch on its front left foot.

"The watch! Dean, she's wearing the watch!"

"I saw."

"So it *is* Muba. Good God, Dean, Muba's *here!*"

Forget the first kiss, the first sex, the first tears of misunderstanding, the first fight. Forget the first amazing gift that says they thought long and hard about what you love. This gift is physical proof they tried their best to get you something concrete, in-the-hand *wonderful* to show the intensity of their feeling for you.

Forget it. Forget it all.

The first great real intimacy between two people begins when secrets are told. The time you stole money from the candy drive when you were a Girl Scout. The time you slept with your ex-sister-in-law after their marriage dissolved. The one shitty self-serving lie you told your boss that changed everything and ended up burning all the bridges you had at the time. To this day you cringe whenever you think about having told that lie. And finally *the* secret about your parents you thought you would never, *ever* tell anyone.

But one day you do—you tell your new partner. No matter what happens to the two of you afterward, they know the truth now and you can never take it back. They have the goods on you and you on them; your life together shifts permanently on its axis. It is impossible to predict whether that is good or bad.

A month after they met, the first great secret Dean Corbin told his new girlfriend Vanessa was about the elephant named Muba.

As a boy Dean had had childhood leukemia. At the time his chances of survival were not good. He spent a lot of time in hospitals getting things like gallium scans and flow cytometry, but the disease persisted no matter what they tried to do to analyze and defeat it. After one particularly grueling chemotherapy session, Dean lapsed into a half sleep, half coma in which he dreamed he met a magnificent red elephant. For some mysterious reason never explained, the animal wore a huge wristwatch and told the boy its name was Muba. Dean asked it if he was going to die. The elephant said no, but there would be many difficult days ahead before he was cured. The most important thing to know was from now on, Muba would keep Dean company throughout his coming ordeal. The little boy was too young to know what an ordeal was, but hearing this red colossus was going to move into his life and be around from now on lifted his spirits tremendously.

He did not dream again of Muba during his successful treatment, but that was all right. He was convinced if he really needed the elephant's help, it would appear.

Years later he sat by his mother's bedside watching her succumb to the same disease. He fell asleep and again he saw Muba in a dream. It was standing in the middle of a mall parking lot. Dean came out of the building pushing a shopping cart. He saw the elephant and walked right over to it.

As before, the animal spoke to him without opening its mouth. It told Dean his mother would die today. Only that and then the dream ended. When he awoke, his mother was staring at him with rheumy eyes full of love and good-bye. Then she farted. Both mother and son opened their mouths in surprise. Dean chuckled. His mother had no energy left but she laughed too and then died. In the middle of her laugh, she passed away. It was the most astonishing, wonderful thing.

Dean was crying by the time he got to this part of his story, but they were not sad tears. Vanessa had never seen him cry before. Not knowing what to say, she scooched over on the bed, snuggled up close, and threw one of her legs over his. They remained that way for a long time. After a while Dean looked over and saw she had fallen asleep. He sighed contentedly. He liked the fact he had grown comfortable enough with this new woman to tell her the story of his cancer, his mother's death, and the spooky red elephant that appeared twice in his dreams to tell him momentous things that later happened.

A week later he was shaken awake in the middle of the night by Vanessa. "What? What's the matter? Are you all right?"

"What does it look like, Dean? What does it look like?"

"What? What are you talking about?" He'd been so deep asleep it took a moment for him to even recognize his girlfriend's voice.

"The elephant—Muba. What does it look like?"

Turning to the clock next to the bed, he tried to get it into focus. The glowing yellow numbers there took some moments to make sense. He grimaced on grasping it was 4:17 A.M. "Umm, it's red. It's big and red. It's an *elephant*. Why do you want to know this at four o'clock in the morning?"

Vanessa was naked, sitting up on her knees. Her arms were crossed over her breasts and her luminous black hair jutted out in all directions. "I *saw* her, Dean. I just dreamt about Muba."

He woke up fast. "What do you mean?" He rubbed a hand over his face to wipe the cobwebs of lingering sleep away.

"I dreamt I was sitting in a restaurant having lunch. I was at a table by the big front window. While eating, I looked up and outside, walking down the street as normal as could be, was an *elephant*—a *red* elephant. I knew exactly who it was so I stood up and raced out of there. I caught up to her and said, 'You're Muba, aren't you.' I said it, I didn't ask. I knew a hundred percent I was right. I just wanted to say her name out loud to make the words real. Do you know what I mean?"

Dean nodded but stayed quiet. He wanted to hear every detail before saying anything. If this was true, if his girlfriend really had dreamed about his Muba, then it was astounding. But after a few moments he changed his mind and thought, so what? Anyone can dream about red elephants. Dreams are the mind's playground, with swings and slides and jungle gyms for every crazy thought in your on-recess-from-reality imagination to spin around on. Vanessa's dream elephant was not necessarily the same one, the same Muba Dean knew.

Fully awake now, he realized something: *her*. Vanessa had referred to the elephant as her. People don't usually refer to elephants as female, but Vanessa had.

"What color were her eyes?"

"You know one of them is blind, Dean. The bad one is totally black and looks burned out. It didn't seem to bother her though."

Propping himself up on his elbows, he stared at Vanessa Savitt as if having just discovered she'd stolen money from his wallet—skepticism mixed equally with shock. It had to be true—if she knew about the one ruined eye then she really *must* have dreamed about Muba.

"Did she speak to you? Did she say anything?"

Vanessa shook her head. "No. She only stood there while I talked and when I was finished she walked away."

"What did you say?"

"I told her about The Skull Farmers."

The Skull Farmers was the band Vanessa sang in at the time.

Incredulous, Dean blurted out, "You told her about your *band*? Why not something important? The animal's an oracle, Vanessa—it *knows* things."

Vanessa slowly pouted, straightened her spine, and tightened her arms across her beautiful chest. When she spoke, her voice had the tone and timbre of a grande dame giving instructions to a gardener. "It was a *dream*, Dean. Illogical things happen in dreams, remember? Besides, the band *is* very important to me."

"Vanessa, you know what I'm saying—you dreamt something from my dreams! When has that ever happened before?"

She wasn't impressed. "Who knows, and besides, how is that relevant?"

He couldn't believe she was saying this drivel. "You might have just contacted some other . . . *realm* or, I don't know, cosmic *level*. It's important and amazing. If you met *God*, would you tell Him about your *band*?"

"Perhaps."

Over the ensuing years to Dean's even greater dismay, Vanessa had several vivid dreams in which she encountered the half-blind red elephant. Dean had none. In her dreams, Muba said nothing while Vanessa did all the talking. And it sounded like she talked only about herself or whatever banal stuff she was doing at the time, rather than anything significant. It drove Dean to distraction to hear his wife merrily describe these encounters the next morning. All the lost opportunities . . .

But today, in this dream or this land or wherever they were at the moment, there was Muba in front of both of them. Dean was going to take full advantage of the opportunity.

Without hesitating, he walked straight over to the elephant and put his hand on its flank. Muba stood still a few moments, then suddenly swung her trunk full force to one side and slapped Dean in the face, almost knocking him down.

"Hey!"

The elephant started to swing her head again. Dean stepped quickly out of the way. "Muba, stop it! What is this?"

The animal didn't speak to him but did not move either.

Up the road in one direction, Jane stood with her arm protectively over the back of the black chair. Down the road, Kaspar Benn and Bill Edmonds watched to see what was going to happen next. Hands on hips, Vanessa shook her head at her husband.

Seeing the look on her face, he bridled. "*What?* What's the matter now?" Dean demanded while cautiously feeling his cheek, which still stung from Muba's slap.

"She doesn't like to be touched."

"Really, Vanessa? How do you know?"

"I remember it from other dreams I had about her. As soon as you touched her I knew there was going to be trouble."

Dean was about to say something snide but then saw the skin, or rather what was written on the elephant's hide. He stopped and frowned. He'd opened his mouth to speak to his wife but instead closed it slowly. Squinting to get a better view, he pointed and asked, "Did you see this?"

"What?"

"What's written on her side. Come and look at this."

Vanessa walked closer. Dean glanced quickly down at the hand he'd touched the animal with. Suddenly some things made sense. None of this made sense, but some of it made sense now.

"It looks like a kind of map, Dean. There—do you see it? It's a map."

An elephant's skin is rough, very wrinkled, and a mix of varied textures. The animal itself is so huge and imposing you're not apt to look at any single part in detail, especially when seeing one up close for the first time in your life. But having noticed it now, both Corbins stared at what was plainly a map of some sort contained within the folds of Muba's skin.

From her safe distance Jane called out, "What kind of map?"

Vanessa pointed to it. "There, do you see it? It's got to be a map."

"What, with names and arrows pointing where to go?"

"Well kind of, but . . . just come look for yourself. It's a map for sure."

Jane glanced at Blackwelder as if for instructions, but the chair remained silent. She walked over to where the Corbins stood.

"There—right there, do you see?" Vanessa pointed but did not touch the behemoth.

While the three looked at the elephant, Edmonds and Kaspar Benn walked back up the road and joined them.

A red elephant stood unmoving in the middle of a country road. Five people stood nearby staring at its side as if it were a movie screen.

"There is definitely something there," one of them said unnecessarily.

The other four nodded their agreement or thought, yes there is.

Kaspar took a step forward and pointed to the elephant. "What did you call it—'Muba'? I've heard that name before; I just can't remember where. Are those mountains there?"

Jane thought he was joking. "Mountains? It's water—probably the ocean. It's blue, Kaspar. Mountains aren't blue. And there are words written on it but I can't make out what they're saying."

Hands tucked in his armpits, Bill Edmonds said, "This is not what I see. It's a forest. Those are trees, not the ocean. And they're definitely not blue."

Jane huffed. "No, it is *not*, Bill—trees are *green*. That is a big turquoise ocean. And look at all the weird symbols. Does anyone know what those mean?"

Edmonds shook his head. "The hell they are—they're trees. I should know a tree when I see one because they were my business for thirty years. I don't see any blue *or* symbols. That is a dark green forest of trees, Jane."

Irritated, Dean pointed at the same spot and said, "I see a letter from the Greek alphabet. What are you two talking about? Show me where you see trees or symbols there; it's a Greek letter."

After more stubbornness, staring, and double-checking to make sure they all saw what they saw, it began to dawn on them that each person saw something different on the elephant's side despite the fact they were all looking at the same place. Eventually the four who'd already had their say looked at Vanessa to hear what she saw.

After a dramatic pause for full effect she said, "Chummie Recel."

Dean looked at the elephant again. "*What?* What does *he* have to do with this?"

Vanessa was unperturbed by the hectoring tone of her husband's question.

"Who's Chummie Recel?" Jane asked.

Vanessa said, "My oldest friend; we grew up together. It looks like a map of the stars he drew when we were kids. We were both going to be astronauts and needed a map to navigate where we wanted to go. So Chummie drew one and it looked just like *that*, as I remember."

Bill Edmonds reached into the back pocket of his eleven-year-old jeans and brought out a small frayed black notebook and ballpoint pen—two things he always carried. Edmonds was an inveterate list maker. He loved everything about lists: making them, reading them, and seeing items lined up carefully one after the other. Lists made life make more sense to him. He'd tried to find his Vedran by listing the objects in his apartment. When he saw things written down on paper in tidy columns it gave him the feeling it was possible to tame some of life's chaos, which was much better than just letting it buzz crazily around you like house flies. "I'm going to write down what each of us sees there. Tell me again what you see. So far I've got: stars, words, ocean, a Greek letter, and a forest." Edmonds kept talking as he wrote. "Everybody keep looking; see if any of these things are on your map too. Maybe there's some crossover. If so, it would be a big help."

Pulling a pair of wire-rimmed glasses out of his jacket Kaspar said, "Say the words again."

Edmonds repeated them.

The five people looked intently at the elephant, searching for signs of anything. None of them noticed the little girl who lived with Edmonds walking down the road toward them. When she reached Blackwelder she sat down on the chair and asked it in a low voice, "Have they figured anything out yet?"

"I don't think so. Not from what I've heard."

Exasperated, Josephine the mechanic rolled her eyes. "Do they even know about . . . ?"

Blackwelder jiggled a little from one side to the other to get more comfortable on the lumpy road. "Maybe they're beginning to understand. They're certainly paying closer attention now, which is a big plus in itself. Look at their faces."

Josephine bent over so her elbows touched her knees and she spoke quietly. "Do you think it'd be okay if I gave them a little hint?"

Indignant, Blackwelder scolded, "No! Don't do it, Josephine. You know you're not supposed to tell them anything. That's not your job."

"I know, but it's taking so *long*."

The chair stayed a scold. "It doesn't matter! Just don't say anything about it. You can talk to them, but don't reveal anything. The whole point is for them to figure it out themselves. You've certainly given them enough hints already."

Kaspar Benn said, "Wait a minute!"

Where do *ah-ha!* moments come from? Those critical but rare, out-of-nowhere heaven's-gift synapses in our brains that bang together like freight cars coupling—*ka-chunk!* Suddenly we frown, look up at the ceiling or down at our feet, our mouth drops open stupidly or closes tight because after the synapse sizzles the mental weld together we instantly finally clearly see how *it* works, or understand how it happened, the right way to do it, or what was there in front of us all along but we were just too blind or dense to grasp it.

Staring at the side of the red elephant, Kaspar suddenly thought of Sivan Ehrenpreis, one of the sexiest women he'd ever known. They'd had an affair a decade ago, but on realizing they had little else in common besides a mutual panting for each other's bodies, they'd split. Afterward he heard about her from different people—she'd gotten married, had children, gotten divorced, remarried.

The only time he'd ever seen her again was years later standing in front of a toy store window at Christmastime in Brooklyn, holding the hand of a little girl. Sivan looked sensational in a black winter coat and long salmon-colored scarf. Kaspar couldn't resist going over and saying hello to his old flame.

Later he wished he hadn't. She'd just gotten out of the hospital after having had a kidney removed. She described in enthusiastic graphic detail how sick she'd been and the medical procedures she'd undergone. When he first saw her that day, even at a distance, he was struck again by her powerful sensuality. Before approaching, he thought with fond longing about the time they'd been together.

But as she spoke about the necrotic parts of her guts that had been cut out, what a laparoscopy entailed, and what "friable kidney fragments" meant, she turned into . . . a hamburger.

Literally—while listening to her speak, in his mind Kaspar could only see this exquisite-looking woman as a series of specific cuts of meat, like those diagrams mounted behind butchers' counters showing customers exactly where the meat they were buying came from on a cow's body. By the time she was finished talking (Sivan had always been a gabber), Kaspar didn't even want to kiss her cheek good-bye because all he could think about was his mother's favorite recipe—braised beef cheeks.

"Wait a minute," he repeated now, his mind racing fast. "Everybody sees something different there, right?" Kaspar pointed to the elephant's broad side. The others looked at him but said nothing, waiting to hear his point. "Bill, would you tear four blank pages out of your notebook please? Who has something to write with? A pen or pencil—I have one." He dug a mechanical pencil out of a pocket as Edmonds carefully tore four pieces of paper from his notebook. Jane and Vanessa had pens. Kaspar took the blank sheets and handed one to each person. "All right, everyone draw as best you can what you see up there." He pointed to the elephant's side. "It doesn't have to be good or detailed. Just a quick sketch to get down the broad strokes of what you see and think is important on your map."

"Why?"

"Because I have an idea; it just came to me when I was thinking about something else. If I'm right it may explain all this." Glancing down the road, he saw Josephine sitting in the black chair and remembered it was the girl who had called him Muba earlier that day in the store. But he was eager to get this thing going right now with the others so she could wait. He handed his pencil to Dean and waited impatiently for his partner to finish.

It took a while. It took much more time than Kaspar had imagined because once they began, everyone wanted to make their drawing look right. None of them knew how to draw so the job was harder. How do you do mountains when you have no artistic ability? Lots of craggy squiggles so stupid-looking and inept that you start again immediately, messing up the paper by scratching things out. How do you draw intricate hieroglyphics with a black roller ball pen and no talent? Lots of unsteady lines . . .

The only person not making an irritated or frustrated face was Vanessa, who actually hummed as she worked. She was drawing both from what she saw on the elephant's hide and from her memories of Chummie Recel's childhood map. Some of her stars had the classic five points while others were just thick black dots. She had fun doing it, but her drawing was awful. When Dean saw it he grinned and gave a scornful snort: leave it to his wife to draw what looked like a third grader's astronomy project.

Sheepish about their efforts but curious to see what he was planning to do with them, they handed their drawings to Kaspar when they'd finished. Bill Edmonds again tore his page very precisely out of his pocket notebook.

Bill's was the best drawn so after collecting them, Kaspar put it on top. Once he had them all, he stacked the sheets together. Like the different parts of Sivan Ehrenpreis's body, he thought if he gathered the different sketches together in the proper order they might combine somehow to show something not there in the five separate drawings.

No luck. No divine lights rose up slowly behind them accompanied by a choir singing Handel's "Messiah." The stack of wildly different drawings did not vibrate or shape shift in Kaspar Benn's hands. Nada. Nothing.

"Well?" Vanessa widened her eyes questioningly.

Kaspar could only shrug. He kept looking at the papers, still hoping something would happen.

Dean didn't notice their exchange because he was looking with interest at the elephant, the girl, the black chair, and then back at the child. "I *know* her." He pointed. "We saw her on the roof the other day."

"That's Josephine—she lives with me. She's my daughter. Well, not really my daughter, but—" Edmonds was interrupted by Jane.

"The daughter you were *supposed* to have but never did," Jane said, more surprised than Bill as the words spilled from her mind and mouth.

"And the chair was in the children's book that saved you when you broke up with your girlfriend," Edmonds answered her right back, just as stunned as Jane at what he said. He had no idea where the information had come from.

"The elephant told you in a dream about the cancer when you were a kid, huh, Dean?" Kaspar said this next, despite never having seen nor heard anything about . . . *Muba*! The little girl had asked him earlier in the store why he didn't remember that name!

How could any of them know the intimate things they'd just said to one another almost simultaneously? Where had the knowledge come from? Why in a flash had they begun to see into the deepest recesses of each other's minds, memories, and places where they kept their biggest secrets? It was as if they were now able to move in and out of each other's heads.

Whatever was happening to them was clearly out of their control. They were given glimpses, peeks under the curtain, flashes of understanding and insight into each other's lives, histories, hearts, and secrets. It was jarring and riveting in its way but most of all unstoppable. As the five people stood there, the most intimate knowledge of each other's lives entered each other's minds in spits and spurts, fragments and odd-shaped pieces like shrapnel.

The five of them reacted differently to the experience. Jane pressed the heels of both hands against her forehead as if suffering a migraine.

Edmonds stared straight ahead, transfixed, as did Kaspar. Dean and Vanessa jerked their heads as if being poked from all sides by invisible fingers.

Sitting in Blackwelder, Josephine clapped her hands and bounced up and down, much to the chair's discomfort. It protested, "Stop that. Please, it hurts!"

But the mechanic who had come to earth disguised as a little girl to help these five people didn't stop bouncing because she was too excited. Finally it was happening—the joining *had* begun.

SEVEN KLEEMS

ONE

He was distraught, alone, exhausted; it was early evening in a foreign city six thousand miles from home. Everything around him was dark and silent; it made the world in the room larger and more ominous. He was bleary eyed, blinking hard, and working to get his full sight back after a two-hour nap to drag his brain out from under the heavy tarpaulin of jet lag. He sat on the side of a spongy hotel bed in his underpants with a cell phone in his hand, trying through a thick head of just-woke-up/not-really-awake to figure out what time it was in the United States: six hours behind or ahead—noon or midnight? Was it all right to make the call now? He knew he must and whatever time it was over there didn't matter. He was cold and only a moment ago realized he was shivering, but whether from cold or alarm he didn't know. It was interesting to watch his free hand quiver on his bare knee. Although he held the phone in his other hand, he put it on top of the shaking one, but it did no good.

Maybe he should pee. Stand up and go to the toilet, have a long satisfying piss, come back empty, and *then* make the call. He'd read somewhere a full bladder raises blood pressure. Right then he felt his blood pressure was probably high enough to lift the *Hindenburg*.

When the phone in his hand vibrated and then a moment later rang he was so surprised he dropped it on the floor, his hand stiffening like it'd gotten an electrical shock. The small blue phone rang a second time, juddering on the wooden floor before he could retrieve it. His heart galloped inside his chest.

"Hello?"

"Kaspar, it's Dean."

"Dean! I was just going to call you. Really, the phone was in my hand."

"I tried and tried before but first you were flying and then I couldn't get through. Anyway, you had the dream too, right?"

Kaspar straightened, swallowed, and answered carefully. "Yes, on the plane ride over here. I don't know how long it lasted. I slept a few hours but who knows how long the dream was. It blew my mind!"

There was rustling and background noise on the other end before Dean spoke again. "Everyone else is here. I've got you on speaker phone so we can all talk about it together."

Kaspar rubbed his mouth. "Why did this happen when I was on a fucking plane to Europe? Can someone explain *that* to me? I'm home all the rest of the year. Why did it happen now?"

In a quieter voice Jane offered, "Maybe there's a good reason for it. Maybe there's something over there you're supposed to find that'll help us figure it out."

"Like what, a Wiener schnitzel?"

In the background Bill Edmonds asked, "Where is he again?"

Vanessa said, "Vienna. Vienna, Austria."

"Why?"

"He's buying loden for the store."

"What's loden?"

"Dean?"

"Yeah, Kaspar?"

"What does everybody else there think? What do *you* say about it?"

"Everybody has a different opinion. Basically the only thing we agree on is *we all shared the same dream last night*. Or all of our dreams were stitched together into one big one that we shared. A lot of what's happening in our real lives was in it, but a lot was also wrong or distorted or just plain crazy."

Vanessa said, "We brought ourselves and our brains *to* the dream and they all got mixed up together in it like they'd been thrown into a blender. . . ."

"Jesus, it's true then; it really *did* happen."

"Plus we figured out each one of us brought an important secret from our lives to the dream too: Vanessa and I brought the elephant; Edmonds his daughter, Josephine; Jane the chair—"

"Wait a minute." In the background Jane's voice got louder. "There was nothing from you, Kaspar. All of us brought something very important from our lives into the dream, some sort of talisman, except you."

Vanessa said, "Wow, right."

"It's true—he *didn't* bring anything."

This talk rumbled back and forth until Dean said, "It's a good point, Kaspar. Why do you think that is?"

Kaspar closed his eyes and squeezed them tight. "Look, I'm sitting here completely goggle-headed in Vienna, Austria, having just shared a dream on an airplane over the Atlantic Ocean with four people in Vermont. And you're asking me why I didn't *bring* anything to the dream? *How am I supposed to know the answer?* I'm lost here, kids, totally lost. Can someone there tell me what's going on so I can keep my head from exploding?"

A silence followed, long enough for Kaspar to regain his composure and speak without any more rancor in his voice. "All right, just tell me what else you discussed. How did you all find out you'd experienced it together?"

"Vanessa woke up this morning in a tizzy and said I had to hear about her dream. Naturally when she described it I went bananas. I told her I had the same one, we flipped out together, and started comparing notes about it. Then Jane called and told us *her* dream."

Jane said, "I called them because Bill called me before. But listen to this, Kaspar—*Bill didn't know my phone number.* He said I gave it to him in the dream."

"Your *telephone* number?"

Edmonds said, "Yes. In my dream she wrote it down in my notebook. I remembered the number when I woke up because it's an easy one— 555-8778."

Jane said, "But my number is unlisted. There's no way Bill could have gotten it unless I gave it to him."

Kaspar rubbed his eyes and blinked hard several times to clear them. "What happened next?"

"We all came here to Dean's house to talk about it. When he couldn't reach you on the phone earlier, he told us to come back later and he'd try again."

"And?"

"And nothing—we just told you what we know."

"But it's not enough! We went to sleep last night and *all* of us shared the same dream—"

Vanessa interrupted. "No, you're wrong, Kaspar. It's one of the things we discovered by talking: we *were* all together in the same dream, but none of us knew what was going on inside each other's head. It's like we were all in the same movie or play. But we didn't know what was going to happen from moment to moment or what the other people would say."

"None of us expected a red elephant or a talking chair. They just appeared and we all saw them," Jane added.

"Or a men's store that time travels back into a news store."

"A little girl who was never born. Oh yeah, and Keebler who was once a two-inch-high statue but came alive and grew," Edmonds added.

Phone pressed to his ear, Kaspar lowered his chin to his chest. "Is anyone there as confused as I am?"

"We all are, Kaspar. None of us have the slightest idea of what's going on or what it means."

Kaspar took his watch off the nightstand and looked at it. "What time is it there?"

"Noon."

"What *are* we supposed to do? Does anyone know? Did the girl tell any of you what to do in the dream? She didn't say anything to me except I had to get going. Then she burned my phone and called me Muba, which only now I know is the name of that red elephant with a map on its side. Not terribly helpful clues in unraveling this mystery."

The four people in Vermont looked at each other to see if there was anything to add, but there wasn't. In Vienna, Kaspar rubbed the back of the phone nervously with his thumb and willed anyone on the other end of the line to say anything that could help.

Dean said, "We have to figure this out. Let's just start from there. What are we supposed to do? Why did we all share this dream and what are we supposed to do about it?"

"Dean?"

"Yes, Kaspar?"

"I'll have to call you back."

"*What?* We just started talking—"

"I'll call you back."

There was a click, a hiss, and the line went dead. Puzzled, Dean looked at the receiver in his hand. "He hung up."

"Maybe he had to go to the bathroom."

"Maybe."

The reason why Kaspar Benn hung up so abruptly was a light went on in his toilet. Moments later someone walked out of there into the bedroom.

Kaspar recognized the person instantly, but that did not make it any better. Under his breath he grumbled, "Shit!" but carefully, so as not to be heard.

"Kaspar."

"*Crebold*. What are you doing here?"

The other man smirked. Both of them knew damned well why he was there. "Kaspar. What kind of dopey name is that? *Kaspar Benn*."

"It's German, so it's just exotic enough–sounding for me to use it as an excuse for whatever mistakes I make here, and I make plenty of them, believe me."

"I've noticed. Do you mind if I sit down?"

"Would it matter if I did?"

"No." The visitor sat on the bed. Kaspar grudgingly extended a hand and they shook. "Well, here we are. Have you been enjoying yourself?"

"I have." But Kaspar's voice did not sound like he was enjoying anything at the moment.

"You're a fool, Kaspar. You really screwed this up. The *dream* last night . . . oh brother, seriously dumb. How did you manage it?"

"I *didn't* do it—it just happened. Don't blame it on me." His voice was small, trying to be smaller.

"What were you *thinking*, Kaspar? I mean, how stupid could you be?"

"I *didn't* do it."

"I told you—"

Kaspar's voice was eager to agree. "Yes, you did. You absolutely did tell me."

"I told you not to come here like this, but you insisted."

"I was stubborn."

"No—you were *stupid*: profoundly, selfishly, blindly *stupid*." Crebold slowly hit the mattress with a fist after every word, as if pounding a nail into wood.

"All right—*stupid*. I get your point—I was stupid. I admit it." He threw up his hands in surrender. "I am guilty of first-degree stupidity."

"Skip the sarcasm, Kaspar. You knew what you were doing. It's part of the job description. We're mechanics—or at least you *were*.

"We know how things work; we fix them or adjust them and then move on. We don't invent them and we sure as hell don't alter them. I can't believe what an idiot you are." Crebold's hands were very animated and expressive as he spoke. They danced along with his words; they pointed and sailed and made fists when the phrases called for it. They conducted the music coming out of his mouth.

"I just thought—" Kaspar's voice was one stop away from a moan.

"You're going to try and justify what happened? Don't—you fucked up—*the end*, okay? Sharing last night's dream with those other people was exhibit A of what happens when you go against policy. It's a catastrophe anyone could see coming ten miles away. Especially you—a *mechanic*!"

Kaspar sat still and stared unseeing into the darkness. "I'm not a mechanic anymore—I'm retired, remember? And I didn't *do* anything! I didn't make them share the dream. The memory—I really believed I could handle it. I thought I could have both."

"You were wrong on both counts, friend. Now we've got a major toxic spill here that needs to be cleaned up ASAP."

Kaspar's phone rang again. He flung it away. It hit a wall, caromed off, and bounced several times on the wooden floor where it continued to ring. Temper flaring, he stood up, intending to crush the thing with his bare foot.

Crebold reached over and grabbed his arm. "Leave it."

Kaspar puffed his lips in frustration. "*Shit.*"

The waiter didn't like twins. He'd never liked them, even though he'd never known any personally. Like Afghan dogs, vegans, and Christian Scientists, all he knew about them was what he read and saw, but it was enough.

Twins dressed the same, wore the same haircuts, and married exactly the same sort of people. Even when separated at birth and moved a thousand miles apart, twins somehow weirdly managed to mirror each other right down to their politics, professions, sports teams they rooted for, religions they joined, and the number of kids they had. It was a fact. Weird, weird, and *weird*. The waiter had recently seen a documentary on TV about twins that reinforced everything he believed: Twins = freaks = stay away from me.

And now first thing on a Monday morning there were a pair of almost identical-looking twins sitting at one of his tables! The only good thing about it was they were dressed differently so it was not difficult telling them apart. In fact they were night and day different. One looked sharp in tip-to-toe expensive everything—the man clearly put serious money, thought, and care into what he wore. In contrast, his brother was dressed in dull and duller. He looked like an East German Trabant salesman in 1967: a cheap-looking, ill-fitting blue suit, thin black tie with a too small knot, and a white shirt with an oversized collar fifteen years out of fashion. The waiter noticed all these details because off duty, he was one spiffy dresser himself and had the ladies to prove it.

"Gentlemen, what can I get you?"

The dull-looking twin ordered—get this—a glass of tomato juice with a poached egg *inside* it. The waiter paused while writing this down to look over the top of his eyeglasses at the man to make sure he'd heard correctly. The guy didn't even have the courtesy to look back. He just continued speaking to his brother. He was not only a twin, but rude too.

Making eye contact with the waiter, the well-dressed one asked for a cappuccino and smiled.

"That'll be one cappuccino and one tomato juice with a poached egg *in* it?"

"Yes."

"Very good, sir."

When the waiter was gone, Kaspar asked his "brother" Crebold, "Why are you doing this? It's not necessary."

"Our waiter doesn't like twins; he thinks we're weird. So I'm going to prove he's right."

"Don't be a jerk, Crebold. Just let the man do his job."

"Oh, like you did yours, huh?" Crebold leaned forward and put both elbows on the table. He rested his chin on his hands. "Kaspar, I do *not* want to be here. I seriously don't. You have no idea how many other things I would rather be doing than sitting in a smelly, smoky Viennese café with you, figuring out how to clean up the mess you've made on Earth. Remember the time you went skiing?"

Kaspar frowned. "I loathe skiing."

Crebold pointed an index finger at him like a gun. "Exactly—and I feel the same kind of loathing being here. But I must be here because of you. So let's work together to fix this as quickly as possible so I can leave and you can go back to selling shirts."

"You say it with such disdain."

Crebold leered. He'd obviously been anticipating this exchange. "Do you really like selling clothes? Is it satisfying measuring men's asses with a tape measure so their new trousers fit correctly? Is the customer always right?"

Kaspar started to answer, hesitated, and chose to go in another direction. "Where are you going when you retire, Crebold?"

"I don't know. I'll let them decide. But when they do, I will be blissfully unaware of their decision. Even if I end up measuring men's asses too, I won't remember where I came from. Unlike you, I will not ask to keep my memory."

They had known each other for ages and worked together almost as long. From the beginning there'd been a mutual dislike, but both of them were completely dedicated to the job, so there was always respect. Dislike but respect—it was sufficient for a professional relationship. Most important, both believed in the work and helped one another whenever necessary.

Kaspar was a natural at the job, while Crebold had to work very hard just to keep up. Of course that was part of what caused tension between the two of them. Everything seemed to come easy to Kaspar: He did the work well and with almost no effort. He was liked and admired; others asked for his advice or wanted to be his friend.

In contrast Crebold was a loner, a glum hair-splitting overachiever who constantly let others know how hard he was working. In general he was the kind of low-key pain in the ass you'd never want to have a drink with even if he was paying.

But both considered themselves no more than soldiers on the front lines, there to protect a system they believed in and to keep things moving in a positive direction. Kaspar was slightly older than Crebold and that was why he was retired now. No matter how dedicated you were to the job, at a specific age you were forced to retire, no exceptions. Kaspar hated to do it, but those were the rules. When his time came he was sad but prepared.

When asked where he wanted to retire, he shrugged indifferently and remained silent. A number of places were suggested. He said any of them was fine. He did have one request though—please don't erase my memory.

They asked why.

"If I don't remember who I've been, I don't believe I'll be able to really appreciate wherever you send me, no matter how long I live there," Kaspar answered, although he knew what he asked for was unusual and against the rules.

For the most part it was a pleasant informative meeting. All parties were reasonable and open to suggestion. Kaspar's request *was* out of the ordinary and would make things more difficult for him in his new life. But quite a few imminent retirees made this same request and a good number of them were granted. Of course memory or not, in the new life they would lose the mechanic's powers as well as the ability to recognize other retirees, including those who'd also been allowed to keep their memory. *Those* rules were set in stone.

By coincidence Crebold was at the meeting. Like jury duty, all mechanics were required to sit on the retirement board periodically and cast a vote. He did not request it but was pleased to learn he would be directly involved in this particular review.

When it was his turn to question Kaspar, Crebold asked in a strong, assured voice, "You don't care where you retire?"

"No, anywhere is fine."

"You only want to keep your memory?"

"Right."

"But it's unfair to the other retirees and likely to cause trouble no matter where you go."

Kaspar remained calm and reasonable. "True, but I didn't think there was any harm in asking. I know quite a few others have been allowed to do it."

Crebold already knew the answer to his next question but asked it anyway for effect. "How long were you on the job?"

"Seven kleems."

"And you've been a mechanic the whole time?"

"Yes."

"You fixed broken things?"

"Yes, mostly. At the beginning I was assigned other jobs like everyone, but for the most part yes, I was a fixer."

"With your experience, don't you think it's likely one way or another you'll disturb things *wherever* you go if your memory is left intact? Haven't you learned anything from this job?"

One of the Deciders sternly scolded, "Enough, Crebold. You're out of line. You're being provocative and argumentative because you two obviously have issues. But those issues are not our concern here and you know it. He made a request, an entirely valid one, which is his right. Be quiet now; you've said enough."

Crebold was livid. Even here, even now, they were siding with Kaspar while at the same time putting *him* down. It was so unfair. His demeanor was placid but inside he seethed.

Kaspar asked, "Am I allowed to know how it works? How I go from this life to the new one?"

"It's instantaneous. One moment you're here and the next you inhabit the new life we've created for you. In your mind you'll have all the information necessary for complete integration. No one there will notice your arrival—we arrange it so whoever you're initially in contact with believes you've always been there."

Unsurprisingly in the end Kaspar was allowed to keep his memory and sent to Earth, of all places. The last conversation the two mechanics had before he left was civil if understandably cool. Crebold asked Kaspar if he knew anything about Earth.

"Not a single thing. They say it's pretty though—very green."

"Aren't you worried at all? It's a big move."

"No, I'm not worried."

Crebold was dubious but from what he could see, Kaspar was telling the truth. He didn't know whether to admire him or think him a fool.

"So here we are again—together just like old times." Crebold leaned back in the scarred bentwood chair. He put both hands behind his head and wove his fingers together. Looking around at the café he loudly sucked air through his teeth. Kaspar smiled because he did the same sucking thing all the time. It drove both Dean and Vanessa crazy.

"You're smiling, Kaspar. Is something funny? Something I said?"

"No, it's nothing."

"I should be laughing at you because I *knew* something like this was going to happen in time. I even said it at your review."

"Yes, you did. You were right."

"But they didn't listen to me, as usual."

"Because you're an asshole, Crebold. Everyone dislikes assholes."

Rather than show anger, Crebold yawned. He stretched it out a long time. Even from the other side of the table Kaspar could see into the back of the other man's mouth.

"Point taken, but asshole or not, I've been sent here because of your mistakes. Somehow we've got to figure out why this happened and then fix things."

Kaspar sat up. "Did they send you only because of this one dream, or have I made other mistakes too?"

Crebold pulled on an earlobe. "I can't answer that."

"You can't or *won't*? Okay. All right, then another question—are they interfering all the time? After we retire they erase our memories and send us empty-headed to nice places to live till we die—"

"No, Kaspar, not empty-headed—*altered*. You're an example: when they sent you to Earth you were reborn here as an early middle-aged man with a human mind. But because of your request, you actually have two—a mechanic's *and* a human mind. A very stupid thing to ask for, because two minds should never be mixed. You knew it. You were a *mechanic*, for God's sake."

"You're not answering my question, Crebold: once 'retirees' arrive wherever they're sent and are reborn, is there ever interference in our lives or do they leave us alone until we die?"

"Gentlemen, your orders." The waiter arrived carrying their drinks on an unusually large tray. Remembering Crebold's rudeness, he purposely put Kaspar's coffee down in front of him first and then the other's tomato juice—with a poached egg inside it. He paused a moment to look at the absurd drink, wanting to make sure the twin saw his slight sneer.

Crebold grinned. He reached for the glass and put his hand over the top of it. Addressing the waiter in perfect German he said, "You think we're twins but we're not."

The expression on the waiter's face said I don't understand what you're talking about but I don't care. Shaking his head, he gave a professional smile.

"Think of an ant farm or a beehive. All ants or bees look alike except for the queen, right? But each has a different duty. Some do the construction, others defend, some take care of the babies . . . but all ants look the same to us, right?" He pointed an index finger at Kaspar and then himself. "The two of us are mechanics. We fix things that break on the ant farm."

Kaspar slid a protesting hand across the table toward his twin. "Don't. Leave the man alone, please. Just let him go, okay?"

Crebold held up a finger to indicate he was almost finished.

Because Kaspar and the waiter were intent on watching his face and waiting to hear what he said next, neither paid attention to the gesture. His hand had been resting on top of the glass of tomato juice. When they did focus on it, they saw it was now completely covered with hundreds of jittering, moving, twisting black ants. Both men recoiled. From the top of the jacket cuff to the very tips of all five fingers, every centimeter of Crebold's left hand was covered with a thick, black, roiling mass of small ants moving busily in every direction.

Still smiling, he lowered his elbow to the table. Looking at it he turned his hand back and forth, admiring it from all angles. Kaspar thought that's exactly what he's doing—admiring his own cleverness. Ants kept dropping off onto the table. But instead of scurrying around after they'd fallen, whenever one fell off it crawled right back up Crebold's arm to the hand of shiny black motion.

"Remind you of the good old days, Kaspar?"

"Take it away, Crebold."

The large serving tray slipped through the waiter's fingers and almost fell to the floor. He caught it at the last moment and pulled it up against his chest as if to protect himself.

Crebold ignored both Kaspar and the ants swarming over his hand. He looked at the gaping waiter. "This is what I'm talking about. All these ants look alike, right? But every single one has a specific job. You'd never know it by looking at all these crazy little fellows now." His eyes moved back to the ants, a slight smile on his lips.

"Crebold, please stop. Leave him out of this."

A woman passing by happened to look down and saw the busy black hand. Horrified, she yelped loud enough so all the people at the surrounding tables glanced over to see why.

Kaspar was furious for two reasons: Crebold was showing off for no other reason than to display his powers to hapless "civilians." Yet one of the most important rules they'd learned and perfected as mechanics was stealth. Under no circumstance should you *ever* reveal to civilians either who you are or what you are capable of doing while on a repair job. It was an imperative of the highest order, one of the first they learned, repeated again and again by their instructors: *Never let others know who you are. Never let civilians know what you are doing or what you can do. Fix whatever you have been assigned to fix and get out as quickly as you can.*

But here was Crebold the asshole less than an hour after arriving, showing off dumb tricks that accomplished nothing other than making the little pisser feel pleased with himself for a few moments in front of an audience of civilians while possibly jeopardizing extremely important matters. It was shameful and inexcusable.

The bitter irony of the situation was Kaspar could do nothing to stop it. He'd been allowed to keep his mechanic's memory but not the powers. Before being sent to Earth he was warned this loss would surely cause him frustration. Times would surely come when he wanted or needed them badly, but a mechanic's powers and insight were always terminated upon retirement.

Exasperated now, he jerked his head away and looked out the café window. He was thinking about how to get this situation under control and stop Crebold from making things worse.

His eyes were caught by a bouncing bunch of orange shapes outside on the sidewalk. Focusing on them, Kaspar realized it was a group of jogging men in identical bright orange tracksuits. On the back of one man he glimpsed the word "Holland." Perhaps it was some team on its daily training run?

Moments later the café doors opened and all of these orange-suited men entered. There were six of them. Without hesitation they came right over to Kaspar's table, pushing the waiter and anyone else aside who got in their way.

On seeing them approach, Crebold's eyes widened. He started to get up but his thighs bumped into the stone tabletop and he was caught halfway between up and down. The men were of various sizes and shapes. Two looked to be Arab, one Polynesian, one black, and two Scandinavians. Each of them had a crew cut and an athletic body.

Surrounding the table in a semicircle, they stared at Crebold and not Kaspar. One of the Arab men, a contemptuous look on his face, shook his head, reached out, and grabbed hold of Crebold's black-encrusted hand. The ants disappeared instantaneously but the man did not let go. Wide-eyed Crebold looked caught and miserable.

Across the room someone shouted out, "Cut!" When Kaspar glanced over, he saw a burly unshaven man with a large camera on his shoulder moving toward them. The cameraman told the shocked waiter they were making a TV commercial here for insecticide. He reached into his pocket and pulled out a wad of bills. Handing the waiter a five-hundred euro note, he asked if it would be enough to cover his participation. The waiter was so thrown by the events of the last few minutes he could barely nod yes and look at the money in his hand.

"Great, thanks. We're finished here, boys. Let's move on to the next shot."

Everyone in the café stared as the orange men, the cameraman, the man with ants on his hand, and his twin all left together. Kaspar would not meet the eyes of anyone in the café because he did not want to see how they reacted to this lunacy.

Out on the street a bright orange minivan with BAGELS AND BEANS RACING TEAM painted in bold blue letters across its side sat idling by the curb in a no-parking zone. Crebold began protesting but to no avail. The cameraman commanded him to get in the van and keep his mouth shut. The disgraced mechanic did as he was told. All the orange men climbed in next, leaving Kaspar and the cameraman standing next to each other on the sidewalk.

"Do you know who I am, Kaspar?"

"Grassmugg."

The cameraman nodded, clearly pleased. They shook hands. "That's right. Good for you, Kaspar. So many years here but you still know. You can still recognize any active mechanics when you see us?"

"Yes, I'm sure you know that was part of my arrangement," Kaspar said quietly, although people passing paid no attention to either of them. "What's going to happen to Crebold now?" He tipped his head toward the van.

"He'll be parnaxed."

"*Really?*" Kaspar glanced warily at Grassmugg.

"Yes. We knew he hated you. It's why he was sent here now. We wanted to see if he could get over his personal animosity and work toward the general good, remember? We need all mechanics to be completely professional now. But Crebold doesn't have the maturity, so he must be disciplined."

Kaspar didn't like Crebold at all, but *parnaxed?* Ow.

Grassmugg patted him on the shoulder, then handed the video camera to someone inside the van. "You've got to figure out why you had the dream last night, Kaspar. It's extremely important you do. Dream sharing can lead to other situations that are not always good. Sometimes it reveals things no one should know about us or what we do." He spoke in a friendly, even voice. There was no scold or aggression in it, which was reassuring.

Kaspar nodded he understood and asked if they would be sending anyone else to help him handle this.

"No, you're on your own now."

Kaspar just said straight out what he was thinking. "Should I kill myself? Wouldn't that make everything a lot simpler? When the people in Vermont hear I died they'll all be horrified. My death will most likely make them forget ever having this dream. It seems like the most logical solution to this problem."

Grassmugg looked with clear approval at Kaspar while thinking over his suggestion. It was a good one and deserved serious consideration. "A commendable suggestion, Kaspar, and I appreciate the offer. It's probably why they let you keep your memory in the first place; you're still willing to sacrifice yourself when necessary. But I don't think it's time for that yet. We need you now—we need you here."

Kaspar's hotel was five blocks from the café. When the orange van drove off, he decided to walk back, which would give him time to think about how he was going to handle this matter. He started to reach for his phone but hesitated, shook his head, and slid it back into his pocket. He still wasn't ready to talk to Dean or any of them yet. Kaspar wanted to organize his thoughts, create some kind of plausible explanation for the dream that would make sense to the others and hopefully assuage their concerns.

Frankly he was surprised something like this had not happened before in his life, or rather in *this* life. At his review meeting they'd said he would probably run into some kind of trouble if he chose to retain his mechanic's memory after being reborn on Earth. As soon as you were retired and "wiped," all of your previous powers were canceled too. That's why most mechanics preferred having their memories erased: best to go into your new life with a mind like a blank sheet of paper just like any other newborn, no matter where you were relocated.

Some time ago Kaspar and Vanessa had been watching television. It was one of those afternoon talk shows; the subject for the day was reincarnation and the afterlife. After listening to three "experts" blab on a subject they knew nothing about, Kaspar said people don't remember their past lives because it would either be too depressing, painful, or confusing. "We don't even get over bad high school memories! How would knowing you were once a slave in ancient Peru, cut into pieces and fed to wild dogs because you were insubordinate, help you to live better now?

"Most lives are either boring or they suck. Do people really think it was any different in the past?"

Vanessa was eating one of the scrumptious raspberry-filled pierogies she'd baked that morning because she would be spending the afternoon with Kaspar and knew how much he liked them. "I disagree—I'd *love* to know about my past lives. I totally believe in reincarnation. Jane told me about my last one. She can do it, you know." A bloop of raspberry preserve fell onto the back of her hand.

"Do *what?*"

"Tell who you were in your last life."

Kaspar looked at her with one skeptical eye closed. "And you believe her?"

"Oh yes." Vanessa nodded while licking the jam off her hand. "She said I was an American bomber pilot in World War II. My plane was shot down over Essen. That's in Germany."

Kaspar bit into his fourth pierogi. The image of Vanessa Corbin in the pilot's seat of a B-17 airplane, flying perilous bombing missions over the Ruhr Valley in wartime Germany, was so preposterous and out of character that he wanted to laugh out loud.

"Sounds very heroic, but what if Jane had said instead you were a

Romanian gypsy street beggar who died of exposure in Bucharest in the terrible winter of 1958?"

Vanessa looked at him and chuckled. "Me? Never happen."

"Why not?"

She fed him the last bit of her pierogi. "Because I'm *me*, sweetie."

She tripped and they met.

That's how Vanessa described meeting Kaspar Benn. It was snowing and the New York streets were icy. She tripped and a big man wearing a very beautiful Chesterfield coat standing directly behind her at the curb caught her by the elbows as she started to fall. They had a little chat there on the sidewalk and she invited him for a cup of cocoa at this cute place she knew nearby. An hour later she invited Kaspar to meet her husband, Dean, who she thought he'd like because both men happened to be in the same business.

Accustomed to Vanessa's sweet habit of collecting strangers who interested her, Dean dutifully went to lunch to meet the man who'd caught his wife. Kaspar liked Dean Corbin immediately, but then he usually liked most people he met. Kaspar liked being human too. Life on Earth had turned out to be an unexpected delight. In his previous life he'd heard horror stories about coworkers being retired to places, to planets, to unimaginably distant stars and other dimensions that were nightmares from the first moment they were reborn there. But not Kaspar; he lucked out. There was nothing unique about Earth, nothing special about human beings either. If he had to draw a comparison, he'd say life here was like a breakfast of bacon and eggs—simple but delicious and wholly satisfying. In fact as Kaspar grew more human, it became his favorite meal of all— bacon and eggs.

At the time they met, he was working selling men's accessories at

Brooks Brothers in Manhattan. Dean was the U.S. representative for an Italian cloth company. The men had a lot in common. They had things to talk about. They became fast friends.

Dean had saved a good deal of money and had access to more through business connections. The Corbins had talked for years about moving out of New York. Then came the mugging and that decided it. Over drinks one night, Dean asked his friend if he would be interested in opening a men's store together in a Vermont college town. Kaspar didn't have money because he spent it as quickly as he made it. But Dean was sure Kaspar Benn would be a perfect partner. He had superb taste in clothes. More important, he genuinely liked people and had a great way with them. Dean had watched him work at Brooks Brothers and always came away smiling. Benn had the innate talent for making customers feel both special and at ease when he was waiting on them. He made their shopping experience pleasant and fun. As a result, people he served frequently bought much more than they had originally intended, and always asked for Kaspar to help whenever they returned to the shop. When Dean made the observation, Kaspar was sorry he could not tell his friend the truth—he was good at his job because he employed exactly the same tactics on Earth he'd used in his former life as a mechanic: ingratiate yourself with the populace, pick your spots carefully, make whoever you're dealing with believe your decisions were *their* decisions, and once you've accomplished the goal, drift away as unobtrusively as a summer cloud. Human beings were so needy in their insecurity. They loved it when you complimented them, purred like just-fed cats when you remembered what they liked or approved of their taste and choices. They liked to be led but didn't like knowing it.

Kaspar was not averse to leaving New York, although he had thoroughly enjoyed living there. Women were plentiful, the variety of available cuisines and delicious meals endless, but best of all he was rarely bored. Sometimes it felt like whenever he walked out the door he was swept along in some kind of entertaining adventure, or an interesting confrontation that the onetime mechanic appreciated. In many ways after his last life, living as a human being was for Kaspar much like a science fiction story where the character is sent back in time with only his wits and bare hands to cope with the undreamed-of limitations and difficulties of a distant past. When he read H. G. Wells's novel *The Time Machine* he grinned all the way through the story.

Then Kaspar Benn fell in love. One fall day, an eighty-seven-pound American blue nose pit bull terrier named Slab marched toward him on Thirty-ninth Street. The dog looked like a molasses-colored sumo wrestler on four short muscular legs, with a huge head shaped like a United Parcel Service delivery truck. The hound appeared to be smiling.

Kaspar was a goner. He liked animals but didn't love them. He was happy to eat them when they were properly prepared. But in all his days as a human being he had never seen a creature like the burly and supremely confident Slab. It really was love at first sight. On the spot he tried to buy the dog from its owner at any price, but no go. However, he did get the name and telephone number of Slab's breeder in Texas. Shortly afterward Kaspar brought home his new roommate—a formidable-looking eight-month-old steel gray pit bull named D Train. Vanessa said the puppy looked like a creature from the underworld in *Peer Gynt*. Dean said it looked like a Samoan.

Luckily D had an exceedingly sunny temperament. Despite looking fearsome, he pretty much liked the whole world and was delighted to make friends with anyone, two- or four-legged. The only problem was his explosive enthusiasm. If some unsuspecting soul came over to say hello, D Train launched himself at the person, a squat sixty-pound muscular missile of flying fervor and love. Cats or small dogs were no different. Strangers were astonished when the silvery beast catapulted himself like a base jumper off the sidewalk into their chest or onto the back of their panicked pet.

Kaspar dutifully took his young ward to obedience school but it was an entertaining bust. D befriended all the other dogs in his class while never learning to obey even one command.

Kaspar couldn't blame him though. In his last life, the pit bull had been a zgloz on Ater, a smelly, dreadful planet. Anyone familiar with Ater knew joy came in mighty short supply there. The puppy didn't know it, but in this new life on Earth he was just showing how happy he was to be away from such a miasma of misery.

At the obedience school Kaspar met an Italian woman who approvingly called D Train *svitato*, which translates as either "screwball" or "unhinged." But as long as words like "joyfully" or "cheerfully" were used as a modifier—joyfully *svitato*—then Kaspar could live with it and figure out how to manage his cheerful screwball.

Several months later the dog was shot. One night after a party Kaspar took D Train out for a late walk. Both of them enjoyed doing that. Kaspar smoked a leisurely cigar while D could sniff around and investigate anything for as long as he wanted because he sensed the boss was in no hurry. Ten minutes along, the puppy suddenly screeched, staggered, and collapsed where he stood. Blood started gushing down his right rear thigh. Walking a ways in front and lost in thought, it took Kaspar several moments to realize D was no longer moving and his dog had cried out. Turning, he saw the animal lying on its side, blood glistening wetly there, illuminated by a streetlight overhead. The hit leg was twitching, looking like it was trying to run away. D tried to twist his head enough so he could lick the wound. Out of nowhere and for no apparent reason someone had *shot* this dear dog.

Luckily a taxi was passing on the other side of the street and the driver saw the whole thing happen. He jammed on the brakes even though he had a fare in the back. Both driver and passenger jumped out of the car and helped Kaspar move the dog in. Blood was everywhere. D Train moaned, cried out when lifted, and whimpered heartrendingly as they shifted him on the seat. He kept looking up at Kaspar with terrified, imploring eyes as if his friend, his big human God who fed and loved him every day, could stop the searing pain. Kaspar was out of his mind with confusion, frustration, and rage. How could this happen? How could someone do this hideous thing to a *puppy?*

The cab driver knew where an emergency veterinary hospital was on Fifteenth Street, a few minutes away. While racing along, he kept yelling over his shoulder to put a tourniquet on the leg and cut off the blood flow. Hold on, we're almost there.

The most frightening part of the experience came when the dog grew gradually silent. Lying on the backseat, D Train still occasionally tried to lift his head and lick the wound, but after a while he stopped moving altogether and made no more sounds. Sitting next to him, Kaspar could almost feel the life energy drain from the puppy's stocky body.

As a mechanic, Kaspar Benn could have healed the dog in seconds. It was maddening now because he'd once had the knowledge to heal anything, but no longer—not here, not in this life. Everything he'd ever known and used as a mechanic was gone except the awareness that once upon another lifetime he could have fixed or healed anything on Earth. If his dog died now, Kaspar knew he would blame himself for being unable to save his small friend.

Fortunately D Train didn't die. After two operations and a slow recovery due to unexpected complications, he walked with a marked limp, which remained for the rest of his life. Otherwise he remained the same rambunctious sweet-natured fellow. The only other real change was his jumping-for-joy (and anything else) days were over.

But the shooting definitely changed Kaspar. While waiting for D's initial prognosis at the animal hospital that night, he decided to leave New York for good. He would move to Vermont along with the Corbins and make a new life in the state the couple seemed to like so much. More important, hard as it might be to accomplish, he would do everything in his power to ignore, or with any luck actually *forget*, his previous existence as a mechanic. He would make every effort to become more human. In many ways it would be analogous to moving from teeming Manhattan to the small mountain town. He would strive to make both "moves" work.

Contrary to what he'd originally thought, Kaspar knew now past-life memories did no good if you could not use or apply them here and now. What agony it must be for people afflicted with Alzheimer's disease. What torment to hold an object in your hand you *know* you know but can no longer name or remember its purpose. Worse, to look at a person some elemental part of your mind recognizes but the rest of you does not. That's how it felt holding the dog on his lap and watching it suffer. Once he could have healed D Train, but no longer. Better to turn away, turn away from this gorgeous city and a past that was fascinating but useless now and thus best forgotten. He did not know if it was possible, but he would certainly try.

So Kaspar Benn loaded his wounded dog, his beautiful wardrobe, and a few other things into a dubious four-wheel-drive Subaru with 83,000 miles on it he bought for his life in New England. He drove north on the twenty-ninth of May, his birthday, stopping often along the way to eat local delicacies he'd read about on food Web sites. He particularly liked the lobster roll in Noank, Connecticut. While driving and while he ate, memories from his life as a mechanic drifted into his head as they always had in the past. Only now he consciously pushed them away, shoved them really, and if some of these memories were persistent or unwilling to move, he tried hard to ignore or at least not dwell on them.

When he worked at Brooks Brothers, Kaspar was friendly with another salesman there, a transplanted Dutchman named Remco Snoerwang.

Remco collected Malaysian parang machetes and Indonesian *golok* knives. He kept every single one of the scary-looking things in his collection razor-sharp. He said sharpening knives and ironing shirts were his ways of relaxing.

One Monday Remco came to work late looking very sad. While he was out of town over the weekend, his apartment had been broken into and his entire knife collection stolen along with some other important possessions. Ironically, the only thing the thieves left behind was the special Japanese sharpening stone for the blades. Kaspar knew what a terrible loss it was because he'd been to Remco's place and listened while his friend enthusiastically recounted how he'd acquired each knife. He was not married, had no girlfriend, and lived simply in a small studio apartment with one window. His knives were his only treasure but now they were gone.

After commiserating about the loss, Kaspar asked Remco what he was going to do about it. The other man held a large paper shopping bag. He brought it up and put it on the counter between them. Reaching in, he lifted out a colorful yellow, red, and blue box. "It took me a while to start breathing again after I discovered the knives were gone. Then after going to the police station and filling out a report, I sat on a bench and thought about it. I ended up going to the nearest appliance store and buying this: the most cutting-edge, high-tech, expensive steam iron I could find."

His answer was so peculiar and unanticipated that Kaspar laughed.

Remco laughed too, shook his head, and patted the box. "It cost a small fortune, but it's the only effective therapy I could think of. I will go home tonight and iron all my shirts to perfection. *That'll* be my way of moving on." He slid the box back into the shopping bag. "My father taught me a good lesson about this, Kaspar. He said, buy whatever you want in life so long as you can afford it: a Ferrari, thirty-dollar cigars, *golok* knives . . . it doesn't matter what. Enjoy the hell out of them, but never *ever* own anything you can't walk away from. Like if your house caught fire, no matter how much you love your possessions, you can still walk out the door without feeling the need to go back for any of them. Let it burn. And if it's gone, it's gone—the end. Sure you love it and of course you'll miss it, but never forget *it's only stuff.* Just walk away."

"Now you're sounding like a Zen Buddhist."

Remco nodded. "All I know is how dangerous it is to wrap your life around objects you own. Because sooner or later everything breaks or wears out, right? It rips, gets lost . . . *or* stolen, and no matter how it happens, when it's gone too often you feel gutted, like someone's cut off one of your limbs. But Kaspar, it's only *stuff.* Aren't we crazy to invest so much of our selves in it? A little perspective please. Own it, yes, love it, but make sure you're able to move on if you lose it. If you can't, then don't get it because it'll end up making you sick and it's one of the few diseases we can easily avoid."

"But you loved your knives."

"I did and I *do*, and I hope like hell they're found. But tonight what I've got is my brand-new super-duper steam iron. So I'm going to have an ironing orgy to make me feel better. And you know what? It will."

Kaspar thought about Remco as he drove out of Rhode Island into Massachusetts and shared donuts from a big bag with D Train, who lay contentedly on a magenta pillow on the passenger's seat. If he could apply Remco's "just walk away" approach to his past life, Kaspar was certain it would improve many things. His time as a mechanic was finished. There was nothing else to do but accept the fact and move on. He resolved to work toward that frame of mind.

For the most part he succeeded. The Vermont town turned out to be terrific—rural and charming but very hip too due in large part to the excellent private college there. Creating the Benn Corbin store from scratch was interesting, challenging work. And to his delighted surprise quite a few intriguing-looking women in the town didn't break eye contact when he crossed paths with them on the streets.

One splendid summer afternoon Kaspar realized he had never been happier in his life or both of his lives, past and present. Not fireworks-orgasms-and-champagne happy, but on waking in the morning he was glad almost every single day to be exactly where he was. He had never before experienced the feeling of genuine, constant well-being and it was a true revelation. The longer the satisfaction continued, the less he thought about his previous life as a mechanic and the extraordinary things he'd once seen and been able to do. Misery may love company but happiness is content to be alone. The funny irony of his existence now was, as long as he was this happy and content with his lot, Kaspar didn't need to make much of an effort to "walk away" from his mechanic's life because now he was sated with *this* one both in mind and heart.

What added to his pleasure was D Train's company. From the beginning the dog loved living in the country. He loved their long walks together, loved to watch the wildlife everywhere around them—the rabbits, deer, and especially the birds. Once they even saw what appeared to be a moose way off in the distance. Man and dog looked at each other and, bedazzled, Kaspar couldn't help saying, "Pretty damned cool, huh?" D never showed the slightest desire to chase any of these animals—watching them was enough for him. For exercise he preferred digging holes, chewing the big bones Kaspar regularly brought him from the butcher, and sniffing the country air, which was always brimming with interesting and exotic new aromas he had never known before.

After work in the store the first summer, Kaspar often walked down the street to the town diner and had them make up a big sandwich for him. Then he'd drive out into the country with D Train, where they would walk for miles, at first very slowly, when the dog was still recovering. Kaspar liked to sit on a tree stump or boulder and eat his jumbo sandwich and drink a beer while watching the sun go down. D sat nearby, lifting his head now and then to sample various breezes or watch any nearby animals. Later when Kaspar started dating women from the town, he invited some of them to come along on these walks, which was fine with D, who always liked company. But Kaspar soon realized it was not the same when another person accompanied them. He had no children and was sure he never would. D Train was the closest to a son he had and these walks in the country belonged only to the two of them, which was as it should be.

Once after hearing Kaspar rhapsodize about a particularly beautiful September trek he'd taken in a forest, Dean suggested he buy camping gear and stay out in the woods for a night or two while the weather was still nice. Kaspar thought the suggestion was hilarious and said so. "I'm not Daniel *Boone*. I like to walk in the woods, but I like sleeping in a bed more."

He rented a small green cottage a few blocks from the section of town where the store was. He and the dog walked to work every day no matter the weather and made friends with most everyone they met along the way. Townspeople were first curious and eventually pleased when they got to know these two new neighbors. Kaspar was always willing to stop and chat with anyone. If asked, he would explain where he was from, why he was here, the name of his pit bull, where *he* came from . . . or basically anything others wanted to know. He never seemed in a hurry to leave.

D Train quickly became so familiar and popular in town, Dean suggested they use his likeness on their store logo, stationery, and business cards. When a customer came in, D would often follow them around the place like a salesman eager to help out. He never bothered anyone or intruded on their space unless he was invited over to be petted. The most interesting thing was despite D's great warmth and friendliness, he was quick to sense whenever someone didn't like dogs or him in particular. Once he'd caught their negative vibe, he would invariably retreat to a far corner of the store until the person left.

One afternoon in late August three women entered Benn Corbin when Kaspar was there alone. They were pleasant-looking but not at all unusual or specially dressed. Long hair down to their shoulders or up in ponytails, minimal makeup, none of their faces were memorable—sort of suburbs-pretty. The type of woman you see driving kids to soccer or band practice in either a big whomping SUV or a politically correct green machine like a Toyota Prius. You might notice her passing by, but mostly because she was blond and well kept.

These women all appeared to be in their late thirties or early forties, casually dressed in jeans and jersey shirts. One of them wore a frayed Baltimore Orioles baseball cap pulled low. Really, the only small detail that stood out was all three were wearing exactly the same kind of black and white high-top sneakers that looked right-out-of-the-box new.

Kaspar was arranging stock in the back of the store and didn't hear them come in. Reemerging with a pair of rust-colored corduroy trousers draped over one arm, he first saw D Train gazing lovingly up at one of the women, who was scratching the top of his head with long, perfectly manicured fingernails. On seeing the women, Kaspar stopped, shook his head, and gave a big smile. "Well, well, *well,* look who's here! What brought you ladies way up north?"

"We weren't sure how you'd react to seeing us," one of the women said.

"We didn't even know *if* you'd react, Kaspar. Maybe you wouldn't recognize us," said another.

"It's always possible," the third added while continuing to scratch the dog's head.

"How could I forget you guys? Come on, sit down on the couch. How long has it been since we've seen each other?" He shifted the pants from one arm to the other and walked forward to shake all of their hands for quite a long time. It seemed an unnecessarily formal thing to do, but the women accepted the gesture.

One of them said, "A thousand years?"

"Yes, about what I figured. And where was it?"

"The Gudrun Asteroid."

"Eee—that was a rough time. Especially how it ended up." Kaspar shook his head and looked out the window, remembering. "Wow, the Gudrun Asteroid. *Truly* unpleasant!"

"Yes, it was, but you didn't stick around to see what happened *afterward*. Even uglier, my friend, believe me."

Kaspar slid the corduroys onto a wooden hanger and hung them on a rack. "Really, it was bad? I had to go to another assignment."

"Brutal. Consider yourself lucky. Lots of blood on the stars after we were finished there."

"More like scorched earth," Number Two added while adjusting the tongue in her sneaker.

The third woman said nothing but her grim look said she agreed.

"Well, thankfully it's over. Why are you here now? I mean, I'm delighted to see you but curious too. Vermont's pretty far from home."

One of the women lifted a purse into her lap and opened it. Reaching in, she brought out a large black squirming shiny disgusting obviously alive, your-guess-is-as-good-as-mine *thing*. Kaspar watched calmly as she broke it into three wiggling pieces and handed them to her colleagues. Politely she offered her section to Kaspar but he put up a hand, no thanks. The women began eating their portions with great gusto.

"Have your tastes changed a lot since you've been here, Kaspar? Do you like food on Earth?"

"Yes, I do, it's terrific. I'm especially fond of coffee."

"How interesting, because none of us do. We prefer our own." The others nodded as they ate with obvious relish their portions of the revolting black writhing mass.

Kaspar wanted to find out before Dean returned why they had come here. Maybe there were things that needed discussing only among the four of them.

D Train lay down on the floor with a satisfied groan.

"You've never wanted to eat it?"

"The dog? No, he's my friend."

"*Really?* He looks very delicious, Kaspar."

"Tell me why you're here."

The dog scratcher said, "There's been a change. I mean, there's going to *be* a change. We were sent to warn you so you can prepare."

Kaspar tensed. "What kind of change?"

The woman in the baseball cap swallowed some food, wiped her mouth with a lilac-colored handkerchief, and said, "A Somersault."

"No! Soon?" Kaspar was stunned.

"Yes."

"They haven't had a Somersault since—"

"We know."

His voice rose into complaint. "But what am I supposed to do about it? And what about others like me? I've been really conscientious the whole time I've been here. Never broke a rule, never told anyone anything—nothing, not a word. Even when my dog was shot and I thought he was going to die I stayed silent and didn't ask for help. I've been good."

"We know, Kaspar, but this isn't only about you, remember. Everything and everyone will be affected—us too. We're threatened by it too."

"Yes, but you're mechanics and this is a *Somersault*. You have your powers; I have nothing but memories *of* those powers. A hell of a difference. When will it begin?"

"They don't know; no one ever knows with one. We all just have to be ready. It's why they sent us out to talk to those who chose to keep their memories. Obviously it's going to be harder on you. It could happen anytime. You're one of the last we have to see."

Slapping his thighs in fear and frustration, Kaspar groaned, "*Jesus!*"

One of the women asked sweetly, "Who's Jesus?"

As testament to his ever-increasing humanity, Kaspar didn't really notice when things began to change, albeit the first signs were small. Of course right after the three women visited he was vigilant and skittish about strange sounds or occurrences, frowned at out-of-the-ordinary anythings or psychic bumps in his road. But when life remained calm and very much same-old, same-old day after day with no suspicious dark clouds looming on his horizon, he was gradually lulled into thinking mostly about other much more pleasant things, like the affair he had begun with Vanessa Corbin, or her heavenly recipe for Polish *zurek* soup.

In a way Kaspar Benn was like the people who reside in areas of frequent earthquake activity—San Francisco, Thessaloniki, Islamabad. Ask them how they can bear living in a place under constant threat, how they can confidently walk around every day on a piece of earth that is not their friend and probably planning at this very minute its next attempt to kill them. The citizens of these shakyvilles say they've got an emergency pack all ready to go complete with flashlight, bottled water, canned salmon, and three flares. Or they get stoic and cite well-worn bromides like when your time's up, your time's up—so live with it: carpe diem. *Or* they turn feisty and annoyed at you for bringing up the ugly, sword-of-Damocles subject. They rebuke you for being morbid. It's not possible to really discuss it with them because deep down they know they're living on borrowed time (or borrowed *Earth*) but have grown adept at keeping the eventuality out of their thoughts. In other words, after Kaspar learned a Somersault was imminent he looked away from the abyss by immersing himself in the many pleasures inherent in being human. There was sex and food, fine cashmere and shell cordovan shoes, and those gorgeous long walks in the woods with D Train.

Kaspar was a man with a sunny nature who liked bourgeois things, not overly bright but so what? He had realized the smarter a person was, the more unhappy they often were for a variety of reasons, both logical and not. Selfish but effortlessly charming, he was especially good at knowing when to take and when to give. He had no qualms about fucking his partner's wife, but he also worked tremendously hard to make Benn Corbin successful. Both he and Dean knew, without his many significant contributions, not least of which was his winning personality, the store would have failed.

Kaspar knew the Somersault had begun when he started sharing others' dreams. These people did not know it was happening, but he did immediately. In essence while asleep, he moved into their heads and witnessed their night dreams along with them. Kaspar fully enjoyed the occurrence and eagerly looked forward to these uninhibited, candid peeks in the windows of others' subconscious. Yes, it was a kind of voyeurism but he didn't care and didn't feel guilty. The experience was good fun, a free ticket to someone else's hidden home movies. The dreamers weren't hurt, and some of the things he saw on these excursions were instructive. He knew for certain this dream sharing had to do with the start of the Somersault.

The first time it happened he actually awoke laughing because what he had just witnessed was funny. He knew the dream he'd experienced belonged to Vanessa Corbin. When he saw her the next afternoon at the store he wanted to ask if she ever really had had sex with an orthodox Jewish rabbi standing up in the back of a moving bakery truck. But he didn't.

Or the time normally placid Dean came into the store one morning. Clapping Kaspar on the shoulder, the first thing he said was a gleeful, "You *dog*." Kaspar knew the correct response was to smile quizzically and ask his partner, why am I a dog? But he already knew. The night before, Dean had dreamed his old college girlfriend Melinda Szep and Kaspar had gotten together. Dean had caught the couple in his college room bunk bed.

But he didn't feel betrayed because in the dream he was already married to Vanessa and Kaspar was twenty years old.

After Dean described his dream and both men sniggered a little awkwardly, Kaspar thought it would be good to ask what Melinda looked like. Dean put up two approving thumbs. He was right—from what Kaspar had seen in last night's dream theater, the young woman was definitely a knockout.

Big as he was, D Train insisted on sleeping on Kaspar's bed with him. As a puppy he was brought up there so the young dog would sleep better and feel more secure at night, especially after being shot. But this turned out to be a bad idea because as he grew older, D took it for granted he belonged on any bed with the boss—a kind of canine eminent domain. In the course of a night he might be pushed off four times but the stubborn soul wouldn't take no for an answer. With the grace and stealth of a ninja, he'd wait a few minutes for the coast to clear and Kaspar to fall back to sleep. Then the wily pit bull crept back up over the side of the bed and settled in until the next foot shoved him off again.

When they moved to Vermont, Kaspar bought an outsized, marvelously comfortable dog bed from L.L.Bean. He placed it three feet across the floor from his own, but D wasn't having it. He only catnapped on this bed when there was nothing else to do.

The ongoing human-dog battle for the Benn bed might have sounded humorous but wasn't very *ha-ha* for any lover who woke up in the middle of the night with a thick gray paw on her cheek or breast, put there in friendship and camaraderie by the other (furry) man in the bed.

Particularly the poor woman—a first-time visitor, no less—who happened to be sleeping over the night Kaspar and D Train shared the same dream. At 4:13 A.M. both fellows came yowling awake and looking wildly around for the horrible creature that seconds before was hot on their heels, its slavering cavernous mouth open to devour them, its breath near, smelling of meat and heat and you're next.

People wonder what dogs dream about; why they twitch, shake, and yip deep down in their REM sleep. Kaspar could tell you why: because they dream they're being pursued by things too awful for words, too big to measure, and too ferocious to grasp by a sane mind. Dogs take everything they know and experience down into their sleep where they blow it up a hundred times. When it's something awful—times a hundred—*that* is what chases them in their dreams and why they're running like hell horizontally to get gone. But sometimes they're outrun. Their dream monsters catch and devour them in crunchy 3-D, feel-your-bones-snap death-o-rama.

This is what canines dream of sometimes, and former mechanic to the stars or not, it scared the wee-wee out of Kaspar Benn. Coming awake, both dog and man sprang off opposite sides of the bed, leaving the poor naked woman cowering half-asleep in the middle, sure the world was coming to an end. The dog barked while her lover snarled at some unseen shared enemy while squatting down in a defensive jiu-jitsu stance.

Afterward Kaspar sometimes shared D Train's dreams but mostly those of his other friends in town. Generally he enjoyed them. Dream sharing was one of the many skills a mechanic needed to learn and develop, so it surprised him when he regained the ability again as a mere mortal here on Earth.

The big difference was in this second life he was powerless to interact. If he didn't like a dream, too bad—he was stuck in it as long as it lasted. Of course a functioning mechanic could change any dream if it was necessary. Right before he was retired, one of Kaspar's greatest challenges and eventual triumphs was the time he wrestled a dream away from a disturbed being near the Gudrun Asteroid and in doing so, helped her perilously unstable planet survive.

But not here. When he shared others' dreams on Earth he was only along for the ride. It didn't matter because most of the time these dreams were enjoyable and frequently informative. He learned things about his friends he was certain they'd never divulge on their own. He learned important lessons about being human. He also learned D Train was for some mysterious reason afraid of carrots.

TWO

After the airplane took off the night before, Kaspar had originally planned to make a detailed list of all the things he needed to do in Vienna. He also wanted to play a new video game he'd downloaded onto his iPad a few days before. But to his mild surprise he felt completely exhausted after eating dinner and decided to nap for an hour or two before doing anything else.

By the time he awoke, the plane was already crossing the Irish coastline. It made no difference because he was too disturbed by what he'd just experienced to do anything he'd originally planned for the flight. Wide eyed and sitting stiffly upright in his seat, he stared unseeing at the blank television screen on the seat back in front of him, all the while trying to grasp what had just happened and, more important, what it meant.

Kaspar Benn, Jane Claudius, Bill Edmonds, and the two Corbins had somehow combined their separate dreams into one and then all five of them experienced the mix at exactly the same time.

Eventually Kaspar got out a large notepad he usually only used for business matters. For the rest of the flight, he wrote on it until the plane landed in Vienna. When a flight attendant walked down the aisle checking to see if everyone's seat belt was fastened, she glanced down to see what the man was writing and paused.

"Wow! What's all that?" She smiled, raising her eyebrows to show how impressed she was while pointing at the notebook.

Kaspar looked up but said nothing, which was very unlike him. His expression would trouble the woman for some time. The flight attendant was usually very good at reading people. It was part of her job and she prided herself on the skill. But what she saw on this guy's face was not only impossible to read, but a contradiction. That was the only word for it. On the one hand the man's face said I'm busy, can't talk now, but thanks for your interest. At the same time his large brown eyes were ice cold, steely and appraising. In an instant she felt like he was looking straight *into* her and seeing things she didn't allow anyone to see.

"It's a map."

"Excuse me?" His glance had unsettled her so she didn't register he was answering her question.

"I said it's a map."

The flight attendant immediately wanted to say, it is *not* a map. The page was filled from corner to corner with detailed, precise drawings of mysterious figures and what looked like hieroglyphics, intricate illustrations, strange alphabets, and abstruse-looking math problems. Also, single words and sentences were written in fine calligraphy. The paper looked like some kind of recondite illuminated manuscript from the Middle Ages.

On the taxi ride into Vienna, Kaspar continued writing on his notepad. But it was a new drawing this time. If the flight attendant were to see *this* page it would have made her even more confused. The entire sheet of paper was covered with seventy-two identically drawn glass ink bottles. They were done in pencil in photo-realistic detail. It was uncanny how much they looked like the real thing. All that distinguished one from the other were the skillfully lettered labels on each bottle describing the color of ink inside each one—cerulean, feldgrau, obsidian, burnt sienna, caput mortuum, gamboge, cerise. . . .

Most impressive about what Kaspar was doing was the speed with which he drew the bottles. There was so much complex detail involved in rendering each one—shadowing, lettering on the labels, and perfectly aligning one right next to the other like toy soldiers. Yet all of the execution took him no more than a minute and a half per bottle from start to finish.

The taxi driver looked at his passenger in the mirror twice during the ride into town: the first time Kaspar's head was down so it looked like he was seriously concentrating on whatever he was working on in his lap. The second time the driver glanced at him Kaspar was staring out the window as they passed the Schwechat oil refinery. What the driver couldn't see both times was how quickly the passenger's hand sped over the page, drawing. Even when Kaspar stared out the car window his hand kept moving. What it drew was as detailed, perfect, and accurate as everything else already on the page.

He had finished by the time the taxi pulled up in front of his hotel in the Sixth District. Tearing the paper off the pad, he folded it carefully in four quarters and slipped it into a pocket.

In his room he took it out along with the one he'd done on the plane. Opening both, he wedged them into opposite corners of a large mirror that faced the bed. After unpacking his bag he sat on an uncomfortable chair and stared at the two drawings a long time. Sometimes he would close one eye and after a while the other. He'd put up a hand to block part of a drawing. In time he dropped his head to his chest and sighed. This was not going to be easy.

Kaspar thought about calling Vermont but wasn't ready to talk with them yet about the dream. He looked at his watch. It was 3:30 in the afternoon, 9:30 in the morning in Vermont. He needed more time to think. If he spoke to Dean or any of the others right now he might say something he'd later regret, and that was dangerous. He knew as little as they did about why they'd shared the dream and more important, why they all knew it.

The three blond women who'd visited Kaspar Benn in Vermont months before were back in town. They sat together now in the same restaurant where he had breakfast every morning. They were all eating the corn chowder recommended by the waitress.

"So anyway, thanks to Kaspar, at least the five of them *finally* shared a dream."

"Here's to Kaspar, poor guy," said the blonde in the Russian fur hat. All three women raised water glasses in a toast to their former colleague. "But will someone please tell me why they sent *Crebold* to Vienna instead of us? Those two guys have hated each other since forever. Crebold made an ass of himself in what, forty-five minutes?"

Her colleagues exchanged glances but said nothing. Fur Hat looked from one woman to the other and scowled. "What? Do *you* know why Crebold was sent?"

Another knowing look passed back and forth between the two others.

"Stop it and just answer my question: why did they send Crebold?"

One woman took a deep breath and said, "Nobody told us specifically, but it's kind of obvious, isn't it?"

Indignant, Fur Hat raised her chin slowly. "No, not to me. You're both making me feel stupid, which is not very nice, so would you please explain?"

The third blonde said, "It was a test: they wanted to know how Kaspar would react to seeing Crebold after all this time. And then if he'd recognize Grassmugg. He recognized both of them right away, just like he recognized us. Humans usually have terrible memories. They didn't know what would happen with Kaspar."

"He remembered everything," the blonde sitting next to Fur Hat added.

"No, not everything; he doesn't know why the five of them shared the dream, so he's still human in one respect."

"True, and that's great; he's reached the perfect mix of the two. It's just what they wanted."

"This soup is good."

"It's *very* good—for human food."

Secretly all three women had specific things they liked a lot about life on Earth, even though they'd only been there a short time. They didn't tell each other though because none of them wanted to appear unprofessional. Whenever they came it was to do a job, not indulge (as individually they had been) in competitive ballroom dancing, the Silbo Gomero click language, or herpetology.

Fur Hat stood up and said she had to urinate—another thing she enjoyed very much about being human. The waitress directed her to the toilet. It was a while before she returned because she spent an excessive amount of time peeing and then reapplying her makeup in the restroom mirror. She loved watching makeup commercials on television. She was by far the vainest of the three blondes. She craved attention and wasn't particular about who gave it to her. Her name was Jezik.

When she returned to the restaurant, her table was empty. She went stock-still seeing this, not believing it was true. These three women never separated without telling each other where they were going. They had worked together for centuries and inseparable was just the way they did things. They were rarely apart at all because they'd found over the years constant close proximity helped them function better and solve problems more quickly.

The waitress passed. Jezik asked her where the other two women had gone. The room was crowded and the waitress was busy trying to juggle many orders at once. She looked at the empty table and thought a moment. "Were you with other people? I don't remember. I didn't see them go, to tell you the truth. Sorry. Should I give you the check?"

Troubled, Jezik nodded and waited while the woman wrote it out. What was happening? Where were the others?

The blondes had been ordered back to Earth as soon as the five human beings shared the dream. Now that it had happened, they were supposed to help Josephine with the gathering when the right moment came.

Some of the dream was true to life, some not. Certain sections were understandable only to the separate individuals. However, the most important part of this shared dream had to do with their past lives as mechanics. All of the people should have recognized those parts instantly.

But it didn't happen. Despite being right there in front of their faces for all five to see, none of the previously very good mechanics noticed or responded to the dream's main message.

At about the same time, something took place in the Fornax Dwarf galaxy. A mechanic doing a task there too difficult to explain suddenly disappeared. Here one moment, gone the next. It was unheard of. Mechanics never just disappeared. Mechanics didn't disappear at all. It was like electrons disappearing from inside an atom. Equally astonishing was that this sudden disappearance wasn't seen by those around her. The mechanic vanished while performing a job in the middle of a large crowd but no one saw it happen.

Later in Vermont two blond mechanics sipped savory soup while waiting for their partner to return from the toilet. And in a blink they were both gone. Not one person in the restaurant noticed.

Plans were going wrong everywhere.

After paying the bill, Jezik walked outside and stood on the snow-covered sidewalk looking around, hoping to see her peers—but they were not there. Next something remarkable happened: for the first time in her very long life, the mechanic felt fear. It was so alien, peculiar, and yet all-encompassing that when it hit, all she could do was stand still and stiff, feeling the force of it grow larger and larger within her. She began to tremble, knowing soon she would be all fear; there would be no more room inside her for anything else.

It was the most powerful sensation Jezik had ever experienced.

And then she too disappeared.

Chaos had arrived in full force.

D Train's greatest and most beloved friend in the world was a yellow sharpei/Labrador retriever mix named Kos, who lived two houses down the street. His owners found him in an animal shelter on the Greek island of Kos while vacationing there. The dogs met the day Kaspar moved to town because Kos was allowed to wander free and he came by to check out the new neighbor. It was big love at first sight and the two became inseparable. This was very convenient because it meant the owners could leave the dogs with each other whenever they went out of town. Except this time all of the owners had to be gone for the week. But Dean Corbin stepped in and volunteered to take care of the dogs at his house. Vanessa loved animals and particularly these two goofy galoots. They were her biggest fans. Whenever the three of them were together, D Train and Kos followed Vanessa around like she was a saint and a movie star combined and they were her fanboy acolytes.

She was addressing them now when Dean entered the kitchen on the day after the dream. Both dogs stared intently at her as if they understood and hung on to every word she said. "I know a *lot* of Debbys. It just dawned on me."

"Who are you talking to?"

"The dogs; I just realized I know a *lot* of women named Debby; not Deborah—*Debby*. Isn't that odd? How many Debbys do you know?"

Dean ignored her question. "Vanessa, what are you doing? Why are you here? We're all in the other room trying to figure out what to do about this dream."

"I *know*, Dean, but we've been trying to *figure it out* for the past three hours and I got hungry. So I'm cooking something for all of us because I assume the others are hungry too."

He sat down on a chair at the table in the middle of the room. "It's good you're in here alone anyway because we obviously have to talk."

Surprised, she looked at her husband. "We do? Talk about what?"

"About what? About the *dream*, Vanessa. About you having an affair with Kaspar. About the fact we've been at each other's throats an awful lot the last few months and things were said in the dream *we actually did say.* I'm wondering now how many other things in there were true."

"Oh come on, Dean. Do you really think I'm having an affair with your partner and best friend?"

"*Are* you?"

She turned to him and made an exasperated face. "Do you own a sled? A seven-hundred-dollar sled?"

"No."

"Well, you did in the dream. So, you don't have a sled and I don't have a lover."

He waggled a finger at her. "No, no—it's not so simple, Vanessa."

"Why not?"

"Because you lie about big things. We both know it and this is a big thing. We *have* been fighting like dogs and cats recently. Sometimes I get the feeling . . . I don't know . . . maybe we are in real trouble and neither of us is brave enough to admit it."

She turned back to the stove and continued preparing the food. "I'm making saltimbocca. Do you know what the word means in Italian? 'Jumps into the mouth.' This recipe is so good that when it's ready, it jumps into your mouth all by itself."

Frustrated, Dean shook his head. "Relevance please?"

Every time one of the Corbins spoke, the dogs' eyes moved back and forth between them, as if they were watching a tennis match.

"Husband, there are very few things in my life so good they jump into my mouth by themselves. I swear to God you are one of them. Yes, we *have* been fighting a lot lately and sometimes it's been mean and ugly. But so what, Dean? Couples who've been together as long as we have fight, and yes, it does bring out the worst in both of us sometimes. *Mea culpa and you're a culpa.* Does it mean I want to divorce you? No. Do I secretly dream about walking out or throwing coffee at you? No.

"I lie about things sometimes, I do, but do you really believe I'd risk our relationship for a few good bonks?"

"Yes, Vanessa, I do. You can be very selfish when it comes to things you want and you don't give a damn for other people's feelings if you want it badly enough. You and I have fought way more in the last few months than we ever did in the past. Times have been rough between us and you know it. Sometimes I feel we really *don't* like each other." Dean's voice was calm and even; there was no hurt or accusation in it. He was simply stating facts.

"Dean, Vanessa—come in here! You've got to see this."

Jane was calling, but they'd never heard her voice sound so loud and shrill. The Corbins often joked Jane Claudius was Queen Poise, stealth itself, the cool ninja. Everything she did—the way she spoke, her languid yet precise gestures, how she moved—most everything about her was the embodiment of cool. But right this minute she sounded like her hair was on fire.

The couple hurried out of the kitchen followed closely by the dogs. In his rush, Dean let the kitchen door swing back hard. It hit D Train smack on the head. Unaffected, the big gray pit bull just kept moving, followed by his pal Kos.

The living room was the largest room in the Corbins' house. When they first moved in, Dean measured it by striding across. On reaching the other side he announced triumphantly, "This room is *big*; it took twenty regular steps to cross it!"

Hovering now in the middle of the big room was a blue-gray cloud about three feet wide by four feet high. It was not low like ground fog or bumping against the ceiling like a regular cloud in the sky. It hung halfway between floor and ceiling at eye level.

"What the hell . . . ?"

"Where did *that* come from?"

Jane and Bill Edmonds stood on opposite sides of the living room. Both had their arms crossed over their chests in exactly the same manner and looked like mirror images of each other.

Vanessa said, "It's an Aurora Cobb."

"Who is? What do you mean?"

"The cloud—it's called an Aurora Cobb."

"Who's that?"

"It's not a *who*—it's a *what*. An Aurora Cobb is a *thing* and I know for sure it's bad."

Dean looked at his wife as if she were insane.

Seeing his expression she said in an irritated voice, "You asked what it is and I'm telling you: *that* cloud is an Aurora Cobb and it's a dangerous thing. Maybe it's not bad but I know for sure it's dangerous. *Finito*." Without looking at anyone, Vanessa crossed her arms too.

While listening to the Corbins argue, Bill Edmonds realized he'd heard the weird name before—*Aurora Cobb*. The three-syllable prettiness of "Aurora" combined with the contrasting ugliness of "Cobb" for a last name was one you'd remember. Had he seen it written somewhere? Seen it or heard it? He couldn't remember, but when Vanessa said the name, it *was* familiar to him.

Tail wagging, Kos walked past Dean and Vanessa over to the cloud in the center of the room. All four people stiffened and felt the same impulse to lunge forward and stop the yellow dog from going any farther because of what Vanessa had said. At the same time, they were curious to see what would happen if the animal made contact with the blue thing.

For a moment Edmonds thought as soon as the dog touched the cloud, out of it would boom a stentorian voice saying something like, "I am the great and powerful Oz!"

Instead, Kos got right up close and stopped. Tail still wagging, he looked straight at the cloud but slowly tipped his head to one side in puzzlement. Then he turned it to the other side, the classic canine sign of "I'm confused." After more head turning back and forth, Kos raised his head as far back as it would go and let fly the longest, saddest howl any of them had ever heard from a dog. It was so distressing D Train and the humans knew the wail had to have come from the deepest reaches of pain in the animal. The mournful bay was uncanny. It went on and on although Kos did not move. Jane thought of the old phrase "to keen," as in a prolonged cry of abject grief. The dog was keening for something—there was no doubt about it.

The only one to move was D Train. He went to Kos and nervously licked his face over and over. It did no good; the yellow dog kept howling. Growing more frantic, D Train moved all around his friend, kissing him, bumping him with his head, trying to stop the other from crying. When he was as close to the cloud as Kos, he looked at it and did exactly the same thing: put his head back and began howling too.

"Jesus Christ. What's going on?"

Above this din, someone's phone began to ring. Dean reached into a pocket and took his out. Looking at the screen to check who was calling, his eyes widened when he saw it was his partner.

"Kaspar?"

"Dean, is a cloud there now? Wherever you are, do you see a cloud nearby, a big one? It's probably at ground level. Someplace it wouldn't normally be."

"Yes! One's right in the middle of our living room. How did you know?"

"Everyone there has to reach into it. Go up and reach right in. Nothing will happen—nothing bad. That's all you need to do. Grab hold of whatever your hand touches first inside the cloud and bring it out. Don't be afraid but make sure everyone does this. I'll explain more after you're finished."

Dean told the others.

"How *does* he know there's a cloud here?"

"I don't know but he said there's no time to waste. Just reach in and bring out whatever you touch first."

Edmonds and Jane said nothing but moved toward it.

Vanessa stayed where she was and shook her head. "I'm not getting near the thing; it's bad. I don't know anything else, but I know it's *dangerous* and I'm not doing it."

Dean told Kaspar. After listening to the other's response he held the phone out to his wife. "He says he wants to talk to you."

She took it hesitantly, as if even her husband's telephone might bite. She lifted it cautiously to her ear.

"Vanessa, the cloud's about three feet high, right?"

She nodded but kept quiet.

"Listen, it's *not* what you think it is. Vanessa, do you hear me? You think it's an Aurora Cobb, but it isn't. I swear to you. I'd be scared too if it was one of those, but it's not. You have to trust me."

"How do you know all this, Kaspar? How do you know its name? How did you know there's a cloud in here?"

"Because I'm looking at exactly the same kind of cloud here in my hotel room now and I recognize it."

"You have one there too?" She looked at the others to make sure they'd heard what she'd said.

"Yes. It's the same as yours. I'm sure of it."

"There's a cloud exactly like this in his hotel room," Vanessa announced before turning her attention back to Kaspar. "But why are they here? What are they?"

Kaspar spoke slowly and precisely. "They hold information and tools. They've brought tools we need now. But you have to get them *yourself*; each one of you has to reach inside the cloud to get what's specifically meant for you. There can be no exceptions because we're going to need anything it gives us—*anything*, do you understand? They're like separate pieces of a puzzle that fit together. If we don't have all the pieces, we won't be able to work out what to do. Please tell everyone they must do it and then I'll explain what comes next. Trust me on this, Vanessa."

She told the others what he'd said. The four exchanged glances, uncertainty in their eyes, all of them wondering who was going to move first. The dogs had stopped baying but both were panting now as if it were a hundred degrees in the room. D Train leaned over and once again started frantically licking the side of Kos's face.

"All right, what the hell—I'll do it. I'll go first." Bill Edmonds walked to the cloud and without hesitating stuck his whole arm in.

Jane rose on tiptoes and put both hands against her chest. "What do you feel?"

"Nothing—it's just . . . colder in there. Noth—wait a minute—now I feel it. There's . . . Yes! I've got something now."

"Something like *what*? What do you mean?"

In Vienna, Kaspar listened intently to this exchange through the bad speaker on his cell phone. He sat on the bed looking at his very own cloud halfway across his room. He'd lied to Vanessa but it was necessary—he needed her to convince the others to do what he said.

An Aurora Cobb *could* be hugely dangerous because they contained every tool a mechanic needed to repair any situation. In the wrong hands, however, those same tools could also cause irreparable damage or horrific suffering. But Kaspar had to chance it now because time was so short. The one thing he had gleaned from the shared dream was that, like him, the others had all been mechanics before they were human. He had to believe any former mechanic, even those with wiped memories, would still have retained some kind of instinctive, primal, or even blood recall necessary to choose the correct tool for them inside the cloud.

He remembered the first time he'd seen an Aurora Cobb. It appeared out of nowhere and despite the fact he and his fellow apprentice mechanics had been well schooled on what it was and the things it contained, Kaspar was still enthralled and frightened to see a real one in front of him. He could only imagine what it was like now for the four in Vermont who, as humans, knew nothing about the cloud or what it could do. The one good sign, however, was Vanessa recognized it although she didn't remember anything about it except the name and its potential danger.

Kaspar sighed, lost for a moment in past memories. Someone on the other end of the phone was speaking. He cleared his head and listened.

"What did you find, Bill?"

"I think it's a . . . it's a figure, a little statue."

Alarmed, Kaspar asked, "What is it? What did he take out? Describe it exactly."

Dean took a while to answer. "It looks like some kind of little wooden figure. I think it's one of those Japanese netsuke figures."

Almost simultaneously both Kaspar and Bill Edmonds said the same thing: "Keebler."

"It's *Keebler*—I can't believe it. This belonged to my wife!"

The figure was two inches high. It was a Japanese sumo wrestler carved out of a tagua nut. Originally ivory colored, some of the paint had worn off here and there so one of the wrestler's eyes was blank while the other was detailed in black.

Edmonds held it out on an open palm for the others to see.

Kaspar shouted, "Put it back!"

Phone pressed to his ear, Dean wasn't sure he'd heard Kaspar correctly. "*What?*"

"Tell him to put it back. Put it back in the cloud *right now!*"

"Why? What's the matter?"

"That figure is what's called a white key. It's dangerous and works very fast once activated. Tell Edmonds to put it back in the cloud, reach in again, and take out something else. Dean, he's *got* to do this. He's in real danger."

"No." Everyone watched Edmonds when he spoke. "I won't do it." He'd heard the telephone exchange between Dean and Kaspar. Bill didn't know how it was possible, but he'd heard every single word they'd said to each other over the telephone and this was his answer: No. He wasn't going to put Keebler back. His wife, Lola, had loved the silly little thing. She'd owned it for years. Its stern frowning face, stubby thick arms held rigidly at its sides . . .

When she bought it at a junk shop in Boston Lola had said it was going to act as a talisman to protect them from all *spiriti cattivi*. At first Edmonds thought the phrase meant "cat spirits." They had a laugh when she explained it meant "evil spirits" in Italian.

But Keebler was neither netsuke nor talisman; it *was* a white key. Mechanics used them to open and release the fatal darkness contained in every conscious being. Fatal darkness, fatal sadness or hopelessness . . . soul toxins contained in a secret chamber of every heart no being knows exists until it's opened and they flood out. Suicide invariably follows. Mechanics used suicide throughout the universe to solve a whole host of logistical problems or perilous situations. Fast, accurate, and efficient, the act was supposed to be voluntary, but "assisted suicide" via white key was used without compunction when necessary.

"He won't put it back, Kaspar. He says it belonged to his wife."

"Tell him it's a *plant, a fake*—they planted it in Edmonds's house on purpose in case . . . I can't explain this stuff over the fucking *phone*. Take it away from him and throw it back in the cloud yourself. Do it, Dean. Do it or else he'll die."

It was too late.

Because they stood closest to Edmonds, the dogs saw it first. Both animals looked at the man and saw the change in his expression as he smiled at the small figure in his hand. But his smile slipped from fond to fragile to fatal in seconds.

Bill Edmonds's mind was inundated by a torrent of memories evoked by seeing his wife's netsuke again. Memories, milestones, mistakes, and moments shared with Lola sped through him faster and faster—some forgotten, some remembered, some cherished and beautiful, some painful. Most had been lost until the moment he took the Keebler figure out of the cloud. For a second, half a second, he remembered Ken Alford talking about his pocketknife named Vedran and how the only way to do justice to a lost love was to try and remember everything possible about the life you'd shared with them. Had Edmonds dreamed Ken Alford and their bus ride together, or had it really happened? Did it matter?

Memories mobbed and mugged his mind. A chaotic seething unsortable mass of pictures, sounds, *smells*, and long-forgotten recollections that had made up a contented fulfilling life with his adored Lola. How could he have forgotten so much of it? How can you go on living without the person who created and shared such a blessed life with you?

A brutal sadness came from encountering these countless forgotten memories. It swept over William Edmonds like a monstrous merciless seventy-foot-high ocean wave of loss and regret. The effect of them coming at him all at once made Edmonds feel the *real* full impact of losing his wife and it killed him. Drowned by grief, his heart said no more and stopped.

At the instant of his death Edmonds vanished. Whenever a mechanic (active or retired) died, all trace of them instantly disappeared no matter where they were. That included all memories others had of them as well. All memories, records, recordings, photographs, possessions . . . even relationships—anything and everything linked to them vanished in an instant. If they'd been married to a non-mechanic and had children, the surviving spouse would suddenly, seamlessly be married to another being with no memory of ever having been with anyone else. The same held for the mechanic's children. From one moment to the next even other mechanics who knew or worked with them no longer remembered anything: a clean sweep.

The three people remaining in the Corbins' living room looked at each other to see who was going to be the first to put their hand into the Aurora Cobb cloud and, according to Kaspar, find something inside that could help them to understand what was happening now. None of them remembered anything about Bill Edmonds or what had just happened to him.

"Dean? Dean, can you hear me?"

"Yes, Kaspar, I hear you."

"You have to do it. One of you has to do it."

"All right." Dean turned off the phone and dropped it back into his pocket. He walked forward and stuck his hand into the cloud. Instantly feeling something, he wrapped his fingers around it. But his hand jumped right back out of the cloud. Not because of fear, but because the thing in his hand squirmed.

"What the hell is it?"

It was black, shiny, and *moved*. It squirmed like a fish just pulled out of the water. It didn't actually go anywhere but wriggled frantically back and forth on the floor where Dean had dropped it the moment he had it out of the cloud.

The three human beings and two dogs watched it move, the dogs captivated, the people revolted. D Train thought it might be good to eat and stepped forward with the intent of gobbling it down. Just in time Dean grabbed the dog by the collar and pulled him back. D Train naturally thought it was because the humans wanted to eat the twitchy thing themselves. He hoped they'd leave some for him and Kos when they were finished. If Kaspar had been in the room he would have told them it *was* food—mechanics' food—the same kind the three blond women had eaten the day they visited him in the store.

Jane said, "I'll go next." She made a wide berth around the moving black thing on the floor and put *her* hand into the cloud. She kept it there five and then ten seconds, not finding anything. The look on her face was intent but not frightened or nervous.

"Something . . ." She pulled her hand out. It was empty but she said warily, "Something just went up my fingers. I don't know how to explain it. But something definitely happened in there, I felt it; I can feel it in my arm now."

"Like what?"

"I don't know—it's not bad. It's . . . something came in through my fingers and went up my arm. It felt cool at first, like a breeze passing over my hand. But there's absolutely something . . ." Jane frowned and her whole body went taut. She looked at the hand that had been in the cloud and flexed the fingers. She glanced at Vanessa, then down again at her hand. Her eyes were all wonder. "Oh my God!"

"What?"

"Holy shit!"

"*What?*"

Jane raised both arms straight out to the sides, wiggled all her fingers, and started laughing. She looked at her arms—left right, left right. She shut her eyes tightly. Opening them, she burst out laughing again.

"What's the matter?"

Without answering Vanessa, Jane Claudius bent down, picked up the black thing on the floor, and bit into it. The move was so shocking and unexpected both Dean and Vanessa gasped. Still smiling, Jane watched them while she chewed. Silently, merrily, she chewed and chewed and eventually swallowed.

The phone rang again in Dean's pocket. He didn't hear it. Jane took another bite of the black blob. The thing jerked in her hands when she bit it. Horrified and nauseated, Vanessa slapped a hand over her mouth.

The phone rang again. Jane pointed a finger at Dean and said out loud, "Kaspar?"

"Yes. Who is this?"

"It's Jane—Jane Claudius." Abruptly she switched to a language neither Corbin had ever heard before. On the other end of the phone in Vienna, Kaspar recognized the words but in the same way an American recognizes Italian or French when it's spoken without comprehending a single word.

"Jane, I don't understand what you're saying. I know what language it is but I don't speak it anymore." He was shocked to hear her speak the secret language mechanics only spoke among themselves. Because his powers had been revoked upon retirement, Kaspar could no longer understand it.

Even more amazing than hearing it again here on Earth was the fact Jane the bar owner spoke it. Where the hell did she learn it? Naturally he hadn't heard it since he was retired. When the three blondes, Crebold, and Grassmugg visited him they all used English. But not now—Jane Claudius had spoken pure Mechanic.

She switched to English. "What do you mean you don't understand? You're a mechanic."

Kaspar couldn't believe she knew this. "*Was*—they took everything away when I was retired. I don't have powers anymore."

"But you remember everything; I know it."

"Remember *what?*" Vanessa demanded to know.

Jane signaled for Vanessa to be quiet till she was finished talking to Kaspar. His voice filled the room when he spoke although the telephone remained closed and turned off in Dean's pocket.

"I *remember* everything but I have none of the powers anymore, Jane. Where did *you* learn the language?"

"When I put my hand in the cloud something came *into* me. It moved through my body. But these words come and go. I understand them and then I don't; it's like they flash on and off in my mind. Sometimes they're there and I understand, sometimes nothing—"

Kaspar quickly cut her off. "Stop—don't say anything else. Don't say any more about what you know or can do now. Not till we've figured this out, Jane. These things are volatile and extremely dangerous if you use them the wrong way. They can kill us all. Really, they're powerful. Don't even try to speak the language if you're not sure of what you're saying.

"I'm going to touch the cloud here in my room now. Let's see what I find inside it. Maybe it'll help. Don't do *anything* until you hear from me again."

While Kaspar spoke, Kos sidled sneakily toward the black thing on the floor. Coming from a Greek island, the dog had eaten lots of fish in his life and loved it. This wiggly thing looked like a fish, which meant good eating. The humans and D Train were all paying rapt attention to Kaspar's disembodied voice. D Train was always delighted to listen to his master, although he didn't understand a word the boss said.

Glancing over at the group once more to make sure no one was watching, Kos swooped down, snatched what was left of the black thing in his big mouth, and bit into it.

In a daze, Jane let what was left of the *udesh* slip from her hand onto the floor. Her consciousness was going through an infinitely complex transformation from human back into mechanic. Otherwise she wouldn't have missed what the dog was doing. By the time she saw it and shouted, Kos had already swallowed twice and was on his last few chews before gulping down what was left. Dean and Vanessa didn't know what the black stuff was but were sure the animal's eating it was *not* a good thing.

People like to believe dogs smile. Maybe it's true—maybe some *do* when they're happy. But when Jane saw Kos smile now, she stepped between the dog and the others, glaring at him as if he were her enemy. At the same time she yelled, "Kaspar! Kaspar, are you there? Kos ate the *udesh*. He just ate the whole thing."

What she said was not "udesh," but that's how it sounded to the Corbins.

Kaspar answered immediately. "Then get out of there! Get everyone away from him. I don't know what happens when an animal eats it. Anything's possible."

He'd seen it happen before and it was horrifying. *Udesh* is mechanics' food. If any being *other* than a mechanic eats the stuff, the best that can happen to them afterward is immediate death. The worst are the effects on them if they survive. Kaspar had twice witnessed survivors. Despite the many extraordinary, often awful sights he had witnessed in his long career as a mechanic, those two experiences left scorch marks on his memory.

While Jane tried to figure out how to handle Kos, her entire being was processing changes beyond measure. It's simple to erase what a mechanic knows, but restoring the knowledge properly and precisely is complex.

What none of these four people knew because none of them remembered him anymore was they needed William Edmonds's help now. As a mechanic his specialty had been as a troubleshooter. He would have known exactly what to do with Kos.

Because Kaspar could do nothing at the moment about the situation in Vermont, he walked across his hotel room to the Aurora Cobb floating by the window. Despite a very real concern for what could happen when he found something inside the cloud, Kaspar touched it anyway. He knew there might be something inside that could help them all now. He also knew the courage needed for this action came from the onetime mechanic in him. Because it's easy being brave when you have nothing to lose. The human being he'd become would never have been able to do it. Part of the joy of being human came from the things he'd grown to cherish and gather close to his heart in this life. His friend Remco had said we need to be able to walk away from things, no matter how much we love them. But what happens when the "thing" you love is life itself?

Earlier at the café, Crebold was correct in comparing mechanics to ants in a colony. They are genetically programmed to do specific jobs. It doesn't matter if a job entails danger, conflict, or even certain death; ants do whatever their job is without thought or hesitation. Because work and the survival of the colony are the sole purposes of their lives. Mechanics are no more afraid of work or death than ants are.

Over the course of his years on Earth, Kaspar had experienced emotions he'd never known before—longing, lust, joy, fear, anger, and surprise being just a few of them. The sensations they evoked in him were both cherished and bewildering. After all this time as a human being, he still could not decide if such feelings made existence better or worse. But things like passion and dogs—irreplaceable.

Plunging his arm deep into the cloud, his fingers immediately touched something. It moved. It was alive and fluttered frantically like a trapped moth in his cupped hand. Squeezing it, he immediately felt its spit-warm sliminess and recognized what it was in seconds—a switterbug. Kaspar had used them before but only when all else failed. They disgusted him as they did most good mechanics. Switterbugs were truly a last resort—the kind of nauseating creature only someone like Crebold at his worst used with no hesitation or compunction whenever it was convenient. Yet another reason why no one liked Crebold.

Kaspar flicked this one off his fingers like snot back into the cloud. He wanted to wipe his hand on his shirt to get all trace of the vile thing off but didn't. His shoulders gave a disgusted shiver.

Groping around again inside the cloud, he found nothing else. How extraordinarily strange! As a mechanic, whenever he'd had to use an Aurora Cobb to fix a situation, *any* situation, the thing he needed came to hand instantly. But this time the only thing he'd found inside was a *switterbug* and he was certain that was not what he needed for this situation.

The cloud vanished. When it happened, Kaspar's eyes were closed while he still groped carefully around inside it. Opening them again, it took seconds to fully grasp the Aurora Cobb was *gone*.

His whole body froze with his right arm extended stiffly out in front of him while the left hand was palm up close to his body, as if to instinctively protect himself from whatever he might find inside the cloud—which was gone.

"Good God." As a mechanic Kaspar had never experienced this before: An Aurora Cobb *disappearing* before it supplied the necessary tool? Impossible. He moved slowly around the room, arms extended, hands feeling the air, fumbling about, searching. Helpless and frustrated, Kaspar stopped, put both hands on his face, and rubbed them up and down fast and hard. His cheeks turned hot from the friction.

Then someone spoke to him. A familiar voice said words he had already heard that day. "So here we are—together again just like old times."

Dropping his hands, Kaspar saw he was once again sitting in a café across a table from Crebold. The mechanic who had chosen for the moment to look like his twin leaned back in the scarred bentwood chair, put both hands behind his head, and wove his fingers together. Looking around at the café, he loudly sucked air through his teeth.

"You're smiling, Kaspar. Is something funny? Something I said?"

Kaspar Benn was not smiling. Maybe it looked like a smile because his mouth *was* twisted up at either end. But it was the kind of tight rictus grin a face gets after a stubbed toe or accidentally running a finger down the mean side of a knife.

"*Crebold?*" Kaspar looked from side to side to make sure he was actually seeing what he was seeing.

His twin snickered. "I should be laughing at you because I *knew* something disastrous like this was going to happen. I even said it at your review, if you remember."

Kaspar frantically threw both hands up to stop him from talking. "Crebold, *shut up and listen to me!* We're in a flip; we've already lived this moment once today but it's happening again. It's a flip!"

Crebold was stopped by the stricken expression on Kaspar's face. The look alone said he was telling the truth. Even the possibility of it being true was disturbing enough to shut the mechanic up at least for the moment.

As much as he disliked and envied him, Crebold still had great grudging respect for Kaspar. Hearing him say they were in a flip confused Crebold greatly. Everything showed in his eyes, one emotion after the other—doubt, distrust, and wonder. Am I being played here or is it really true? Because if it *is* true, we're in no-man's-land/zero gravity/everything up for grabs/uncharted territory, even for a mechanic. All those conflicting feelings showed as he stared at Benn, still appraising him, still dubious.

Kaspar pointed at Crebold's hand. "When the waiter brings our drinks you're going to cover that hand with ants so you can show off your powers to the guy. You're planning to do it right now, aren't you?"

The right corner of Crebold's mouth twitched but he fought to keep the rest of his face expressionless. "How do you know?"

"Because this *is a flip*—I'm telling you, we're in a flip right now. You've got to believe me. We've been here before, Crebold." Kaspar slapped the stone tabletop. "We've already done this whole scene once before today. You're gonna show off to the waiter by covering your hand with ants. It'll gross him out and cause a scene. Then whether you believe it or not, Grassmugg himself is going to come through *that* door over there with a bunch of other mechanics in orange suits. They're going to haul you out of here because of your stunt. You know stealth is the first rule of mechanics, but you couldn't resist. They're going to parnax you for showing off in front of these people, Crebold."

Although Crebold flinched on hearing the word "parnax," he still wasn't convinced. Not because he thought Kaspar was lying, but because the idea was so contrary to everything he knew or had ever learned. "Come on, Kaspar—a mechanic is never *inside* a flip. You remember: we make them happen. Then we stand back and watch the results. We're *always* outside; a flip happens to *them*, never us."

Kaspar said, "I know, but this is different—this one *is* happening *to* us. We're both inside it. You know the Somersault has already started. I think it might have caused this to happen. Anything goes when one of them hits; even mechanics aren't exempt.

"Look, were you planning to do the bit with the ants on your hand? Yes or no?"

Crebold hesitated. He answered in a tight voice, "Yes."

"And you know I don't have any of the powers anymore, do I? You know it better than anyone because you were on my retirement review. Crebold, look at me! How could I read your mind now if I don't have any powers? How could I know about the ants on your hand? *Because this has happened before.* We're just doing it again, right this minute. It's a classic flip."

"They're really going to parnax me, Kaspar?"

"Yes, if you go ahead with the stupid stunt. Grassmugg told me—not some underling—Grassmugg himself is coming here to get you if you do it."

"Gentlemen, your orders." The waiter arrived carrying their drinks along with other orders on an unusually large tray. Remembering Crebold's earlier rudeness, he purposely put Kaspar's coffee cup down in front of him first and then the tomato juice with the poached egg inside it. The waiter paused a moment to give a long look at the absurd drink, wanting to make sure the unpleasant customer saw his slight smirk.

Crebold's hand lifted off the table. He watched, absorbed, while it rose.

"Crebold don't, *please*—"

"I know, I know."

"Will there be anything else, gentlemen?"

Kaspar smiled at the waiter and said no, thank you.

With effort Crebold lowered his hand again and stared at it until the waiter was gone. "I didn't do that."

"Do what?"

"Raise my hand. It went up by itself, Kaspar. It rose by *itself.* I had to fight myself to pull it down again and keep those ants away. *What is going on?*"

THREE

Jane said it slowly, with particular emphasis on the last word. "It's called a flip."

"*What* is?"

"What's happening to us right now."

"A *flip*, really? Sounds stupid."

Jane made fists against her thighs and looked at the floor. She wanted to throttle Vanessa but knew she couldn't lose her temper now because she needed to keep the lid on things as best she could. Jane was completely unmoored by everything that had taken place. If moody Vanessa went sullen or ballistic right now it would be disastrous. "It's not really the name but a term they use for it here. It makes it easier to refer to."

"What do you mean, here? Where's *here*? And who are these *they* you keep talking about?"

"Here is Earth and *they* are what are called mechanics."

Vanessa shook her head and glared at Jane Claudius as if she'd just farted long and loud.

Jane touched Vanessa's shoulder and pointed to a bench nearby. "Let's go sit over there. I'll try to explain it better."

"I have to go to the toilet first. I'll meet you there." The big woman walked off and disappeared into a restroom nearby.

"Was that Vanessa Corbin you were talking to?"

Jane turned around and saw Felice. A wave of happiness and calm rolled over her. As always, Jane was delighted to meet her partner. But on this occasion it was different because she knew the encounter was part of a dream in which they'd already had this meeting once today. Now was just a repeat—part of the *flip*. "How'd you know I was here?"

Once again Felice handed her a brown paper bag containing a fresh blueberry muffin and steaming hot cup of black coffee—Jane's favorite breakfast. Felice said, "I was getting something to eat in the food court and saw you two down here talking. Then I remembered you said you were coming here this morning to buy a skating helmet."

Jane put a hand on her lover's elbow and squeezed it. "I can't talk now, Felice. I'm kind of in a crisis with Vanessa and we've got to work the whole thing out."

Felice nodded and said, "Of course, sweetie. But are you okay? Is there anything I can do to help?"

Looking at her partner, Jane remembered how earlier in the dream they'd sat here by the fountain, knees touching while contentedly eating breakfast together. How nice and right it had been. How fulfilling it was to have this generous thoughtful woman in her life.

"No, I can handle it. But I love you and thanks for asking."

"I love you too. If there's anything I can do, I'm just up there. You know where." Felice pointed to the bookstore where she worked.

"I know." Jane touched Felice's cheek. Smiling, Felice took the hand and gave the back of it a quick kiss. "See you at home."

Watching her love walk away, Jane wondered if that would happen— if she'd ever see Felice or their home again after this flip. She sat down on the bench, put the bag with the coffee and muffin next to her, and took a very deep breath.

A few moments later her eyes were closed while she tried to rebalance her inner gyroscope, without success. She jerked on hearing Vanessa ask, "Oh, is this for me? Thanks, I'm starved." Jane looked to the side and saw the singer sitting on the end of the bench holding the coffee Felice had brought and trying with her free hand to open the bag with the muffin in it.

"Let me do it for you." Jane took the bag, pulled out the muffin, and handed it over.

"Thanks. I'm ready now, tell me about flips."

"Okay. But first you *know* we're back in our dream from last night now, right? The one we all shared? In it, you and I met here at the mall and you told me Dean wanted to separate."

Vanessa nodded and took a giant bite of muffin.

"Simply put, a flip is when you're sent back to moments or periods in your life you've already lived. But this time you experience them with all the knowledge you have now. So when you go back to that specific experience this time, you already know what will happen next. It's like an instant replay in sports but *with* the added knowledge of how the game turns out."

"Why?"

"Why what?"

"Why do we have them? What's the point of these flips?"

Jane was surprised Vanessa hadn't first asked who or what caused them.

"To help you see your life more clearly in retrospect. All memory lies, Vanessa. It paints nice colors over the ugly or disturbing things. Or it cleverly distorts them, bends and twists them, so they fit better into the convenient history we're all continuously writing and amending of our lives. That fact applies to every conscious being in the cosmos: no matter what you are, your memory is always and for *everything* an unreliable witness. Never trust it to tell you the truth about who you are or how you got here."

"How do you know all this, Jane?"

"I'll explain in a minute; one thing at a time." Jane took the coffee out of Vanessa's hand, had a sip, and gave it back.

"So why are we back *here* in the mall? Is it important? Should we be looking for something?"

Jane shook her head. "I don't know yet."

"Who put us here?"

"I think I did."

Vanessa didn't seem surprised by any of this. She took another bite of muffin and sipped coffee, all the time watching Jane. "It kind of reminds me of the movie where the guy keeps re-living the same day again and again."

"*Groundhog Day?*"

"Yes."

"Vanessa, this is different. Because once a flip takes place, your life is never sequential again. One day you're forty and the next thing you know, you might be fifteen again. There's never any way of knowing what will be next."

"You mean from now until I *die* I'm going to move back and forth between the different years I've already lived?"

Jane kept her facial expression neutral. "Yes, I believe that's what will happen."

Vanessa's voice rose. "I'll *never* go back to living a normal—what did you call it—*sequential* life?"

"No."

The women looked at each other, Jane letting this news sink in before moving to the next fact, which was going to be even harder for Vanessa to believe, much less accept.

"Did I die, Jane? Is that what all this is now, death?"

"No you're not dead. But—"

"But *what?*"

"Your life won't progress any farther than today. This is as far as it will go: from now on, today is as old as you'll ever get. Think of it as coming to the end of a cul de sac when you're driving: when it happens, you have to turn your car around and go back the way you came.

"You're forty-three, so everything you experience from now until you die will be your life up *until* today. You'll travel back and forth across it, setting down here and there but never knowing what age you will be next. No matter where you travel in your life, you'll always have the mind of the forty-three-year-old you are now. It's what happens with a flip."

"This is *ridiculous*, Jane. You're crazy."

"I'm not finished, Vanessa. Remember when I ate the black shiny stuff before?"

"That was disgusting. I thought you were crazy to do it and now I know you really are!"

Jane ignored the insult. "Remember how you knew the name of the cloud in your living room?"

"The Aurora Cobb? Yes, but I don't know how I knew it. It just came to me."

Jane nodded. "The name came to you because in a previous life you were what's called a mechanic. Eventually you were retired and your mechanic's mind was wiped clean. Then you were moved here to Earth to live with a whole new identity as a human being.

"But they need something from you now, they need something from *us*, so we're all being reawakened, if it's the right word. They're making us aware again of our past as mechanics."

Vanessa barked a scornful *ha!* "So you're one too? We're all mechanics? How comforting. Is it like an elite club or a *cabal?* Do they have a secret password?" She hissed the last sentence like someone nearby might be listening.

Jane knew she'd have to handle this explanation carefully because it was plain Vanessa was close to overload or shutting down and dismissing completely what she was saying. Would it be better to use reason or simply make a dramatic demonstration to convince the singer she was telling her the truth?

"Choose a special day in your life. A day in your past where something very important to you happened."

Vanessa frowned and put the coffee cup down on the bench. She'd had enough of this crap.

"Please just do it, Vanessa. It'll show you I'm telling the truth. You want concrete proof? I'm trying to give you some right now. Choose a day or an experience that for whatever reason was significant to you. But don't tell me anything about it. Just bring up as much of the memory as you can."

"Is this a card trick, Jane? Are you going to take out a deck of cards and show me which one I chose?"

In her best cajoling voice Jane said, "Please—think of one important day or event in your life."

Vanessa brushed muffin crumbs off her lap. This was ridiculous. She was scared by everything going on but okay—she'd think of a day. What other choice did she have?

Unexpectedly the first thing that came to mind was her Omi baking. Her grandmother used to bake the greatest cookies, cakes, and pies Vanessa had ever eaten. Watching her make these treats instilled in the young girl a lifelong interest in cooking. A happy part of Vanessa's childhood was spent in the white-haired woman's kitchen as this alchemist with a rolling pin and a Mixmaster transformed flour, water, sugar, eggs, and spices into endless miracles for the mouth.

Almost as delicious as eating them was inhaling the smells wafting out of the oven while they baked; each treat had its own distinct gorgeous aroma. Vanessa could usually tell by each heady scent what today's gift was. Cinnamon, vanilla extract, lemon zest, brown sugar, cloves, and oranges . . . they all had their own signature perfumes. Over the years the little girl became so adept at recognizing and distinguishing between them that Omi would often play a game: she'd open her apartment door but not let the child enter until she'd correctly guessed by sniffing the air what was baking in the oven.

Vanessa's grandfather died long before she was born so it had always been just Omi and little V together doing stuff. Which was exactly how Vanessa liked it because from the very beginning she was a selfish child who wanted all the cookies, all the kisses, and all the attention.

One day she and her mother went to visit Omi. When the door opened, Vanessa took her usual giant dramatic sniff of the air inside the apartment. Apple strudel—an easy one. The aroma of baking strudel was heavy and pungent even out there in the hall. But Vanessa's eyes slowly widened while her mouth set into a hard bratty moue.

Yes, an instantly recognizable aroma was in the air, the delectable sweetness of strudel with its cinnamon, butter, baked apples, raisins, and nuts all melting hotly together inside fresh homemade *teig*. But other smells were there too, new and unfamiliar ones. They were what made the girl glare: alien smells, harsh, *masculine*: Aqua Velva aftershave lotion, tobacco, and the slight funk of human sweat. Her Omi's apartment had never smelled of any of those things before.

Little Vanessa put her hands on her hips and looked at her grandmother reproachfully, as if the older woman had messed up. She demanded to know why it smelled so weird there today. Omi glanced at Vanessa's mother, who said, "You might as well tell her now. She's going to find out sooner or later."

It was the day the girl learned about Omi's new fiancé. Vanessa was outraged. She was too young to know about loneliness or sex or companionship, so for the first time in her short life she felt betrayed. Because as far as the seven-year-old was concerned, Omi's home and everything in it belonged to her. All the cookies were only for her. She chose the color of the toilet paper in the bathroom, her own pink flamingo drinking mug sat easy to reach in a kitchen cabinet, and she was allowed to watch whatever TV shows she wanted when she visited. Vanessa had long ago staked her claim to so many things there. She knew she was the queen of her grandmother's heart, so Omi's apartment was Vanessa's kingdom and refuge all in one. But now to her bitter dismay she learned someone else had been coming here *by invitation*.

Thirty-six years had passed since then. The memory of the day and the disappointment had naturally faded from the mind of adult Vanessa Corbin. But smells are unlike any other memories. They remain with us fully a hundred percent forever on some remote desert island of the mind where they keep the lowest profile. If they're not shaken awake by something, they lie silent and still like sleeping dogs under the table. But once roused, they return as completely as the moment we first encountered them.

Having recalled this memory now, Vanessa looked at Jane and said, "Okay. I've thought of something."

Jane put both hands out in front of her and rubbed them briskly together as if they were cold and she was trying to warm them up. Abruptly stopping, she turned palms up and lifted them together toward Vanessa.

"What? What are you doing?"

Jane said nothing but kept them lifted.

Vanessa looked at the thin black hands. "I don't understand." She was so busy watching and wondering what Jane was doing, she'd forgotten to breathe. When she did again, Vanessa inhaled a smell she'd encountered only once in her life: a mixture of sweat, men's cologne, tobacco, baking apple strudel, old carpets and dust on the sills of closed windows, her grandmother's Jungle Gardenia perfume, and other Omi things—all combined in one. *That's* what Jane was doing with her hands—conjuring the exact smell of Omi's apartment the day of that first betrayal thirty-six years ago.

But it was impossible because Vanessa hadn't said anything about the memory or the ingredients comprising the singular odor. She'd only said, "Okay, I've thought of something." So how could Jane have known? How could she have recreated the smell thirteen thousand days later?

To her continuing disbelief, Vanessa breathed in and there it was again. Unexpectedly a powerful flood of other completely forgotten childhood memories washed over her. She wanted to say something about it but the deluge was so intense and wonderful she couldn't gather any words to speak. She closed her eyes, covered her mouth, and let these forgotten parts of her past live again, even if only for seconds.

Watching, Jane said nothing. From the expression on Vanessa's face, she saw the other woman move beyond the surprise of experiencing that specific childhood smell again to consternation in both her mind and heart on reencountering so many lost pieces of her history. How could I have forgotten these things? Where have these memories hidden in me all these years?

How volatile and untrustworthy memory is. How naive we are to depend on such a fragile, temperamental mechanism to keep our most important records straight.

Vanessa started to shake and cry at the same time. Jane reached over to touch her but the singer shrank away and threw up her arms to keep the other away. She shook her head again and again, tears sliding crooked paths down her face. "I don't know what to do. I don't understand any of this. What is going on?"

"Look at me. Vanessa, *look* at me!"

Vanessa looked but her eyes were skittish and wild—the eyes of an animal about to bolt.

"I'm going to explain everything I know to you now, but you *have* to calm down first. Take deep breaths and try to relax, understand? I need your head clear. Breathe slowly, clear your head, and when you tell me you're ready I'll explain everything I know. The rest we're going to have to find for ourselves." Jane tried to make her voice sound even and calm, assured. She didn't want to give even a hint she was just as frightened as Vanessa.

But before she could say another word, she was flipped again.

"Who's the old guy?"

Kaspar and Crebold walked down the country road toward Dean, Vanessa, Jane, and Bill Edmonds. Kaspar had just explained who the others were.

"I don't know; I've never seen him before."

In a voice as close to a dismissal as he could muster, Crebold scoffed, "What do you mean you don't know him? This is *your* dream!"

Kaspar jammed his hands in his pants pockets and stopped walking. "Crebold, you've done *nothing* but complain since this started. You haven't helped nor have you told me anything helpful. You're a fully functional mechanic who's supposed to know how to fix situations like this. Instead you've been acting like a nine-year-old pest. So either shut up or help me— one or the other. I've got enough questions of my own about what's happening. I'm trying to figure this all out as fast as I can. Believe me, if I knew what was what I'd tell you."

Down the road the Corbins were also watching Bill Edmonds and wondering who he was while he spoke to Jane Claudius.

Kaspar and Crebold approached the group. Kaspar felt no inclination to introduce the mechanic to the others.

Jane turned to the Corbins and said, "Bill was with us before."

"Before *what?*" Dean asked the white-haired stranger.

Edmonds looked at him and answered, "I had the dream too. I was in it with the rest of you."

Dean piped up, "But why don't we remember you? Jane does, but only because she said she knows you from the bar."

Jane said, "Bill was also a mechanic. That's why he's here now, not because I know him. He shared the dream last night too. We're in another flip now, so something must have happened to him after the dream and he was erased from our memories."

Without thinking Crebold said, "Sounds like he found a white key. Works every time if you want to disappear someone completely."

Kaspar nodded. "How do you know these things, Jane?"

"I ate the *udesh*, remember? After I did, details started coming back to me. They still are—so much is bombarding me right now I feel like I need two heads to hold it. But I know for certain all of us were once mechanics. It's why we shared the same dream."

Kaspar asked Crebold, "Did you know that?"

"Yes."

Dean tipped his head toward Crebold. "Who's he?"

"Another mechanic."

"Why's he here? I didn't dream him—did anyone else?"

Kaspar said, "He's part of *my* life, part of my last flip."

They were silent a while. Jane had explained to Dean and Bill Edmonds both what mechanics and a flip were. She'd already told Vanessa these things at the shopping mall right before the next flip brought the two women back here to the part of the dream on the country road with the others.

"Wait a minute—where's the . . . ?" Jane turned around looking for Blackwelder, the chair from the children's book she liked so much. It was twenty feet away on the side of the road. "So there's the chair, which means the elephant with the map or whatever on its side should be here soon. Maybe we'll be able to read that map now and it'll help us figure things out."

Dean's voice was sad but firm. "But we don't know how long we're going to be here, Jane. The next flip could happen any second and then what? We'll all be shot off like buckshot to different parts of our lives. Who knows if we'll ever be together again? I may be five years old next, which means none of you will be around. That's what a flip does, right? You said we keep bouncing around different years of our lives like a pinball."

"Yes, that's right. But maybe not this time—*he* might be a clue." Kaspar pointed a thumb at Crebold. "If this were a normal flip, he wouldn't be here; mechanics are never in flips—they just cause them. I should have had my experience with him in the café but when I flipped from there, Crebold should have remained. He wasn't in our dream—he came after we woke up, when I got to Vienna. But he's here now. Why? How did it happen?" Kaspar said this while looking at Crebold because he was the only active mechanic among them. If anyone would know the answer to these questions, it had to be him.

Crebold said, "I don't know."

"You *have* to know—you're a mechanic."

"No, I really don't, Kaspar; I'm flying blind here, just like you."

"I don't believe that."

The two men glared at each other; they looked ready to fight.

Dean stepped forward and touched Crebold's arm. "You're a mechanic but you really don't know what's happening?"

Crebold looked angrily at the hand touching him. "No."

Dean turned to his partner. "Then what do *you* know, Kaspar?

Look—this is a question for us: If we *were* all mechanics, then some of the knowledge must be inside us somewhere still. It's obviously beginning to show itself but not fast enough. So what *do* we know? What *do we know* right now? Let's try to pool our knowledge and see if there's something helpful."

"I did it already, sort of." Jane pulled out a piece of paper and skimmed it before speaking. "Dean said he doesn't remember anything from his days as a mechanic. Vanessa's spotty—she recognized and knew about the Aurora Cobb, but nothing else. For me, lots of stuff has been coming into my head since I ate the *udesh*. I know it's connected to this but I can't process it all yet. There's just so much and it's overwhelming me. Lots of it I simply don't understand.

"Bill, what about you?"

Edmonds shook his head and looked at the ground. "Nothing. Forget me in this—I don't know anything."

"Kaspar?"

Kaspar Benn, retired mechanic and until recently contented occupant of planet Earth, looked at Jane and said honestly, "I remember almost everything, but it's no help now because I can't *do* anything with what I know. I have no power—only the knowledge. It's like having an airplane with an empty gas tank. I know about Aurora Cobbs and flips and lots of other things mechanics know, but as far as putting any of the knowledge to use, I can't." Something dawned on him and he said to Crebold, "But *you* can. Try red slap. Just try it. Why not? You have nothing to lose and it might help us."

Edmonds spluttered, "*Red slap?* What the hell is that?"

Crebold pulled on one ear and looked at the fingers to see if anything was on them. "It's a translation. Mechanics speak the language of wherever they are; 'red slap' is a human translation of a mechanic's phrase."

Before Edmonds could ask what it meant, Dean asked excitedly, "It's a mechanic's phrase? Then say it in your language."

"Say what?"

"Say 'red slap' in Mechanic language. Maybe some of us'll understand now and it'll help. We have nothing to lose."

Crebold shrugged. "Okay." Putting his hands on his hips he looked straight ahead and spoke what sounded like high-pitched gobbledygook. Vanessa, Kaspar, and Jane immediately flew backward and fell sprawling on the ground as if they'd been flung in the air by a cartoon giant. Vanessa squawked like a crow while Jane staggered and stumbled back to her feet as fast as she could.

"I was afraid of that." Kaspar stood up and brushed off his pants. "Damn it."

"I knew it would happen."

"Shut up, Crebold, you did not. If you're so prescient and informed, tell us why you're here in my flip, Mr. Mechanic. Huh? Why? Just shut up and let me think about this because you obviously haven't."

"What happened?" Dean asked while trying to pull Vanessa back to her feet. She wasn't doing much to help him.

"I think I might have broken something," she whined.

Crebold looked at Vanessa Corbin. "Landing on *that* fat ass? I don't think so." He shifted his glance to Dean. "It happened because *those* three know *a few* things—words, elements . . . about mechanics but not nearly enough to fully understand them. As soon as I spoke our language, they hit what you would call our 'firewall.' It's a form of protection around mechanics, our language and knowledge, so nothing can make sense of how we work or destroy us. It's a protection against Chaos. For example if someone has even the slightest inkling of what our language means, like you three do now, when they get even close to real comprehension the firewall repels them."

Dean asked, "Did you know it was going to happen, Kaspar?"

"I was afraid it might, yes."

"Then why did you suggest it?"

Frustrated, Kaspar made an exasperated face. "Because we've got to explore all possibilities now, Dean. Normally mechanics can fix any problem that arises no matter what it is. But this is different; look at how confused Crebold is about what's going on.

"Even mechanics don't understand how to handle what happens when a Somersault hits or how to fix everything it breaks. It's like being in an Alaskan blizzard with hundred-mile-an-hour winds and zero visibility. You're stuck in the middle of it while trying to get your bearings and find a way out, or at least to shelter."

Crebold added, "But there's no shelter from Chaos until it passes by."

Kaspar looked at him. "There's *got* to be. There simply has got to be, Crebold."

Dean's voice dropped on the weight of his next question. "So are Somersaults just pure Chaos or Evil and mechanics Gods? Or God?"

Crebold said in a quiet voice, "We're more like fireflies."

"Fireflies? What do you mean?"

Surprised by the peculiar answer, Kaspar repeated Dean's question. "Yes—what *do* you mean?"

"Human beings love the daytime because they love light; it's where they flourish. Some say they prefer the night, but not most. Because night is when you let your guard down and are most vulnerable to the disturbing things—like doubt, sorrow, or regret. People *bruise* more easily at night.

"During the day you're busy with your lives and have little time to let your minds drift, wonder, or worry. But at night most people turn off their busy selves and rest. Or they go searching for things to keep themselves busy and diverted until the next day comes. By running into the night, they're running away from it."

All five people listened closely to Crebold, waiting to hear where he was going with this. Particularly Kaspar, who had never heard the other mechanic talk this way before.

"I've noticed most people are at their best during the day, in the light. Night fascinates you with its mystery and potential, but it's ominous too because things are easily hidden or lost in the dark, especially control. Most species I've encountered are powerless there. No matter where that dark is—inside or out—you are all at its mercy. It's harder to lose things and easier to find them, including yourself, in the light."

"What does any of this have to do with fireflies?"

Crebold nodded, agreeing he'd gotten off track. "Think of the times you see fireflies. Think of when they appear—always on late spring or summer nights. They only show up in beautiful weather and always right before nightfall, ushering in the real dark.

"Children notice them first because they're more attuned to such things—the first snowfall, the colors and shapes of stones, or when fireflies show up on summer nights. Kids are usually the first ones to shout, look, fireflies! Or the child *in* you is the one who notices them.

"Fireflies stop the dark for a moment with their fire, like someone lighting a match, which is then quickly blown out. But it's a fragile fire, weak and brief. That's what makes fireflies so dreamlike and endearing: like creatures from a fairy tale that delight you a while before they go away and you return to the tasks of real life."

"Crebold, you sound completely different."

Ignoring Kaspar, he continued, "I think mechanics are similar to fireflies, only our little flashes of light come from the jobs we do. We go around fixing things Chaos breaks. But in the end it's absurd because nothing ever *stays* fixed and of course in the meantime ten more things break and need repair. What we do is like fireflies—our work gives off tiny blinks of 'light,' which last a few seconds but fade back into the dark again.

"When we're faced with something huge like a Somersault, we're useless. It's like a billion fireflies trying to light up the night." Crebold paused, took a breath, and continued in a low sorrowful voice. "This is what I, as a mechanic, think is going on here. But don't take my word as anything more than one opinion from someone as confused about all of this as you are." He swallowed and began speaking again. Only this time what came out were words none of them understood, including Jane and Kaspar.

Kaspar *recognized* the words but had no idea what they meant.

From the look on his face and the calm way he was speaking, it was plain Crebold thought he was making perfect sense and the others understood him.

Dean frowned. Edmonds's mouth dropped open a little while he listened to the unintelligible language. Vanessa just stood there looking peeved as hell at Crebold for his cruel remark about her big ass. She didn't pay attention to what he was jabbering about.

"Crebold?"

"What's he saying? Why is he talking like that?"

"I don't know. Crebold, stop! We don't understand you. You're speaking in the Fourth. Do you *know* you're speaking the Fourth Language to us? Can you hear yourself?"

Crebold stopped. Looking at Kaspar, he shook his head no. Hesitantly he touched his mouth as if checking to see if it was the same one that had spoken the words.

Jane asked, "What's the Fourth?"

Kaspar said, "The Fourth Language is a mechanic's last line of defense. Remember he described the firewall around their regular language? The Fourth is used by them to communicate with each other only after all their other firewalls have been broached. It's not something you learn—it's part of a mechanic's DNA. But it can never be accessed voluntarily; it kicks in by itself when all other systems fail and we need a totally secure way of communicating with each other to solve a problem. I recognize the language but don't know what he's saying. It can only be *understood* when the mechanics handling a problem are at the same level."

"Why's he the only one speaking it but none of *us* understand? Don't we need it now? Why *can't* we understand if we were all once mechanics?"

"I don't know, Dean. I don't know the answer. Maybe because obviously we don't have it all back yet—all the knowledge and abilities mechanics have and need to do their job. Every one of us seems to be on a different level of awareness. Jane has the best understanding but she can't put it all together. *You* say you remember nothing about being a mechanic. Vanessa only knew what an Aurora Cobb was. And I recognize Crebold's speaking the Fourth Language but don't understand it. Like recognizing when someone's speaking German even though you don't know the language. I think he's being blocked from telling us things only mechanics are supposed to know."

Edmonds raised his arm like a student in class who knows the correct answer. "*I* understood him. I mean, I understood maybe every third or fourth word he was saying."

"You *did?*"

"Yeah, but like I said, not everything."

"What *did* he say?"

Crebold spoke again. Edmonds listened to his fast spew of incomprehensible words, craning his head forward, trying to follow everything. Finally he held up a hand to stop Crebold from saying more.

"I believe he's saying it's partly your fault." Edmonds pointed at Kaspar. "He says you knew your whole life you were a mechanic, right?"

Kaspar didn't move or respond. The others looked at him with varying degrees of curiosity.

"He says you knew this thing, this *Somersault*, was coming so you should have prepared everybody for it."

Kaspar shot back, "No, not true! I didn't know about it until recently. Anyway Crebold, you know there's no way to prepare. It's *Chaos*; you can't prepare for chaos or know how to handle it when it comes." Kaspar turned to the others. "I have known all my life I was once a mechanic. But that's irrelevant because I had none of the powers. I couldn't have done anything to stop or fix what's happening to us now. Neither can Crebold and he *is* a mechanic."

"Kaspar, what *is* a Somersault? You said it's Chaos?"

"You know Halley's Comet? It's visible to Earth every seventy-five years or so. Travels on an elliptical, two-hundred-year-long orbit toward and then away from the sun. They call it a 'short period comet' in contrast to long period comets whose orbits last thousands of years.

"Somersaults are like comets, only instead of being made up of ice and dust like dirty snowballs, they consist of only one thing—chaos. Because of that, their orbits are wildly unpredictable. We never know until the last minute when they're approaching and it can be eons between appearances."

Still pissed off at Crebold's slight, Vanessa asked belligerently, "What's an eon?"

"Technically, a million years. But if you want to be poetic—*eternity*. In other words an eternity can elapse between one Somersault and another. Or it can be a lot shorter, you never know."

"What do they do when they come?"

Before Kaspar could answer, Crebold started speaking the strange language again. Edmonds leaned in and put a hand behind his ear to catch every word of the bizarre language. He thought the more he heard, the better chance he had of understanding.

Kaspar was glad for the interruption because he really didn't know how to answer the question without causing even greater alarm. What do Somersaults *do*? As far as he knew (and had heard from those who'd witnessed the last one), they were like tornadoes the size of Jupiter that tear everything in their path into the smallest confetti and toss it indifferently in the air.

Chaos doesn't *do*, it *undoes*.

What *was* a moment ago now *isn't* when Chaos comes to town. What *was* solid is now liquid or soft or gas or gone. Things that were a hundred percent certain, definite, or guaranteed become instantly suspect once chaos arrives.

"He says chaos doesn't *do*, it *undoes*."

It took Kaspar a beat or two to come out of his mind-cave and register what Edmonds said. "What—*what* did he just say?"

Bill repeated the mechanic's words. "He said 'chaos doesn't *do*, it undoes.'"

"Crebold, I thought the same thing! Two seconds ago I thought those exact words—the *exact* same ones."

Jane heard the urgency in Kaspar's voice. "Is it important? Does it mean something?"

Kaspar and Crebold stared at each other knowing damned well it was *very* important, although neither wanted to explain why to the others.

But Kaspar knew it was his responsibility. "We need to be straight with each other now and hold nothing back. No bullshitting around or mincing words. I don't know when the next flip will come. As Dean said, it's likely to send us off in different directions. We might not ever be together again. So if we can brainstorm right now, maybe we'll come up with valuable and helpful things.

"What Crebold and I just experienced is something you could call 'same-ing.' We thought exactly the same thing at the same moment and used identical words to describe it: 'Chaos doesn't *do*, it undoes.' Same-ing is a method mechanics use to fix certain problems, but neither of us used it this time—it was used *on* us. Right?" Kaspar looked at Crebold, who nodded.

Jane asked, "What does it mean—it was used *on* you?"

"This is the first time it's ever happened to either of us. If it continues it could mean all of us are soon going to be thinking the same things, as if we have exactly the same mind. Six people, one brain."

Crebold spoke again. Everyone looked at Edmonds for a translation. It was obvious from the stressed expression on his face he was having real trouble keeping up with the words. "He says the things mechanics do, like making those flips happen, understanding the Fourth Language, or this same-ing—it might be out of their control now. Like maybe the powers of mechanics have been taken away from them and are controlled by something else." Edmonds looked at Crebold, who wiggled a hand back and forth to indicate Edmonds had gotten the gist of what he said right but not exactly.

"Controlled by what?"

Kaspar said, "This Somersault would be my guess. It's Chaos. Wherever Chaos goes it causes havoc. Look at the craziness of what's happened to us today: five people have the same dream. That in itself is insane—the same dream, five people? Then we're *all* flipped and end up back here *in* the dream again, plus Crebold. But from one moment to the next he can only speak in the Fourth, which no one understands except—"

Crebold interrupted Kaspar. Edmonds listened to his babble a while before putting up both hands and almost yelling, "Slow *down*, man! It's hard for me to understand; when you talk so fast I can't get any of it. Slow down—just slow down."

"Dean, look, it's Muba."

Dean Corbin faced away from his wife when she spoke so he had to turn around to see what she was talking about. Down the road the giant red elephant walked toward them. It clumped along at a slow steady pace until stopping twenty feet away. Crebold froze the moment he saw the beast. The expression in his eyes looked like he'd just been electrocuted.

"Look for the map on its side again. Maybe we'll understand it now. Remember before we each saw a different one? Maybe something's changed."

Panicked, Crebold grabbed Edmonds's arm and spoke quickly again. Bill shook his head and said, "Don't worry—it's okay, it's safe. We saw it before and it's friendly. You don't have to be scared. Just don't touch it." Bill looked at Dean and smiled, remembering how he'd been hit in the face by the elephant's trunk before.

Kaspar looked at the mechanic. "Oh *right*—you hate animals, don't you? I remember once—"

Crebold glared and put his hands together as if praying or begging the other man to shut up. Kaspar stopped, despite a mean glint in his eye. He waggled an "I've got the goods on *you*" finger at his onetime colleague. "I own a dog now, Crebold. Did you know? A gray pit bull named D Train. Wait till you meet him—you two will get along great."

Crebold gave him the finger.

"Kaspar, could you come here?" Vanessa stood with the others near Muba. The others were looking intently at the map on the side of the elephant. It swung its trunk lazily back and forth but otherwise stood still. Vanessa pointed to something on the map for Dean to see. A few steps away Edmonds and Jane watched. While Kaspar walked over, Crebold slowly took as many steps backward as he could without being too conspicuous in his retreat from the elephant.

"Yes, yes there! *Now* I see it! Kaspar, come and look at this." Dean pointed to a spot on the map, although careful not to actually touch the elephant's red hide.

Kaspar got up close but not before looking to see if Muba was okay with that—he remembered it whacking Dean in the face.

The Corbins and Kaspar Benn stood together, Jane and Edmonds just behind, all five of them studying the distinct markings on the animal's side.

"*There!* Do you see that?"

"No, show me."

Dean stabbed a stiff finger at different parts of the map.

Kaspar nodded slowly.

"Vanessa saw it first. She's the one who pointed it out."

"*What?* What is it?" Jane went up on tiptoes for a better look.

"Yes! I see it too." Edmonds's voice was high with excitement.

Whatever "it" was on the map, everyone saw it now but Jane. Distraught, she wailed, "*See what?* What do you see?"

FOUR

The next thing she knew, Jane was perched on one of the leather stools back at her bar. The place was very hot, packed with people, full of movement, and *loud*. It looked like it usually did on a weekend night, filled mostly with lively couples laughing and flirting. Some were dancing to a Billy Joel song on the sound system playing in the background. The few singles in the thick crowd scanned the room with faces full of high hope and desire while at the same time trying to look as cool and removed as actors in a French New Wave film.

Naturally after this latest flip Jane had no idea what day or year it was in her past. But it had to be fairly recent if she was in the bar and everything around her looked familiar. As casually as possible, she asked Tiko the beautiful bartender what the date was today. Tiko glanced at her hefty black rubber wristwatch. "Friday the twelfth."

"The twelfth of what? I'm really out of it today."

"September. Do you want anything to drink, Jane? Something to clear your head?"

"Yes, a very good idea. Could I have a large glass of that Ardbeg single malt please?"

"Wow, sure." Tiko smiled because Ardbeg was their most expensive whisky and her boss usually drank only club soda.

Jane wore the black ski parka she had on in the dream. It was so hot in the room that she quickly took it off and draped it over her lap. But first she slid her hand into the pockets. In the left was a large folded piece of paper. She felt it a moment to see if touch alone would stir a memory of what it was but nothing came to her. She thought it was the list she'd just been reading to the others. Pulling it out, she unfolded it on the bar. Her fingers had lied—there was not one but two folded sheets.

The first was filled with detailed precise drawings of mysterious figures and what looked like machines, single numbers underlined several times, symbols, and abstruse-looking scientific formulas. Also strings of words and sentences written in several languages Jane didn't recognize except for one in Cyrillic and several in Greek. As a whole, the paper looked like some kind of recondite illuminated manuscript from the Middle Ages.

She did not know it but this was the first drawing Kaspar Benn had done on the airplane after he woke up from last night's shared dream.

The second page was covered with seventy-two identically rendered glass ink bottles. The pencil drawings were done in photo-realistic detail. It was uncanny how much they looked like the real thing. The only thing distinguishing one from the other were lettered labels on each bottle naming the color of ink contained inside—celadon, cerise, burnt sienna, periwinkle . . . It was the drawing Kaspar had done on the cab ride in from the Vienna airport.

Tiko brought the whisky and lingered to see how her boss was going to drink the liquid gold. Only one customer had ordered it in all the time she'd worked there and he was reputed to be one of the richest men in the state. Jane ignored the glass and kept smoothing the drawings on the bar as if she could eliminate all the wrinkles if she just kept sweeping her hand across the two papers.

"What are those?"

So intent was Jane on studying Kaspar's papers that she glanced up and peered at Tiko as if she were a stranger. "Oh, um, I don't know. But they're really interesting, don't you think? I found them in my pocket."

"How weird, Jane—you don't *know* how they got in your pocket? Did someone put them there?"

Jane reached for the whisky. "Dunno—maybe." She took a swig of the Ardbeg and pouted as it slid strong smoky spices down her throat. Then she went back to examining the wrinkled papers. Tiko walked off to serve a customer, gesturing to her from the other end of the bar.

A few minutes later someone nearby asked in a fast rat-a-tat voice, "Are you doing your homework?"

Jane turned and was almost nose to nose with Marlena Salloum peering shamelessly over her shoulder at the papers. A bar regular and casual friend, Marley was a professor of religion at the college. She had a good heart but was skittery as a hummingbird and just as easily distracted. She was also a big snoop who always wanted to know what was going on in your life.

"Marley, look at this paper and tell me if you see anything on it that makes sense to you." Jane slid the first Kaspar sheet with the numbers, enigmatic figures, and unrecognizable words on it down the bar to her friend, who now sat on an adjacent stool.

The professor dug a pair of glasses out of her faded jean jacket and slid them on. Immediately she pointed to three figures near the middle of the paper. "*These* three are letters from the Phoenician alphabet used around 1,400 BC. This letter is a *zayin*, which the Greeks called 'zeta.' It was also commonly used to represent a weapon of some sort, like a sword. The middle letter is a *kaph*, the eleventh letter of that alphabet. It also represents the palm of your hand. And this last one is a *daleth*, which means a door or a portal. The Greeks turned it into 'delta.'" Marley spent more time looking over the paper before sliding it back. "I don't recognize anything else there. Have you taken up the study of ancient scripts? I'm impressed. You should enroll in one of my classes."

Jane smiled and tipped her head from side to side. "Do those three letters or signs or whatever they are together mean anything in that specific order?"

Marley took off her glasses. "You mean in between the mishmash of all the other stuff on the page? Not necessarily. But looking at them with modern eyes I *might* construe it as some kind of manic, three-thousand-year-old suicide note or last will and testament.

"Oh, there's Dru and Ryder. I've got to go over and say hello to them. See you later, honey." Marley bustled off across the room to her next meet-and-greet.

Jane sipped whisky and continued studying the two papers, her eyes constantly moving back and forth between them. Where had they come from? Had one of the other dreamers put them in her pocket? If so, for what reason?

The bar grew louder and more raucous until it finally overwhelmed her. She decided to go outside for fresh air and silence. Maybe it would be easier to think and make connections out there. On her way an idea slid into her head. Jane said a loud "Yes!" and pumped her fist. Veering left she went into the office. Beneath the desk in there were her Rollerblades and they were exactly what she sought.

If it was September outside and not winter with its snow-covered streets, she would go rollerblading through town and maybe a ways into the countryside. It was the best method she knew to clear her brain and let it take long deep breaths of clean air, which was exactly the tonic it needed right now.

Toting the blades, she exited via the back door, which opened onto a small parking lot. Next to the door out there was a lovely old maple wood bench Felice bought at a church yard sale, had refinished and weather-proofed, then given Jane on the first anniversary of her bar. Jane had work-men set bolts deep into the ground to anchor it and keep the bench from being stolen. Surprisingly little graffiti had been written or carved on it since she had it installed there for bar employees to use when they took a break. Felice said it was because the bench was a gift of love, thus it held special magical powers to keep vandals and evildoers away.

The night was the kind of not-quite-chilly that lives during mid-September. A tricky cold, you can't decide whether to go out in just a sweater or throw on a coat just in case. It was perfect skating weather be-cause you'd start out cold but soon the physical exertion warmed every bit of you to a perfectly toasty temperature.

Jane lay her jacket down on Felice's bench after making sure the draw-ings were zipped safely inside one of the pockets. She needed both hands free to put on the Rollerblades. They were a professional model with a complicated system of lacings and clips, which required both dexterity and concentration to do up. Sometimes it took her two or three tries to get it right. She was always so eager to start zooming down the street on her blades that she often left patience and caution in her street shoes after slipping them off.

While changing now she kept thinking about the comment Marley had made about the figures on one of the papers possibly being a last will or suicide note. Jane wondered if there were other things on the papers that, if she were able to translate them, would shed further light on what it all meant.

And what was the significance of the ink bottles on the second sheet? Nothing about them seemed mysterious or ambiguous—just beautifully rendered drawings of many bottles. Did the different color labels have special meaning—or the order in which they were placed in the drawing?

With her brain sizzling with so many thoughts and her fingers busy with the proper lacing, it took Jane a while to notice someone was sitting on the other end of the bench. And she didn't realize *that* until her eyes slid to one side and saw a pair of Rollerblades exactly like her own—make, model, and color—on another's feet. The same skates, only much smaller, worn on a pair of little feet down there on the corner of *her* bench.

Jane's eyes moved up from the skates to the person wearing them: the girl she'd seen before moving across town roofs at night who had also showed up in the dream. She recognized the child immediately but for some reason wasn't surprised to see her sitting so close by, wearing exactly the same Italian Rollerblades. Jane had to wait seven weeks for those skates to arrive after ordering them because the brand and model were so hard to find in America.

"Do you mind if I join you?" The girl spoke in a surprisingly deep voice, which sounded almost adult, a voice both comical and disturbing coming out of such a small child. Jane looked at her again to make sure she wasn't a midget or dwarf, then went back to lacing her skates. "What if I said no?"

"I guess I'd join you anyway."

"I thought so. Why did you even ask?"

"I was being polite."

Jane finished and stood up. "Polite is for nice people; I already have a feeling you don't fall into that category. Are you a mechanic? Is that why you're here?"

Josephine nodded and stood up too.

"Can you skate? Because I'm not waiting for you."

"It's not a problem." The child wiped her hands on her jeans.

Jane sped off across the parking lot, Josephine right behind her.

From the first instant it felt magnificent to be skating again, moving fast, flying along, her body deliciously pushing against the slight night breeze instead of standing around talking to people about things in a world and a life completely out of her control. Jane even found herself smiling at this odd time but she didn't care. Everything was so confused and chaotic now; what difference did it make if she was able to have a brief few minutes of happiness? She was sure the appearance of this girl was only going to add to her confusion one way or another.

"Do you want to know answers? Because I can tell you if you want." The girl was nearby but the only trace of her until she spoke was the sound of her skate wheels on the asphalt.

Jane said angrily, "Could you shut up for a while? Can we just skate and not say anything for now?"

"Sure—not another word."

Past the bakery, past the diner where Bill Edmonds and Kaspar Benn ate breakfast, *shoosh shoosh*, the thrilling dip and long curve in the road right before you rocketed into the radiantly bright lights of the only gas station in town that stayed open until midnight. Sometimes when night skating, Jane stopped in there to buy a couple of energy bars to eat along the way. The owner of the station, Roberta Zaino, stood in the office door now and waved as Jane swept past. Roberta called out, "Where have you been? I haven't seen you in ages."

Jane shouted, "Crazy busy," waved with both hands, and kept going. The girl stayed right at her heels.

They skated in and out of the darkness, across crinkly dead leaves, through different shades of shadow, in and out and in and out of the orange glare of overhead streetlights, back into the dark again, more scratchy leaves beneath their feet, more shifting shadows. The air smelled of smoke from burning leaves, wet trees, earth, and a sudden stiff chemical reek of exhaust fumes when cars passed in both directions going fast or slow. The skaters' moving bodies caught for a moment in the headlights. Jane was breathing heavily by the time they started up Villard Hill.

As they chugged up the steep hill together, too many nagging questions and worries zoomed around inside Jane's head, distracting her from enjoying the moment. Would she see the others again? Would her life ever return to any kind of normal?

Jane stopped and put both hands out to the sides to keep her balance. She looked straight at the girl and said in a voice filled with both wonder and fear, "Your name is Josephine."

The girl's face lit up. "Yes, that's right."

"You came here as Bill Edmonds's child, or the child he was supposed to have."

"Yes."

An instant ago she knew only the life of Jane Claudius. Now she also knew explicit details of the life of William Edmonds, grieving widower, former tree surgeon, cheapskate who gave his beloved wife lousy presents. Jane knew what Edmonds believed about God, what he dreamed when he was asleep and when he was awake. She knew the words he used when he prayed and what he'd said when he caressed his wife. She even knew some of his most secret fears, the ones he never told Lola when she was alive. In an instant, an infinitesimal fraction of no time at all, Jane knew almost as much about the life of William Edmonds as he did.

Josephine smiled; she beamed. It was plain by her smile she knew precisely what was happening to Jane and it made the girl very happy.

"You know what's happening inside me, don't you? I can see by the look on your face."

Josephine nodded. "Yes, I know."

A very loud sports car came roaring down the street. They waited in silence until it had passed.

Jane saw something a few feet away resting against the curb beneath a street lamp. She rolled over for a closer look. It was a baseball, but completely black and shiny; it looked like it was made of patent leather. As the sound of the car faded, she picked up the ball and turned it over a few times in her hand. The contrast of something as familiar as a baseball but colored so "wrong" made it look like two separate objects existing in the same space.

"What do you think, Jane—is it still a baseball?"

"Huh? What?"

The girl rolled over and put out her hand, gesturing for the glossy black ball.

Jane gave it to her. "Sure; it's a baseball that's just black."

Josephine said, "Maybe not . . . baseballs have to be white so you can see them. You can't play with a *black* ball; it'd be too hard to see. Imagine a high pop fly to deep centerfield with a black ball? Or using one in a night game—it'd be almost invisible." She gave it back.

Jane tossed it up and down in her hand. "Did you put this there?"

The girl ignored the question. "Maybe with a *black* ball, you have to create a whole different set of rules, or even a new game. Maybe you need a whole different pair of eyes to keep track of it."

"Look, Josephine, I'm not a fan of gnomic sayings or double meanings. I flunked metaphor in college. So just tell me what you're getting at and skip the analogies." To emphasize her point, Jane let the ball drop onto the street. It bounced and rolled slowly into a small puddle by the curb.

"That's not a good idea. You'd better keep it because you might need it later."

"Why?"

"What color is it?"

"Black."

"Not really black, Jane, there's something more to it, something else just as important."

"It's shiny?"

"Right. What else has the same kind of shiny blackness?"

Perplexed, Jane went over and picked the ball up again. It was wet from being in the puddle. She dried it with a small handkerchief she kept in her coat pocket. While drying the ball, she looked at it and felt the texture. The name flashed into her mind: "Obsidian."

Josephine said, "One of the ink bottles on your drawing is labeled 'obsidian.'"

Jane pushed the ball and handkerchief into a pocket and pulled Kaspar's drawings from the other. Scanning the bottles under the overhead streetlight, she saw nothing at first glance. Forcing herself to slow down, she looked again more carefully. In time she noticed it—in the lower left corner of the picture, a bottle labeled OBSIDIAN. Without looking up, she said to the girl, "Okay, I found it, but what does it mean?"

"Why don't you ask Bill?"

Jane shook her head, confused. "What do you mean?"

"*Ask* Bill. It's simple."

"I can't—he's not here."

Josephine pointed to Jane's chest. "He's there. How do you think you recognized *me* before? How did you know my name and all those other things about Bill? He's *in there*—he's part of you now, for at least a little while. Take advantage of him, use what he knows." She pointed again at Jane's chest. "You're becoming a mechanic again, so use the powers!"

Jane nodded. She already knew those things from discussions with the others.

Josephine continued. "All retirees are being recalled because you have two things now—your past lives as mechanics and *this* one you've lived in a completely different environment. It's happening to retired mechanics everywhere in the universe; you've not been singled out."

Jane had questions about this but wanted answers to other things first. "Why do I know so much now about Bill Edmonds?"

"You were the only one of the group to eat the *udesh* when you saw it.

When you swallowed and it entered your system, naturally the process of you regaining your powers sped up."

"The powers of a mechanic?"

Josephine nodded. "Yes."

The girl started to speak again but Jane cut her off. "Wait a minute—Bill *killed* himself, didn't he? He got the white key and walked into the Aurora Cobb."

Josephine smiled. "See? You're beginning to remember things too. The transition is happening quicker than I thought with you."

"So the only reason why we saw him alive just now is because we were flipped back to the part of our dream where we were standing on the road together?"

"Correct."

Jane expected the girl to say more, to explain why Edmonds was permitted to kill himself if they needed him back as a mechanic.

As if reading her mind, Josephine said, "They need to know about *that* human experience too, grim as it is. They need to know precisely what one of you feels and what you're thinking when you commit suicide. It's very significant information.

"Humans treasure life; they cherish it like few other beings do. What happens inside a human psyche for someone to willingly give up the thing they value most?"

Jane wasn't having it. "The white key caused his death. It showed him parts of his life that broke his heart. The effect of the key made him give up; if he hadn't found it in the cloud those memories would never have come back all at once and he would have gone on."

She heard a cough behind her and turned. An old woman stood nearby with a big black Newfoundland on a leash. Both of them were staring at Jane. The woman asked, "Who are you talking to, dear? Sounds like you're having a lively chat with the wind. Don't let me interrupt." She finished with a loud self-satisfied "Ha!" and toddled off down the street behind the giant dog.

Jane turned back and looked for Josephine but the girl was gone. This didn't bother her. Alone again, she would be able to think clearer about everything.

She started skating again, one leg in front of the other faster and faster, the sound of the spinning wheels and the gusty wind in the trees her only companions.

A few minutes later she was rolling down the hill toward Bill Edmonds's house again. The last time she'd been there was in the dream and the house was on fire. Bill and Kaspar Benn stood outside watching it burn. But the house she saw now had neither burned nor was it in flames. Lights were turned on throughout the small building and gave off a warm yellow light. It looked very cozy inside on this crisp fall night.

Tiko the bartender had said it was September, but was it this September or last, or even three years ago? It had to be either this year or last because Jane's bar was three years old and Felice had given her the wooden bench on the first anniversary of the place.

Having reached Bill's house, she stopped at the driveway before moving up it as slowly as possible without losing her balance on the skates. She wanted to look in the windows to see who was there and what they were doing.

A familiar song by the group ABBA came drifting faintly out of the house. Both Jane and Felice liked ABBA and often played their music at home.

Above the song she heard a great woman's laugh, which went on and on. It was the kind of happy uninhibited cackle you like to hear because it's neither fake nor forced. The laugh of someone who isn't afraid to let loose and *ha-ha* right up to the rafters.

Jane moved closer to the house and saw in one of the lit rooms the back of a green couch with a television on a table in front of it. Several seconds passed before she recognized the film *Mamma Mia!* playing on the screen. Meryl Streep and Pierce Brosnan were singing a duet together. Jane grinned because she and Felice loved to cuddle up on their couch and watch it, especially whenever either of them was feeling blue and needed cheering up. It was almost a given they would start singing the score about halfway through the movie.

Sitting on the green couch and facing away from her toward the TV were two men, or what she thought were men until one of them stood up and turned to say something to the other. Jane caught her breath when she saw the face: It was a woman with almost no hair on her head. She was wearing a plaid hunting jacket several sizes too large for her. It was wrapped tightly around her and held in place by her arms across her chest. The film froze on one frame. Obviously it was a videotape or DVD put on pause.

The woman's face was appallingly thin. Her skin was stretched tight over her forehead and cheekbones. In grim contrast, there were ugly dark bags beneath her eyes. They broadcast to anyone who saw them, "Yes, I am gravely ill. You don't want to know the details." At once Jane thought of photos of starving children in Africa. The difference being those kids' eyes always appeared to be locked in some kind of otherworldly, thousand-yard stare combining their imminent death with an almost saintly expression that said, I am still here but I am already gone.

In contrast, this woman's eyes were powerfully alive, all here and *now*. She looked at whoever was on the couch with love, laughter, and flirt, but most palpably *delight*. It was almost unbearable for Jane Claudius to watch those eyes burning like a bright, bright flame on top of the very last bit of melted candle.

The woman dropped her arms to her sides and the heavy jacket fell open. She was wearing a yellow sweatshirt with SIMMONS COLLEGE across the front. But even though the bright shirt fell like a tent around her, Jane could tell at a glance she was skeletal and frail.

This was Lola Edmonds, Bill's late wife. Watching her move out of the room in a sick person's slow shuffle, Jane knew more and more about her with each step. Lola Dippolito Edmonds was self-absorbed, great company, highly sexual, happily directionless, and adored a husband who had disappointed her for years. As a young woman in Italy Lola had always believed her life would turn out to be prime time but it never did. She'd come to America as a college exchange student and fallen in love with the way the United States supersized everything. She thought, *this* is where I belong, center ring, and in many ways America was the perfect fit for the exuberant young woman. She did a number of things well but came up short of great in any of her pursuits. She could hold a room's attention with funny or charming stories and anecdotes but inevitably they went on too long because she never knew when to stop. She was a terrific cook but only knew how to make six dishes. A competent albeit unimaginative painter, her college teachers had given her good grades more for her warmth, *grandezza*, and three-ring-circus personality rather than for her brains or talent.

She peaked at twenty-two and like so many good-verging-on-great athletes who never finish higher than fourth place in the big race, eventually slipped back in the pack. By thirty she knew she didn't stand a chance of being a contender anymore for any kind of role in the spotlight. So she married a nice stingy man who loved her every day of their life together but never tried very hard to understand her.

The most heartbreaking thing Bill ever did for her was, soon after Lola was diagnosed with cancer, he came home one day with a book he'd ordered from the town bookstore entitled *Italian for Beginners*. In his fear and frustration about what to do, he thought by learning her native language it would strengthen their bond and enhance their ability to fight her new enemy together, which was already well on its way to eating her alive. But Bill had absolutely no talent for language. To watch him sit hour after hour, day after day at their kitchen table with his fat brown Italian book, taking notes and slowly mouthing the beautiful sonorous words from her homeland (*per sempre*) caused Lola to love her husband more than she ever had. Her impending death opened her already large heart until her love of Bill and her life became both exquisite and almost too much to bear. She had never been happier, ever. She had never been more afraid.

Lola was unaware of it but this was her one great, genuine talent in life—loving people. The image of her man with the Italian book in his meaty hands looking so damned serious made her smile when they lay in bed at night holding hands, knowing "forever" was no longer a word either of them owned in any language. In Lola's increasing dependence on him, Bill learned how to be generous, thoughtful, and fully present in the limited days they had left together. Perhaps that was the greatest achievement of her life: without trying, she taught her husband to be a much better person. And then she died.

Jane didn't realize how deep a fugue state she'd fallen into as all of this information revealed itself and then the effect it had on her. Minutes might have passed; it easily could have been longer. She was standing at the window with head down and eyes closed, reviewing everything she'd experienced, when she heard the voice behind her.

"It's beautiful, no?"

Turning, she saw Lola Edmonds standing nearby with arms across her chest again, hugging Bill's heavy mackinaw coat to her body. Up close in this dim light coming from the window, she looked even sicker than from a distance.

"You *knew* I was out here?"

"Yes, that's why I came. We dead are like mechanics—we can move wherever we want in time. Before when you saw me inside the house I was still alive but I died a week later. It's why I can talk to you now. Do you see the color in there yet?"

"No, *what* color?"

Lola smiled and said excitedly, "It's the best part of what's in that room, Jane! Even when I am not inside with him, the color is still there because it's so strong when Bill and I are together. Look closely and you should be able to see it. Try again."

Despite having just been told what to do by a dead person, Jane was fascinated by what was happening and looked again into the Edmondses' living room. Bill was still sitting on the couch with *Mamma Mia!* frozen on the television screen. Jane looked everywhere but noticed nothing more than what she had already seen. She shook her head. Lola said, look harder.

Eventually she saw it on the ceiling over the door Lola had used to leave. A kind of faint-colored wash across everything in that particular section of the room made it look like an old photograph exposed to the sun too long so the individual colors were fading into one.

"I think I see it—a sort of burnt sienna, right? What is it?"

"*Esatto*—that's right—Italians call it *terra di Siena*. It was the first color used by the cavemen who painted on the walls. But do you know why they chose it first? You're getting your mechanic's eyes back so you begin now to see the colors of human emotion again. Burnt sienna is the most important one.

"Did you notice the little bit of orange still in there? Of course orange is the color of passion, the desire people have for each other when they fall crazy in love: Fireworks! Explosions! The hunger at the beginning of all great romance for sex and physical closeness. *Pow!* It's delicious and torture too. *That* crazy first passion always goes away, no matter who you are. But when love is *real*, the orange fades into a quieter color, which is much more nuanced and beautiful.

"After I got sick, the little orange left in my relationship with Bill disappeared. For a while the only color we shared was the shiny black of me dying, the same color as the obsidian ball you have in your pocket.

"But black taught me a lot too. At the end, in those last days we had together before I died, we moved *through* the black to the most important color—burnt sienna. It is what you are seeing in our living room now, even when I am not in there, because it remains: the color of the greatest love humans can feel for each other. It comes only when all others have burned off or faded away and what remains is a hundred percent pure. Like the color of the earth in direct sun on a late fall afternoon. It is the color of the truest human passion."

Jane was taken aback. "Burnt sienna actually *means* something?"

"Yes, it means immortality, or as immortal as human emotion can be. We only live a few years, so our forever is pretty short." Lola grinned. Her voice sounded strong and healthy, not the voice of a dying woman. "*You* brought me out here, Jane. Maybe you don't know how you did it yet, but your mechanic side told me you were here."

"Why? Why would I?"

Lola rubbed the top of her almost bald head like someone who's just gotten a short haircut and enjoys the bare feeling up there. "So I could tell you what to look for in our living room? And burnt sienna is one of the most important colors on the drawing of bottles you have. Obsidian is important too because it is the color of death, which you must teach yourself to move *through* to get to the burnt sienna."

Instinctively Jane touched the pocket holding Kaspar's two drawings and the black baseball. She took out the ball and showed it to Lola, who nodded as if she fully understood why Jane had it with her.

"What *are* those other colors on the drawing? Why specifically those?"

Lola took the ball. Hefting it in her hand she said, "The colors on the ink bottles are the most important sentiments of the whole human experience;

it's like a chart showing the letters of the alphabet. A detailed chart of what make us most human."

"Is it supposed to help me fight this Somersault thing?"

Lola shook her head. "Maybe, I don't know—you'd have to ask the person who gave it to you, but I would guess so. The colors on those bottles are for sure telling you important things about being human. Since you were a mechanic, maybe you can put the two together in some way. . . .

"Whether they will actually help fight against Chaos I don't know; some things work better than others. But the problem is Chaos always returns sooner or later and just . . . destroys.

"I'm going back into the house now, Jane. Do you mind if I keep this ball? I am where it belongs. I want to be with my husband now." Lola tightened the coat around her, lifted one hand in a small wave, and left. A few moments later she reappeared in the living room and sat down next to Bill. The image on the television unfroze and *Mamma Mia!* started playing again for the last time in Lola Edmonds's life.

FIVE

All the lights were off inside Kaspar Benn's house when Jane arrived ten minutes later. To her surprise, Kaspar's lovely dog D Train and his blond pal Kos were sitting side by side on the steps leading up to the small front porch, looking like two old philosophers watching the world go by. She remembered the last time she'd seen these two: Kos had just gobbled up the *udesh* and no one knew what to do about it. If she were ever flipped again back to that moment in the future, what could she do to save him?

On seeing her approach now, the dogs rose together and ambled over to say hello. She knew Kos's owners let the dog come and go as it pleased. She often saw the gentle fellow walking around town by himself. Although it was against state health regulations, Kaspar sometimes brought D Train into Jane's bar where the pit bull sat quietly at his master's feet, happy to shimmy his body hello to anyone who greeted him.

Scratching both dogs' heads as they pushed their big bodies up against her legs, she thought, Kaspar's not here so I can't talk to him about this. What now? Then there were sounds from inside the house—laughter? Moving closer to the building, for the second time that night she found herself looking in windows like a peeping tom. She walked slowly around to the back of the house where she noticed a dim light flickering inside one window. She moved closer for a better look.

More laughter, sexy laughter, the kind from lovers who have just finished or are about to begin. The light inside came from candles—a bunch were placed all around one room, dimly revealing it with their shy sway and flickers of pale yellow. By all indications Jane expected it to be a bedroom but realized after squinting hard for a better view it was the kitchen.

Sitting across from each other at a small metal table in the center of the room were Kaspar and Vanessa Corbin. Both were fully dressed and the table between them was covered with plates of food.

Jane put her hand on the side of the house. In the short time traveling from Bill's house to here, her mechanic self had awakened further so she knew now by doing this, she would be able to hear everything that was said inside. To her surprise and amusement, the two were only talking about food. Sex took no part in their conversation. She'd heard rumors about something going on between Vanessa and Kaspar but the talk neither fazed nor interested her. Jane had enough trouble dealing with the singer on a professional level. She didn't care what Vanessa did in her time outside the bar. Besides, gossip was like junk food: you ate it with a kind of fanatical glee, but then felt like shit when you realized you'd emptied the bag and your guts were now stuffed with lard. If there was any truth to the rumor, the only one she felt sorry for was Dean Corbin, who was a very decent, stand-up guy.

While the dogs kept her company, Jane listened to the conversation inside Kaspar's kitchen. The more she heard, the more she enjoyed it because it sounded like two swooning gourmands talking food porn rather than red hot lovers hungry only to jump each other's bones. Eavesdropping on their chat, she could tell right away there was between them the kind of easy intimacy longtime lovers have with each other. But whether those two were physically intimate was another question. However, the most interesting thing she learned came from the dogs.

D Train kept walking over and rubbing his head against her legs. While doing this, he'd look up at her and doggy-grin while his whole body wriggled affection and desire for a pat. Jane was torn between listening to the conversation inside the house and giving the friendly dog the attention he craved.

Squatting down to D's level, she briskly rubbed his head with both hands, then up and down his back and sides. His gyrating body grew frantic with love and appreciation. On noticing that his friend had the woman's attention and caresses, Kos came over for his share. The two goofy dogs were nothing if not enthusiastic in competing for her hands. Their squirms, head tosses, paw whacks, and body bumps eventually got the best of Jane's balance and knocked her from a squat onto the ground. The dogs loved that and engulfed her with kisses and big feet all over her. Grinning, she tried to stand up but was still on skates. They were no good for getting her balance gyroscope back on track.

"Come on guys—help me up." Using their muscled backs as leverage, she pushed hard enough to rise. Neither dog seemed to mind.

While her fingers were still on their backs, Jane suddenly began to experience the world through the dogs' brains and not her own. Mechanics can enter any mind they choose. The difference here was she didn't choose to enter D Train's and Kos's minds—it happened on its own.

The world as they perceived it was very similar to the human world except for one key difference—dogs know what comes after death. In the brief moments Jane Claudius lived as a canine, she saw and understood for the first time what death was and what came afterward.

It was not bad.

This is the primary reason why most dogs are so merry and resilient:

death is no more frightening than traveling to a distant land where the landscape is lushly tropical or glacially polar or simply unlike anyplace you've ever been. Just the smells alone . . .

Jane and Felice had once gone to Marrakesh. The first thing that crossed her mind now was the smells of the markets there: so extreme, exotic, and mysterious. The whole time they were in Morocco neither woman could get over the constant barrage of unknown, wildly *foreign* tantalizing scents. They kept asking each other, "Do you smell *that?* What is it?"

Whether as a mechanic or a human who had been enlightened, Jane knew for certain now what death was and it was not to be feared. She assumed it was why Lola had been so cheerful when they spoke outside the Edmondses' house. Overcome by this epiphany, she brought both hands to her mouth and squeezed her eyes shut to hold back grateful tears. Her connection to the dogs was broken and instantly she was herself again. But it took a while to mentally digest and accept what had just been revealed. She opened her eyes after hearing voices on the other side of the house.

Looking in the kitchen window, she saw the candles were still burning and the table was covered with plates, but no one was in the room. Listening to the voices, she heard Vanessa say good-bye. Footsteps clomped down the wooden porch stairs. Both dogs took off to investigate. Jane didn't move until she heard a car start and move off down the street. Then she walked around the house and rang the front bell.

Kaspar answered the door holding a plate piled high with wedges of cheese, crackers, and glistening black and green olives. Working on a mouthful he said awkwardly, "Jane! This is a surprise—come in." He seemed happy to see her but mildly perplexed.

He flicked on lights as they walked down the narrow hall and into the living room. It was the first time Jane had been in Kaspar Benn's house and she liked what she saw.

He collected things. Black-and-white vintage photographs covered the walls, all of them interesting enough on first glance to make her want to stop and examine each one. A handsome hanging brass and smoked crystal lamp spread a warm buttery light over the hall. Kaspar said he'd bought the lamp at the Viennese flea market. On a long industrial-looking brushed aluminum table were arranged a quirky assortment of found and flea market objects: two old street signs peppered with what looked like bullet holes, an array of pocketknives, a gouged and scratched wooden bocce ball, a large crudely made copper bowl holding battered old pool balls. Next to it were metal toys, and in the middle of the table was a large white display window head of a handsome man that appeared to be from the 1920s or '30s. When they walked by the bust, Kaspar tapped it and said, "my personal Jay Gatsby." Jane wished she could linger and look at everything more carefully but once they reached the living room Kaspar gestured her to a leather sofa the color of an old brown football. He sat down in an equally worn Eames lounge chair facing it.

"Nine o'clock on a Tuesday night in the middle of my life the mysterious Jane Claudius shows up out of the blue at the door. This is a surprise. How'd you know where I live? How come you're not at the bar?"

"Kaspar, I know about mechanics. I know you used to be one. I also know about the Somersault that's coming."

He stiffened but said nothing, only put the plate he was holding slowly and carefully down on the floor next to his chair. Bending forward he looked up, appraising her.

She didn't wait for him to answer. "I'm in the middle of a flip right now and don't know how long it's going to last. So I need to get some answers from you fast."

Hearing that one word convinced Kaspar she was telling the truth. "You know about flips?"

"Yes. I have so much to tell you and I will if there's enough time, but first I have to ask my questions. You've got to give me some answers. As I said, I don't know how long I'll be here; the flip has already happened twice to me."

Nodding, he tried to hide his bewilderment and worry behind a placid face. But his insides were going off like an explosion in a fireworks factory. "If it's true and you are in a flip, Jane, you can ask me anything because I won't remember any of this after you've gone. It's how they work."

"I know, Kaspar."

"*How* can you know?"

"Because I was a mechanic too." As fast as possible she told him about how the other three people—Dean, Vanessa, and Bill Edmonds—had been mechanics too, their shared dream, and what had happened to them since the dream. She knew Kaspar needed to know these facts in order to have some kind of background before she asked her questions. But she was petrified that in the middle of her explanation another flip would occur and she'd lose the chance to ask them. At the end of her brief account he started to speak but she brushed it aside and begged, "Please—*please* just let me ask my questions first."

"Okay, Jane, I understand. What do you want to know?"

She took the drawings out of her pocket and put them down in front of him. "What do these mean? Do you know what they are?"

He'd never seen them before but after a brief glimpse at both he knew what they were. "I do, but I can't tell you what they mean."

She grimaced. "Why? You *have* to."

"It's not that I don't want to—it's because I *can't*, Jane."

"*Why not?*"

He put his hands down flat on the papers. "Have you seen hieroglyphics?"

"You mean like the Egyptian ones?"

"Egyptian, Mayan, Cretan . . . it doesn't matter which. The word 'hieroglyph' is actually Greek and means 'sacred carving.' These pages *are* sacred too in a way because they were definitely drawn by a mechanic and I know they're instructions of some sort. This I *can* tell you. I'd recognize Egyptian hieroglyphics if I saw some, but I wouldn't *understand* them. The same thing goes with these drawings."

"How do you know they were drawn by a mechanic?"

Kaspar quickly pointed to four things on one sheet, then tapped the page with his thumb. "These figures tell me who wrote it and the fourth says, look at this drawing in combination with the one of the bottles on it."

In a worried voice she asked, "*Why?* What do they mean? What do they say? This drawing is only a bunch of ink bottles."

"I agree."

Frustrated and almost angry, she latched onto something he'd said. "But those figures—how come you recognized them but nothing else?"

"Because they represent my name—the name I had as a mechanic. Plus it's my handwriting; *I* did these drawings, Jane. That's what the third figure says—this one here. I haven't done them *yet* obviously, but if what you're telling me is true then we have to assume I *will* sometime in the future. That future me made these drawings and gave them to you, probably thinking they'll help once you decipher them." Kaspar shook his head and looked at the papers again. "It's so strange to get a glimpse of your future no matter how unclear it is. I have no idea what these mean but I drew them, there's no question about it."

"Maybe I can help."

Huddled together over the drawings, neither Jane nor Kaspar had seen the man now standing in the doorway.

Kaspar did a double take—this wasn't possible. "*Crebold?*" He hadn't seen him since their mechanic days. "What are you doing here?"

Crebold pointed at Jane. "I thought I'd make a guest appearance in her flip. Glad to see me?"

Kaspar said nothing but didn't like it. What *was* he doing here? Jane had told about the others in the dream but said nothing about Crebold because she'd forgotten him. Who was he anyway? As far as she knew, just a guy who'd been with Kaspar Benn on the country road along with the others—and the elephant, and the talking chair. . . .

Kaspar got up and warily made himself shake Crebold's hand. Then he asked if Jane had ever seen this man before.

"Yes, he was with you in our dream."

The mechanic nodded. "But we haven't been formally introduced. You can call me Crebold if you like, or"—he said something incomprehensible. Seeing the blank look on her face he said, "Ah too bad, you don't understand our language yet. But any time now I'm sure you will, Jane."

"You were on the road with Kaspar."

"Right."

"Why are you here?"

Crebold pointed to the drawings. "I need to take those with me; they shouldn't be here." He leered at Kaspar. "You don't know what we're talking about, do you, old friend? I cannot express how much that pleases me. Jane and I are talking about *your* future and events you know nothing about yet."

Ignoring the taunt, Kaspar asked, "Why do you want these drawings?"

"You remember the rules, pal—mechanics can never divulge the future to mortals."

Kaspar wasn't having it. "The fact you're here in *her* flip, making your presence known to both of us, is breaking the rules, Crebold. Both of those things are taboo for mechanics. Rule number one: stealth. Remain unseen—anonymity at all costs."

"Yes, well, some of those rules have changed since you retired. Just give me the drawings and I'll go." He wore a smug smirk that Kaspar wanted to slap off his face. The arrogant little prick.

Jane asked, "Why do they matter to you?"

"Kaspar cheated back there on the road. He slipped those drawings into your pocket because he wants you to decipher them and use the information if you can, no matter what happens to him."

Kaspar couldn't resist asking. "What are they? What do they mean?"

"In part they're instructions—instructions about how mechanics function. They're also a kind of map of the human heart, translated into a visual language humans can understand."

Jane glanced at the drawings in Kaspar's hand as she processed this information. "But why not let me use them? Aren't we *supposed* to become mechanics again to fight this Somersault thing?"

"Is that really what it's called—a Somersault?"

"No, it's a"—Crebold spoke again in the mysterious language. "But we call it a Somersault so humans understand."

Kaspar folded the drawings along the lines already scored in the paper. He tapped them on his open palm. "Why would I do such a thing, Crebold? Why would I want to give her instructions? There's something about these papers you're not telling us."

Jane kept staring at Crebold, searching for something different in his face, his voice, his demeanor; something unique or special to set him apart from others. But she saw absolutely nothing; he was simply a man in a suit. Although he wore a different face now, Crebold looked much like he had in Vienna when he appeared as Kaspar's twin brother. But despite the different face, he still looked like the kind of forgettable functionary who handled your ticket at an airline counter. Or the waiter who takes your order at a theme restaurant: the guy in a starched white short-sleeve shirt wearing a name tag too small to read: KEVIN. He looked like a Kevin. Or a Bruce. Hi, I'm Bruce. Are you ready to order?

Kevin/Bruce/Crebold now asked, "Jane, do you know what Pipetoe is yet? Or Tenbrink?"

"No. Say the words again."

"They're not words—they're names: Pipetoe and Tenbrink."

"No, I've never heard either of them before."

The mechanic looked at Kaspar, who shrugged—he didn't recognize the names either. Crebold was genuinely surprised. "Really, *you* don't remember them?"

"No."

Crebold pointed an accusing finger at him. "I thought they let you keep your whole memory."

"They did. But I don't remember those names."

"It's not possible, Kaspar—you *were* a Tenbrink."

Kaspar was unimpressed. "Which is what?"

Crebold couldn't contain himself. "Are you joking? Do you expect me to believe that bullshit?"

"Believe it or not, it's the truth; I don't know what a Tenbrink is. Sorry."

Jane spoke to divert the mechanic's attention. "Tell *me* what it is; tell me what those names mean." Distracted, Crebold looked at the woman with angry eyes before registering what she'd asked.

"Each mechanic has a specific job to do. Tenbrinks do this, Pipetoes do that. Kaspar and I were Tenbrinks. You were a Pipetoe."

"Pronounce the two names in your language."

Crebold said the mechanic names aloud but they sounded like gobble-dygook to Jane and Kaspar. "Now just give me the drawings and I'll go."

Still holding them in his hand, Kaspar looked at the floor and shook his head. "I don't think so."

Crebold considered crossing the room and taking the damned papers. He could do that easily but it would be no fun. Besides, he had a perfect chance now to stick it deep into his old rival and watch his dismay. Crebold wouldn't miss that for anything. Turning to Jane he asked, "Do you really want to know why I'm here?"

She nodded, curious but suspicious of what he would say.

"Okay, I'll tell you in just a moment. But first I need to tell Mr. Pants Salesman here something. Remember Jezik? You liked her, right?"

Kaspar's memory flashed back to the three blond women who'd come to his store last summer to warn him about the Somersault. "Yes, of course I remember her."

"Gone. Jezik and *all the others* are gone, Kaspar; every single one of them—poof! They're wiping out mechanics. Soon it'll be just me and a few others left to tell the tale." Crebold flashed a triumphant smile. "Shocking, huh? It's a whole new ballgame."

"The Somersault—it's here." Kaspar said it as a statement of fact, not a question.

"Correct—and has been for a while. It's just moving more slowly this time."

"If the others are gone, how did you survive?"

Crebold answered quickly. "I'm going to tell you the truth even though it makes me look bad. But I'm okay with that now. Chaos's representatives came to those of us who never fit in very well as mechanics—I'm sure you remember which ones I'm talking about, Kaspar.

"They said it was here now and everything is going to change. Any kind of old order is out and Chaos is *back*. They said we could either bathe their lion or try to fight it. But if we fought, sooner or later it would eat us like it did the other mechanics. It's very simple—choose one—bathe or fight." Crebold took a deep satisfied breath. "I may not have been the best mechanic, Kaspar, but I'm a *fucking* good survivor."

"You're with Chaos now?"

"I am." Crebold bent forward in a small mocking bow. "My guess is your shared dream was one of the last things the mechanics were able to make happen before they started being wiped out. Your dream and flipping all the retirees at the last minute. Just imagine right now everywhere in the universe, confused ex-mechanics are bouncing around the days of their lives like they're on some kind of treasure hunt to find *anything* to help stop the Chaos rolling in all around them. If you ask me, it's ridiculous for them to try to stop it, but you gotta give them credit." He broke eye contact with Kaspar and looked at Jane.

"Something in Kaspar's dream must have inspired him to do the drawings when he woke. To sum up on paper everything he knows from the two lives he's had and pass it on hoping it'll help. Then he slipped those little maps of his soul into your pocket, Jane. He must think very highly of you."

Since the Kaspar Benn who was there now had not had the dream yet, Jane couldn't ask him anything about it or why it had inspired him to make the puzzling drawings.

A tense silence fell on the room as Kaspar and Jane digested what Crebold had said.

Before any of them spoke again, there was a scratching sound at the front door and Kaspar left the room. Crebold looked at Jane and smiled.

"Isn't it strange being in two time frames simultaneously? I never get over this unsteady feeling I have whenever it happens, no matter how many jobs I've done. It's like having each foot in a different canoe on the water and trying to keep your balance."

Confused, Jane stared at him. "What do you mean?"

"Well, as soon as you and I leave here tonight, Kaspar won't remember any of this. He'll go on living his useless life exactly as he has been. Not until he shares your group dream a few months from now will he experience any of the stuff we've just been talking about. So while you and I are literally existing in both his present and his future, he's only in the present. He must feel left out, huh?"

Jane had other concerns. "Can I ask you a question?"

"Sure." Crebold straightened up, fully expecting something nasty from this impressive-looking woman. With her poise and stature, she could have been some kind of CEO. It was almost too bad she would end up like the others eventually—a real waste of talent.

Jane was careful the way she phrased the question—she wanted it to be both clear and concise. But when it came out, her confusion and need for an understandable answer made her gush. "All those things that happened in our dream—what were they? What did they all *mean*? So much was true and real, even down to specific details, but just as much was a confused jumble or simply not true.

"There were so many different stories and unconnected details . . . it felt like a hodgepodge of all our experiences scrunched together without any kind of filter to keep the stories separate. There was no through line; I can't make sense of it."

Crebold couldn't resist asking in a snarky voice, "Sort of like human life, eh?"

With loud fanfare the two big dogs came bounding into the room happy and eager to greet and kiss everyone. Crebold forgot Kaspar had said in the dream he owned a dog. Now here were two big slobbery brutes coming straight at him. Without a second's hesitation he lifted his hand and killed them both. D Train and Kos dropped to the floor as if they'd been shot point-blank in the head.

Horror-struck, Kaspar howled and falling to his knees, grabbed up his great and beloved friend D Train. The pit bull was heavy and warm and rubbery in his embrace, as if it had no bones at all. Its large head hung over one of his arms. "No!"

Crebold's mouth tightened. He was sort of sorry to have done it but not really—an instinctive reaction. He loathed all animals and Kaspar certainly knew it from their previous work together. As a result he never should have let the dogs into the house; he should have remembered Crebold's hatred. Yes, it was Kaspar's fault they were dead now.

"You can't do that," Jane said in a calm authoritative voice, which showed no sign of either shock or fear. It was a clear challenge to Crebold.

Crouching down next to Kaspar, she gently pulled him away from his dog. He struggled at first but after a few seconds let go. Kos was lying inches away. Jane touched D Train on the chest and Kos on the head—D with her right hand, Kos with her left. With what knowledge she'd gained from petting them while outside the house and those brief moments when she actually *became* the dogs, she immediately located where their souls were now and positioned her hands over them. Luckily the souls had not left the dogs' bodies yet.

"What are you doing?" Crebold didn't like this one bit. He didn't know how much Jane knew now about being a mechanic or what powers she'd regained. But what he was most wary of was suddenly very possible; they had warned him about it. If that was the situation now, he had to flee immediately if he wanted to survive.

"You can't change the past, Crebold, and you know it. Not even Chaos can do that—the past is fixed forever. So you can't kill these dogs now because they were both alive when we had the dream that happens months from today."

Crebold tried to bluff her. "You don't know anything—Chaos can do whatever it wants to do. If it wants to kill those dogs yesterday, it can."

Jane shook her head. "Nope, not true. The only time the past 'changes' is when we twist it in our memory or in whatever subjective histories we write about it. Hitler was Hitler. What he and the Nazis did was *fact*; how those facts are seen and *interpreted* is up to the different people and their various biases.

"But by itself the past is permanent, written in stone. Chaos can't *undo* or change the Big Bang, any more than you can kill these dogs yesterday."

Kaspar was silent throughout this exchange because he no longer remembered exactly what a mechanic or Chaos *was* capable of doing. Was

Jane right about the past being permanent and unalterable, even by something as powerful as Chaos? Oddly he kept thinking about *algebra*. Because at the moment he felt like a middle-aged man who'd learned algebra back in school and forty years later was trying to remember even an iota of what he once knew about it.

Crebold stared at the dogs and his eyes smiled. "If it's not true, why aren't they moving?"

Hands resting on the bodies, Jane said, "Because I won't let them until you're gone. I'm holding their souls until then."

Crebold spat out, "Bullshit!"

Slowly lifting her hands off the animals, she turned both palms up. Kaspar craned forward, desperate for a miracle, a sign, anything to prove what she'd said was true. But he saw nothing on Jane's pink palms and the two dogs remained still. Frustrated, he let out a small, strangled sound, an anguished cry from a grieving heart.

Crebold also looked at her palms, but obviously he *did* see something significant there because he quickly stepped back: one, two, three.

Watching him, Jane touched the dogs again. "Kaspar's not giving you his drawings because I won't let him. If I take my hands away again these two will come alive and tear you apart. I'll tell them to do it and you know I can—you won't be able to stop them because nothing can change the past.

"The only thing which *can* be changed here, right this minute, is *you*, Crebold, because you're the only thing that doesn't belong. You can't kill the dogs but they *can* kill you because they lived this moment. Ironic, isn't it? The past is our only safe refuge from Chaos."

Crebold's voice hardened. "Kill me? A really bad idea. You have no idea what'll happen if you do it."

It was Jane's turn to smile. "I don't care. If all you've said is true, we're doomed anyway. So why *not* kill you after what you just did? It'll be my small protest against Chaos. You kill these lovely animals, I bring them back to life and they kill you. Poetic justice: mate and checkmate."

The dogs' eyes opened but were blank, the look any creature has when it reawakens after having been knocked unconscious. The men saw this and were stunned.

Kos's legs quivered and twitched, then he sat up. His eyes were still unfocused. He did not try to stand. His blue-streaked tongue, slick with drool, lolled out the side of his mouth. D Train remained lying on his side but slowly started licking Jane's hand and the part of her arm he could reach by lifting his head a little.

Kaspar roared, "My boy!" and asked if he could hold the dog. Jane shook her head no, not yet.

In the moment when they glanced at each other, Crebold was gone.

"Do you want some wine? I've got all kinds."

"No, but I'd love a glass of very cold water, please."

Jane sat at the table surrounded by plates of food. Kaspar buzzed around his kitchen like a summer fly, the events of the last half hour still blasting red-hot survivor's adrenaline through his amped-up body. He couldn't be still so he brought more and more food and put it down in front of his new hero. He needed to do something to thank Jane for saving his dog's life, so when she had said she was hungry, he sprang into action and started gathering.

"Jane, I thought it was over; I thought for sure D Train was dead."

"Me too."

At the sink Kaspar looked over his shoulder at her, his mouth open in surprise. "*What?*"

She nodded it was true. "I knew mechanics had the power to bring things back to life. But I didn't know if *I* had it yet or if I'd use it right. I was flying blind, Kaspar, completely on instinct."

"Well, your instinct proved to be a good friend, which is even more impressive, Jane. You looked so cool, in *complete* control of the situation.

I'm certain it was part of what scared him off: Crebold saw you weren't going to take any shit from him because it sounded like you knew exactly what you were doing. Then when you actually brought the dogs back . . . he knew he'd met his match."

"But did you see his eyes, Kaspar? The whole time he talked, I could see in his eyes he wasn't sure we'd do what he wanted. When I saw that insecurity, I knew your drawings had to be incredibly important and worth protecting."

"But we don't know what they *mean*, Jane. What good are they if—" He sighed in frustration. Kaspar didn't need to finish the sentence because she knew exactly what he meant.

She picked up a small knife and cut a piece of Stilton cheese off a big hunk Kaspar had brought to the table. Jane loved any kind of cheese. Placing it on a cracker, she dipped the knife into a cup of shiny red condiment Kaspar had insisted she try on the Stilton. Apparently it was his invention— cranberry sauce mixed with wasabi mustard. She loved it from the first taste—the startling combination of very sweet in contrast to horseradish-sharp went perfectly with the cheese's own strong tang. It was a whole new and unexpected taste treat for her.

Looking at it now, Jane realized she'd eaten almost the whole serving of the oddly delicious stuff while chatting with Kaspar. She was still staring at the empty cup when he came over with a glass of water filled to the brim with ice cubes. He waited for her to take it but she just kept staring at what was left of her dip.

"Are you okay?"

She didn't respond.

"Jane, is something wrong?"

The dogs lay on the floor nearby. Although they appeared to be pretty much back to normal by then, neither had any energy. Usually when Kaspar was at the refrigerator D Train was right beside him. It was one of the few things the pit bull was smart about—he knew the big cold silver box held endless yummy treasures. So D always made it a point to station himself in the vicinity when it was opened in case any of the goodies inside came his way. But not this time, because he was completely pooped; death and resurrection had emptied both dogs' tanks for the day.

"Sit down, Kaspar. I think I might have just figured something out." Jane picked up the condiment cup and wiggled it. "Your dip, right?"

He gritted his teeth, preparing for criticism. "You don't like it?"

"I love it, but that's not the point. How did you know it'd taste so good? I never would have thought to combine those two flavors."

His mind paused and sat silent seconds thinking over her question. "How did I *know*? Um, well, I like wasabi and I like cranberry sauce."

Jane shook her head. "Lame answer. I like them too but never would have thought to mix them."

He looked relieved. "Okay, then maybe because I'm a culinary genius?"

She gave a fake smile, which died a moment later. "Close, but not quite." Putting the cup down, she wiped her hands on a napkin. She took a long drink of water, stopped, drank some more. " You said Crebold compared mechanics to ants in a colony, right?"

Kaspar nodded.

"After everything I've heard, this is what I've figured out: like ants, every mechanic has a specific job to do—only one task until you die."

"Well not *die*, Jane—retire."

"Okay, but *until* you're retired you do one job and nothing else, right? According to Crebold you were trained to be a 'Tenbrink,' whatever that is. A worker ant's sole job is to carry a load from A to B. When the task is complete, it carries *another* load from A to B, ad infinitum. It does the same job its whole life long. I know nothing about ants but assume they're born with the job already programmed into their genes."

"What's your point, Jane?"

"Like ants, a mechanic's single purpose is to do one job to help the colony survive, which in our case is the universe. Mechanics weren't taught to think but to *do*. I know I'm oversimplifying things, Kaspar, but humor me. As a mechanic, do you remember *ever* being told to use your imagination?"

"No, we were given powers and specific instructions on how to use them. It was rare to encounter a situation we couldn't handle. If it ever happened, our directive was to call in another mechanic and together we managed it."

Jane clapped her hands. "Exactly as I thought!"

Kaspar waited for her to say more, to draw this all together into some kind of brilliant *ah-ha!* revelation that would drive a stake through the heart of his questions and confusion about what was going on.

Instead she reached for the saltshaker. She took it, the cup holding the wasabi mix, and her water glass. She lined them up one, two, three next to each other on the table. Pointing to the water she said, "Think of this as the mechanics—they represent order, stability, and the greater good of the cosmos at any cost, okay?"

Next she pointed to the saltshaker. "*This* is the Somersault—Chaos, Randomness, and Disorder. The opposite of everything a mechanic is and works to prevent."

She picked up the wasabi cup. "And your delicious mix here stands for the humans. Let's not limit it only to humans and Earth, but to all beings in the universe with the capacity to think and choose for themselves." She drew a large imaginary circle around the three different objects. "What do they have in common, Kaspar? Mechanics fix things broken by Chaos. They keep things running right in the universe. But they can't *create* because they have neither the aptitude nor the tools.

"In contrast, Chaos *can* create but it's always a by-product of the havoc it causes; it's never intended. Think of a tornado or a hurricane: they create wild and imaginative things like putting a car on top of a tree. But it's never *deliberate*. A storm blows in and whatever mess it makes, creative or not, is all incidental."

Jane placed the wasabi cup on her open palm. "Now we get to the humans. Chaos and the mechanics have nothing in common. They're at opposite ends of the spectrum: anarchy and order.

"But human beings contain elements of *both*; sometimes they're chaotic, sometimes organized. Using their imaginations they have the ability to keep order, or create, *or* cause mayhem and confusion. Most importantly, it's usually a conscious choice which one we do."

Kaspar thought out loud: "Chaos isn't afraid of mechanics because they're only capable of keeping order?"

Jane nodded. "Right, it's like being afraid of a vacuum cleaner. But it *is* wary of humans because it knows they're creative and have the potential to think and act outside the box." She grinned. "But I believe what Chaos most fears is the *fusion* of the two—the mechanic and the human: *us*. Or the mechanic and whatever other combinations are made when they're retired and given second lives. They become like binary weapons." She crossed her index fingers in an "X" in front of her face.

"Retirees are *mutts*, Kaspar, mixed breeds, and I think Chaos is most afraid of what we're capable of doing. Former mechanics who have experienced second lives as humans or Martians or Alpha Centaurians? It doesn't matter where they've been because I'm guessing the same holds true for mechanics retired anywhere and like us are now being called back." Jane drank the rest of the water thirstily, as if what she'd just said had squeezed her dry.

Kaspar laid the drawings on the table. "What if it was planned, Jane? What if they knew all along Chaos was returning and lied to us when they *said* we were being retired? But it wasn't true—they knew full well that one day they'd call us back after we'd experienced these second lives. Assume your theory about mutts is correct. Imagine countless numbers of retired mechanics gathered together, millions of *mutts*, with all the knowledge and experience they've gained from years living as mortals. Reawaken their mechanic, mix it with their mortal side—"

"—and you've got an army," Jane completed his sentence.

It wasn't the word Kaspar had planned to use but it was a good one. He bowed his head in deference to her. "An army—*exactly*."

Kaspar looked at the drawings again. "I just saw something else here I recognize."

"Really, what?" Jane leaned forward to see what he was pointing to on one of the papers. It was the same three figures Marley Salloum had singled out back at the bar: the three letters from the Phoenician alphabet. Kaspar remained silent a long time and just kept tapping his finger back and forth between different things on the two papers.

Jane held back until she couldn't stand it anymore and blurted out, "*What?* What do they mean?"

"This is a will, Jane. It's my last will."

The same thing Marley had said after examining the drawings.

Kaspar's voice was soft and calm, no worry or upset in it. "I don't know what the other figures mean, but I recognize these three now: If you put them together they say I'm going to die soon and Crebold was right—all the rest of what's written on this sheet is a summing up of what I've learned and want to pass on of that knowledge; what I *need* to pass on." He pointed to the paper covered with the drawings of ink bottles. "I still don't get what these signify, though."

Jane countered, "Maybe I do." She described skating with Josephine and finding the black baseball that the girl called "obsidian." Then about her conversation with Bill's dying wife and seeing burnt sienna on the wall of the Edmondses' living room. On the drawing Jane pointed out the ink bottles labeled OBSIDIAN and BURNT SIENNA. "Mrs. Edmonds said each of these colors represents the most important emotion people experience; she called them the letters of the human alphabet."

"The colors are our *emotions?*"

"I guess—that's what she said. Then she described how burnt sienna represents the purest, best form of human love. She was very convincing."

Kaspar stared at the drawing of bottles and spoke in a voice just above a whisper, "The human alphabet." He glanced at Jane and said, "I'm going to *die* soon—*die*. It says so right there on the paper and I wrote that."

"Does it say when or how it will happen?" Jane looked at him but could not look for long. She dropped her eyes to the drawings.

Kaspar licked his lips and shook his head. "As soon as they flip you from here again I'll forget everything that's happened tonight. I won't remember *any* of it—Crebold coming, these drawings and what they mean, this talk we're having . . . I'll forget it all, Jane. I'll just think I've had a quiet evening at home by myself. It's what happens to anyone who's left behind after a flip; they have total amnesia about the experience and go right back to their status quo.

"It's so wrong because if I at least remembered I was going to die, I'd have the chance to change some things in my life now. Not many because I'm happy with the way it's gone; I've had a wonderful time. But yes, I'd do a few things differently; anyone would.

"I even thought before about writing notes to myself about your coming here and what's happened this evening. I'd put them in a drawer where I know I'd find them after you're gone. But it doesn't work that way—once *you're* flipped, everything vanishes, even secret notes to myself.

"If I *am* going to die soon, at least let me know when so I can walk in the woods with my dog a few more times and . . ."

As if on cue both dogs lifted their heads and looked in the same direction. D Train growled. D Train never growled.

Looking at the door Kaspar folded the drawings, handed them to Jane, and told her to put them somewhere safe. She slid them into an inside pocket of her parka and zipped it shut.

There was a knock at the front door. They looked at each other. Kaspar shook his head as if to say no, he wasn't expecting anyone. He got up to answer it. Jane didn't know if she should go with him or not. He left the room with the dogs close behind.

Moments later Jane felt a kind of tingle in her right elbow that grew quickly into a sharp pain. As she reached to touch the spot and rub it, she vanished.

Kaspar opened the front door not knowing who or what to expect on the other side. After his conversation with Jane, it could have been anyone or anything. If he knew she was gone now he would have been even more on guard.

"*Dean!* What are you doing here?"

His friend and partner stood on the top of the porch stairs. "I brought you something, Kaspar. Can we talk a minute?"

"Of course; Jane Claudius is here."

"No she's not."

"Excuse me?"

"She's gone; she was just flipped."

Kaspar looked back into the house as if to check on her whereabouts. "I don't understand."

"Jane was flipped; you know what it means. What's not to understand?" Dean shrugged.

"Then why do I still remember everything that's happened tonight? How come my memory hasn't been erased?"

"Because I'm here, Kaspar; I came to talk to you."

"Why?"

Dean waved him over. "Come outside. It's a nice night and I'd rather talk out on the porch."

"Wait a minute." Kaspar went back into his house. After checking the living room he walked to the kitchen, but there was no sign of Jane anywhere. Standing in the hall, hands on hips, he tried to figure out just what the hell was going on. No matter what happened now, at least she had his drawings, his small legacy. It was what mattered most. Hopefully those drawings would eventually lead her to something important, once she was able to decipher them.

When Kaspar returned to the porch Dean was sitting on the top step with his arm around D Train. Kos was nowhere in sight. Kaspar sat down on the other side of his dog. "What's up, Dean? Why are you here?"

Dean Corbin looked over the top of the dog's head and smiled at Kaspar. It was a nice smile, the smile of a friend who likes your company and wants only the best for you. "I assume Jane told you everything?"

Kaspar nodded. "Everything she knew, which wasn't a hell of a lot. We figured out some more stuff together by comparing notes."

"Did she tell you about us, about you and me? Did she tell you we're both gonna die before this is over?"

Hearing these words, Kaspar had a peculiar first reaction—he didn't know whether the fact scared or interested him. "I knew I was going to die soon, yes—just not *how*. Jane didn't either."

"I do." Dean reached into a pocket and brought out a jazzy-looking cell phone. He tapped it a few times. Kaspar started to speak but Dean cut him off: "Hold it a second. Let me just get this working." He tapped the screen more times and then nodded he was ready. Handing the phone to Kaspar, he said, "Watch."

An obviously homemade video clip jittered on. The view was jerky at first but quickly steadied. It held on an ugly giant insect, black as pitch, scuttling from left to right across a gray cement floor. When the bug was halfway across the frame, a hand holding a thick brown work boot smashed down on top of it, crushing the bug into instant black and yellow goo. Kaspar winced but what happened next made him gasp: instantaneously hundreds of tiny black bugs streamed out from beneath the boot in all directions—pregnant mama's surviving babies running for their lives. Kaspar was so revolted he instinctively opened his mouth and stuck out his tongue.

The clip ended and the screen went black. Dean put the phone in his lap. "*This* is what's going to happen to us, my friend."

Disgusted by what he'd seen, Kaspar asked sarcastically, "A big boot's going to come down out of the sky and crush us?"

"We're disposable, Kaspar, like the bug. They're going to let us die and then take whatever they need from us. Nice, huh? I don't know what's going to happen to the others, but I know this is our fate. No, they're not going to stomp us with a boot; they're just going to leave us for roadkill."

Kaspar looked at the phone in Dean's lap, remembering what he had just seen there. "How do *you* know about this?"

Dean pulled a folded piece of paper out of a shirt pocket and handed it over.

When Kaspar saw what was on it he started: it was identical to one of the drawings Jane showed him, a drawing *he* had purportedly made in the future.

"Where did you get this? It's exactly like one I did."

Dean nodded. "I know; but I made this drawing. In the dream, all five of us copied a map we saw on the side of an elephant. This is what I drew. Now I realize every one of us drew exactly the same map; we just didn't recognize it in the dream because none of us had the powers back yet." Dean stopped and touched a temple with his fingers as if to slow the buzz in his head. "We *thought* we'd all drawn different things, different maps.

But that was only because each of us was at a different level of conversion back to the mechanic mind. And we still are, Kaspar; it's like we're all in different grades at school. Even Jane isn't complete yet—if she were, if she'd regained her full powers by now, she could have refused this last flip and stayed here.

"I was able to make myself come after I deciphered some of these figures on this paper. It's like the more you grasp what you were once capable of doing, the more power you have."

Kaspar pointed to what he recognized on the page. "But these symbols—these exact three—say *I'm* going to die and the rest of what's here is a list of things *I've* learned about life as a human; not you, *me*."

Dean nodded in agreement. "I totally agree—it *is* the same map, believe me, but we perceive the images differently. Every one of us interprets it in their own way because we have all lived different lives both here and before.

"For example I saw the fact of my death down here." Dean pointed to figures and numbers on the bottom right corner of the paper, far away from Kaspar's three. Then he pointed to other things on the paper. "*These* say something about *fruit*, which I don't understand, and these are about you, me, and Edmonds all dying. It doesn't say how or when, just that we will and soon.

"*This* group of figures told me specifically how to come here." He pointed to the middle of the page where a bunch of what looked like ancient runes and Internet icons were lined up.

"What about the women, Dean? What about Jane and Vanessa? Does it mean they'll die too?"

Dean shook his head. "I don't know, Kaspar. I only understand some of what's on my map. I don't know what's going to happen to them."

SIX

Vanessa Corbin never told her husband, Dean, she'd once killed a man and gotten away with it. That's not to say she didn't want to tell him; it's just whenever a moment arrived when it would have been suitable to make the admission, to tell, to come clean to the one person on Earth who understood her better than any other, something always stopped her. After their third year together she decided *not* to tell. The right moment had come and gone at least ten times but she'd always found excuses not to do it. Her reasons for that failure varied from the reasonable to the very selfish, but the result was the same. So once and for all she chose to stay mum and let her deepest secret live on the skin of their relationship like a precancerous lesion, and hope nothing ever caused it to turn malignant.

Looking at her now, Crebold said the dead man's name, "Barry Rubin," then waited to see how she would react to the verbal hand grenade dropped in her lap.

She didn't. To his dismay, although it was the first time she'd heard the name in years, Vanessa's expression remained placid. Nor had it changed earlier when Crebold walked up to her table in the restaurant and asked if he could sit down. She said nothing but gestured lazily with a finger at the empty chair across from her.

He sat but kept silent, waiting to hear what she'd say about his abrupt reappearance in her life. After a few seconds of staring coldly at him, the chubby woman went back to eating the piece of pecan pie in front of her. Vanessa's clear indifference offended Crebold, so he chose to do away with any niceties and just drop the Barry bomb on her and watch the smithereens it blew her into.

Nothing—not one smithereen.

With a fork she cut off a small piece of pie and brought it up to her mouth. She paused it there to admire the deep caramel color and sugary glisten over the shard of nut. Then she slid the sliver into her mouth and closed her eyes so she wouldn't be distracted from giving her tongue's full attention to the tasty treat.

"Did you hear what I said? *Barry Rubin.* Doesn't the name ring a bell, Vanessa?" This time Crebold pronounced it slowly and precisely, as if repeating his own name to the maître d' of an exclusive restaurant who had just asked him to repeat it because there didn't appear to be a table reserved in that name.

Vanessa put the fork down and patted her lips with a green napkin. "Crebold, you have learned nothing—absolutely fuck-all *nothing*. What is it like to always, *always* come in last? My God, if you had a soul it would look like an old shriveled potato chip by now.

"I have something for you; it'll make you feel good for five minutes." She pulled a large black leather purse onto her lap and rummaged around inside it. "Here you go. I assume it's what you came here for." Vanessa handed him a piece of paper—the map she'd copied off the side of the elephant in the dream.

When Crebold saw what it was he hesitated to take it, as if the paper itself might be poison-coated or booby-trapped in some way. "Why are you giving this to me?"

She shrugged one shoulder. "Because it's what you came here for, right? I don't need it anymore."

"Why not? Do you know everything on there now? Are you *enlightened?*" His arrogant, mocking voice said he didn't believe her for a minute.

Instead of answering, she put the map on the table. "You're a mechanic, or at least you were once. Do *you* know what all of these things mean?"

He ran a hand down his necktie. "No, because some of them are human." There was no reason to lie to her, plus Crebold wasn't aware of how much mechanic knowledge she had regained by then. If she was already up to a certain level, she would see through any lie he told now anyway.

"Do you recognize this little fellow?" With her finger she tapped on a symbol toward the middle of the page that looked vaguely like a fire hydrant. Crebold said nothing.

Vanessa nodded. "I didn't think so." She placed her hand over the symbol. Seconds later it rose up off the page until it became a solid three-dimensional figure beneath her open palm. Picking it up, she turned her hand over so the thing was held in the middle of her bunched fingers. She moved the hand toward Crebold. "Eat it."

"What?"

"Take this and eat it." Seeing the incredulity in his eyes, she asked, "Are you afraid it's poison?"

He answered too loudly: "How should I know? I don't know what it is."

"You never were a big adventurer, were you, Crebold?" Without another word, Vanessa popped the figure into her mouth and chewed while looking straight at him. In a while she swallowed and smacked her lips. "I *really* like the taste of that one—sort of cinnamony."

"What is it?" He'd been watching her mouth and not seen what her hands were doing. She lifted an identical "fire hydrant" up to him from the paper. "Here's another one just like it—*try* it. I promise it's not poison."

He took it slowly from her, like a shy dog taking a treat out of a stranger's hand. "What *is* it?"

"Just put it in your mouth and then I'll tell you. Go on, Crebold—show you have at least one ball."

Still dubious, he opened his mouth and cautiously licked the thing once, twice: nothing. Vanessa had said she liked the taste but this one had none. He licked it again. "Nothing—I don't taste anything." His already suspicious mind raised more red flags.

Vanessa sighed, snatched it out of his hand, and popped it into her mouth. Crunch crunch crunch—swallow. Then she offered him yet *another* one. Crebold took it without hesitation, put it in his mouth, and bit down. Or tried to but it was like biting a stone—nothing, no give at all. No taste, no give—it really *was* like trying to eat a rock. He took it out of his mouth and shook his head. "I can't."

She showed no surprise.

"So what is it, Vanessa? You said you'd tell me."

"Humor."

"What?"

"Try this one." She held out a different figure she'd lifted off the paper. He tried but it was impossible too.

"*That* one's grace." She took it out of his hand and placed it on the table although it was still wet from his mouth. "I could give you hope or generosity or a bunch of others off this map but the same thing would happen: you can't eat any of them, Crebold; you couldn't even bite into them."

"But you can?"

Vanessa nodded. "Yes, because I'm human, or most of me still is." She rubbed the paper with her fingers. "These maps are records of what we've seen and experienced and what we find most important about this second life we've been living. Some of what we've seen has been through the eyes of the mechanics we once were, but we weren't aware of it until now."

Crebold said nothing because Vanessa was right.

She held out another figure to him. "Now try *this* one."

"This is a waste of time—"

She made an exasperated/amused face. "Just *do* it—trust me."

If Crebold had been Bill Edmonds he would have instantly recognized the figure she offered now as Keebler, the netsuke sumo wrestler Lola Edmonds had owned and loved for years.

Crebold took it but again first licked the figure before putting it in his mouth. Delicious! Startled, he bit off the head of the little sumo. It was as soft as a piece of jellied candy. He couldn't resist gobbling down the rest of what was in his hand. Scrumptious.

Vanessa said approvingly, "Great, huh?"

"Fantastic! But why can I eat this one and not the others?"

"Because it's made of only mechanics' food—*udesh* and other things. They planted one in Edmonds's life when he retired. You're still mostly mechanic so you can eat their food. There are other things on this map you could eat too because they were also planted in our lives.

"But watch this now—" Again Vanessa put her hand on the paper. Another Keebler materialized beneath her fingers. She held it up a moment for him to see before slipping it into her mouth. As if knowing what was going to happen, she gingerly tried to bite it but could not.

Crebold craned forward for a better look, to make sure he was seeing what he was seeing and it wasn't a trick. It *wasn't* a trick. "Why, Vanessa? You were a mechanic; and now at least part of you is turning back into one."

She put it back on the table. The two of them looked at the Keebler figure until Vanessa said, "Petrichor."

"What's that?"

"The smell of the earth just after it starts to rain."

Crebold made a *huh?* face. "Clarify please."

"People think petrichor is only the combination of rainwater, earth, and stone. But it's really a mixture of at least *fifty* different compounds, all blended together in an oily essence like perfume."

"Answer the question, Vanessa."

"It answers *everything*, Crebold. All of us, all the retired mechanics, are different kinds of petrichor now. We've become mixtures of who we were and what we are now. We're no longer only stone or water—single things. Mechanics and Chaos are single things, *pure*, but we aren't anymore.

"Do you know why you couldn't eat humor? Because it's a mix of *mortal* things, fallible, flawed things. Humor, grace, generosity, even sadness—all of them are mixes.

"Single things, things with hard edges and fixed boundaries, will never be able to understand how such weird, contradictory elements combine so well. Black and white can't understand gray."

Crebold wasn't having it. "You're talking about *mechanics* and *Chaos*, Vanessa. Between the two of them, they pretty much understand everything."

"Wrong—they only have *power* over everything. They control it but don't necessarily understand it.

"Here, I'll show you." She raised another figure off the map and offered it to Crebold. Without hesitating he took it, tried to bite it, couldn't. "What is this?"

Vanessa took it out of his hand and gulped it down. "The dream we shared. Five people shared the same dream, each one adding different parts from their lives to it. All those parts got mixed together like in a thick vegetable soup. A great, fantastic-tasting *zuppa di verdure* with every kind of vegetable imaginable in it. Five lives—our hopes, fears, secrets,

joys . . . bits and pieces of everything that we are, human *and* mechanic—
went into the soup."

"So what?"

She reached over and patted his cheek. "So could you eat our messy
human dream? No, but you just saw I could."

Crebold disliked him on sight. The man was too tall, too handsome, too cocksure of himself with every step he took approaching the bar. It was as if his whole physical presence announced, "Out of the way, world—a god is coming through." Crebold had seen versions in all places of this kind of egomaniac, and not just on Earth. All of them seemed to take it for granted life was both their friend and fan. And why not, the proof was everywhere—look at what it had already given them without their ever having had to ask.

The man sat down at the bar a few seats away. He shot his cuffs and adjusted his sevenfold silk tie. His beautifully tailored navy blue suit fell just so and didn't scrunch up anywhere like most men's suits do when they sit down. Even the damned suit loved him!

Naturally he and the bartender shook hands warmly and appeared to be old buddies. Without taking an order, the barman prepared a drink, put it down in front of him on a round red coaster, and said admiringly, "Lagavulin, twelve years old, one cube."

Mr. Handsome put a hand over his heart and bowed an exaggerated thanks to the barman for remembering what he liked to drink.

"Do you have a Balvenie, fifteen-year-old double wood?" Crebold was sitting just close enough for Handsome to hear his request. Clearly impressed by the choice, the bartender said indeed he did and went to the far end of the bar to get the expensive, rarely ordered drink.

"Balvenie? I've heard you should drink it with a piece of gingerbread. Supposedly the combination of the two makes the cake taste more spicy."

Crebold turned his head slowly toward the other man and raised his eyebrows in casual interest. "Izzat right? I never heard it before. I haven't eaten gingerbread in twenty years."

Handsome moved down to the seat next to Crebold's and extended his hand. "You are a man who obviously knows fine scotch. I'm Barry Rubin."

"Crebold."

Rubin smiled, waiting for him to say more. When he realized nothing more was coming he dipped his head forward and back like a nervous bird. "*Crebold?* That's it, only one name?"

"I'm from Macedonia."

From the immediately shifty look in Rubin's eyes it was plain he didn't know what the hell Crebold was talking about but didn't want to admit it or ask what coming from Macedonia had to do with going by a single name. Baffled, Rubin nodded sagely as if he totally understood. "What do you do, uh, Crebold?"

The bartender brought the Balvenie and as a sign of respect, gave the bar a quick wipe with his rag before putting the glass down on a coaster in front of Crebold. Instead of answering Barry's question, the Macedonian picked up the glass, closed one eye, and carefully sipped the very expensive whisky. To the mechanic the stuff tasted like skunk piss but he pretended to savor it as if it were ambrosia. Rubin let him have his moment.

"I'm a singer."

"A *singer*, really?"

"Yup."

"What kind of music do you do?"

"Polka."

Rubin hesitated, nonplussed. "I didn't know polka music was sung."

"Only in Macedonia; but it translates surprisingly well into English." Crebold was talking complete crap but it was the first thing that came to mind and he wanted to mess with Rubin a while to see how he'd react.

The room around them slowly began to fill. It was after six and the city wanted its first drink of the evening. The next time Crebold looked up from the conversation, he noticed two bartenders were at work and both were very busy.

This was the night years ago Vanessa and Barry Rubin slept together for the first time. Crebold had chosen to return here not because of the event, but because he simply wanted to meet this Rubin character and see what kind of fellow he was. What kind of person would bring out the killer in a woman like Vanessa Corbin? Crebold knew he had a good hour before she was to arrive here for the date, so there was time.

"And what do you do for a living, Barry, besides drink good booze?" Crebold lifted his glass in a toast to his new friend. Rubin did the same and they both took small sips.

"I'm a designer. I helped create *Lightcage*." Endearingly there was immense pride in Barry's voice. He sounded like a little boy telling his parents he'd gotten a good grade in school.

With one finger Crebold rubbed a circle around the top of his whisky glass. "Lightcage? Is it some kind of lamp?" He made sure to inject just the right soupçon of derision into his voice to make it plain whatever "lightcage" was he didn't give a shit.

Rubin raised his chin, startled and offended by the other's remark. "No, it's a video game; one of the bestselling games of all time, actually."

"Interesting, but you're talking to the wrong guy; I'm not a *gamer*." The way Crebold said that last word was like a bully's poke in Rubin's chest.

Without missing a beat, Barry fired back, "Well, I guess we're even then because I don't have any *polkas* on my iPod; never been a big *fan* of the genre, you know?"

The mechanic grew a sly grin. "Touché, Barry." It was the first time he'd liked anything about Rubin.

"Here you go, gentlemen." The bartender gently laid two plates down on the bar in front of them. On each was a long golden brown baguette filled to overflowing with different kinds of meat, cheeses, and colorful vegetables. Oozing tantalizingly out the sides (the sandwiches were wonderfully warm to the touch) was what looked like a brownish mayonnaise but turned out to be a sensationally good piquant sauce that enhanced the flavor of every single thing in the sandwich.

Both men looked at the bartender for an explanation. "Orders from the management: everyone in here tonight gets one and they're all on the house." He moved down the bar and placed two more plates in front of a couple sitting there. The woman lit up when she heard the bartender's explanation, clapped her hands at the unexpected gift, and without a word picked up the sandwich and took a big bite. A few chews later she let out a loud long groan of pleasure that was half sexual and half joy. "My God, Bryce, you've got to *taste* this; it's a work of art."

Her companion needed no further urging. He took a couple of big bites and chewed with eyes closed, all the while nodding his head, then held the sandwich out in front of him and pointed to it. He shook his head in wonder and appreciation. "Unreal! This is without a doubt the *greatest* thing I've ever eaten. I am not exaggerating." His girlfriend, mouth full, could only nod in eager agreement. "But what's just as amazing is my sandwich doesn't have any meat in it like yours. How did they know I'm vegetarian?"

The woman shrugged and kept chewing.

Crebold and Rubin looked at each other. Rubin said, "Never look a free meal in the mouth." Both men lifted their sandwiches and set to.

The couple was right—it *was* the most delicious thing either man had ever eaten. But how could that be when it was just a sandwich? It really confused Crebold, because he loathed human food. Anytime it had been necessary for him to eat it in the past had been a horrible experience.

But not this sandwich: how was it possible? He kept examining it as he ate, turning it this way and that, opening it several times to see what exactly was inside, recognizing ingredients he'd always found revolting before—waxy capocollo ham, slimy avocado, viscid Brie cheese . . . disgusting stuff. Normally just the thought of these textures on his tongue sent a slick shiver of revulsion down his spine. But not this time, not when they were combined with all the other ingredients inside this magnificent sandwich. And what the hell was in the dressing that fused everything together so perfectly?

While he ate, Crebold swiveled on his bar stool and scanned the noisy room behind him. It was absolutely packed full; there must have been over a hundred people in there. It was loud, but a sexy intimate loud—murmurs, laughter, plans being made, plots being hatched, phone numbers exchanged, the tinkling of glasses, women saying yes. He watched waiters hurrying from table to table bringing trays of sandwiches to everyone. They kept moving in and out of the kitchen to get more.

"It's a very strange idea to give these out during cocktail hour, don't you think? Everyone in here is about to eat dinner; they're going to ruin a lot of appetites. Sort of reminds me of the free lunch tables bars used to put out during the Depression." Rubin wiped his mouth with a napkin. His face was flushed from eating too fast. There was something small and green stuck in his front teeth. "But hey, I'm not complaining, far from it.

Whatever the reason for this grub, I am now officially in love with the management of this place."

At a nearby table a very beautiful woman was served a sandwich but didn't want it. She smiled sweetly but kept shaking her head, no thanks. She and the waiter talked back and forth until he finally got the point and just left the plate in front of her on the table. In contrast, the man with her devoured his sandwich with great gusto. Crebold watched this couple a while, wondering if the woman would give in and take a taste, but it didn't happen.

"Do you know who she is?" Barry leaned in and spoke quietly to Crebold. "I've been watching her too; it's Riley Rivers, the porn star. Isn't she gorgeous? They say she's never had one bit of plastic surgery done to her body, which is pretty hard to believe when you look at her, especially in person like this.

"I think the guy's she's with is her boyfriend. His name is Duck Tape. He's the drummer with some famous band. I forget which one."

Crebold narrowed his eyes and stared at the boyfriend, who although festooned with ornate, mostly illegible tattoos wore thick black eyeglasses, which made him look intelligent. "*Duck Tape?* Are you serious? That's really the man's name?"

Rubin nodded. "It's probably really something like Joe Smith, but Duck Tape is what he goes by. I guess it's his stage name."

Riley Rivers saw the two men were watching her and her companion. Something about them caught her attention. Smiling slyly she stood up and walked right over despite the fact her boyfriend was still talking. Rubin was so surprised by her approach that he moved on his stool until his back was pressed up against the bar.

The woman ignored him and got right up close to Crebold. Unfazed, he didn't budge even when she was only inches away from his face. Her chutzpah intrigued him.

"You fool, Crebold, don't you recognize me? *Really?* Or are you just being a dick?"

Crebold was about to eat the last bite of sandwich but dropped it on the plate and brushed crumbs off his hands instead. "Why would I recognize *you?* I don't watch porno."

Ignoring his insult the woman reached forward, took the last bit of food off his plate, and ate it while watching him and waiting for a reaction. After she'd swallowed she turned to Barry Rubin and in an ice cold voice told him to get lost. Confused and surprised, Rubin picked up his drink and moved way down the bar.

Poker faced, Crebold blinked twice watching the sexy stranger. But gradually the look in his eyes changed. His whole body gave a twitch, as if it had been shouted awake out of a deep sleep. When he spoke again to her his words were full of both wonder and unease. "*Milnie?* Milnie Odle?"

The woman licked crumbs off her fingertips. "*Yassou patrioti.* Nice to see you haven't lost *all* your perception since you've been here. You had me worried there for a minute."

Crebold could not believe what he was seeing. "What the hell are you doing here, Milnie? And what's with the porn star thing?"

She pushed a lock of long auburn hair away from her eyes. "Well, since I had to be here I thought it would be interesting to sample their flesh, so it was either porn or cannibalism. I tried both, but porn feels better."

From their respective places Barry Rubin and Duck Tape watched this exchange. Once they glanced at each another but neither man had a clue as to what was going on.

"Why are you here in this place tonight?"

"Why are *you* here?" she taunted, clearly enjoying his confusion.

Crebold slid a quick look down the bar to see how close Rubin was. "To check him out; I wanted to meet the guy Vanessa Corbin killed."

With a wave of her hand Riley Rivers dismissed this idea and shook her head. "Don't bother—he's unimportant."

"What do you mean?"

"Why do you think those sandwiches were given out to everyone—because they think we're hungry? They're a metaphor, baby. How do you make a great sandwich? Load it up with the perfect assortment of ingredients—diverse tastes and spices and sauces.

"That's us, Crebold—*we're* the ingredients; Rubin too, despite the fact he's a total fuckup. They're taking all us retirees, all our lives both here and as mechanics. Everything we *are* now and were and combining it into one big . . . sandwich." She put her open palms side by side as if she were holding a book or two pieces of bread. She closed them together. "Think of it, Crebold: see this room as a microcosm of what's going on all over the universe. Almost everyone in here is a retired mechanic. Like Mr. Rubin over there and Vanessa Corbin. All these lives, all these brains, all these individual experiences combined into one—"

Crebold put up a hand to stop her. "Wait a minute, I'm not retired."

"Yeah you are, pal—or rather you *were* after that dumbshit stunt showing off with the ants at the café."

Shoulders slumping, his mouth dropped open in dismay. "No, really? I *was?*"

"Yup—they parnaxed you immediately while you were being taken away in the van but you didn't feel it. 'Twas all part of their plan. They've been collecting whole ranges of experiences and thought a secret parnax would be a good one to add.

"So some of us knew when we were retired, others didn't, like you."

"Then what have I been doing here this whole time since I was parnaxed?"

"Living, experiencing, following your instincts, doing what you thought was right—or at least right for you. It's why you cut the deal with Chaos, or *thought* you did. That was funny." She slapped him playfully on the arm and shook her head at his impudence.

Eyes wide and caught completely off guard, he whined, "I didn't?"

Riley sneered. "Hell no! They really enjoyed watching you pull *that* stunt. You've got a big fucking ego, Crebold—did you honestly believe Chaos would specifically come and court *you*? Uh, no! It was some of our people who made the offer. They just wanted to see how you'd react to the bait. Of course being you, you took it. And yet another little notation was made in their big book about Crebold.

"Chaos *is* coming, there's no doubt about that. Mechanics have begun disappearing everywhere. You can see and feel it already in a million different ways, but obviously the worst hasn't arrived yet. What's here now is mostly the grumble of thunder before the real storm comes rolling in.

"So they decided to harvest the fruit now before the Somersault really gets going." Having said this, Riley tugged up the front of her dress, which had drifted alluringly low. When she saw Barry Rubin staring at her while she did this, she stuck out her notoriously long tongue at him.

Crebold put a finger to the side of his head and twisted it back and forth to indicate the whole situation was crazy. He stood up. "What do you mean, *fruit*? Wait, don't answer yet—I have to pee. I can't stand it anymore; I have to go right now."

Riley shrugged. "So go pee—enjoy."

"Enjoy? I hate pissing. I hate *bodily functions*. Why do they call them that? It's *pissing* and *shitting* and is there a bigger waste of time?"

Riley giggled like a young girl at his anger. "What *don't* you hate, Crebold? Go, take your piss, and don't hate it too much. At least enjoy the relief it brings and see it as a little intermission in our conversation.

"Remember Jezik? Before they got her she loved to piss. It was one of the things she liked most about being human. So be nice to your dick; give it half a chance and it can be very nice to you in the right situation." She reached out and squeezed his shoulder. "It *is* true though—you do seem to hate everything. Have you ever noticed it about yourself? Maybe it's just the type of fuel you run best on. You drive into a gas station and tell them to fill it up with hate." She shook her head and gave his shoulder another squeeze. Crebold didn't like being touched but in light of what she'd just said about him, wasn't about to mention it.

Walking across the room now he looked at the various faces in a new light. He didn't recognize any of them but that didn't mean anything. He hadn't even recognized Riley Rivers when she first approached him yet he'd known *her* forever. Did it mean they had already taken away some of his powers or—

"Crebold!"

He looked for whoever had said his name loudly and distinctly. No one. No one was looking at him or walking toward him. Checking again, he turned every which way just to be sure. No one.

Continuing to the toilet he pushed on the door to go in. No one was there. It was a surprisingly large room with what must have been ten stalls and as many urinals. Walking over to the closest, he unzipped his fly as quickly as possible and fumbled his penis out of his jockey shorts. He was in the middle of an obscenely pleasant piss when he heard it again.

"Crebold!"

Glancing left and right while urine hissed urgently out of him, he was afraid he'd have to stop and still dribbling, stuff himself back into his pants so as to be presentable to talk to whoever had said his name.

Crebold spoke cautiously, "Hello? Who's there? Where *are* you?"

"Right here," said a woman's voice. "Did you really come here to spy on me, Crebold? Has Barry Rubin been giving you all the dirt on me?"

Vanessa Corbin.

"Vanessa, where are you?"

"In your head—I told you. All of us are in you now, Crebold: Riley, me—everyone in the place. You're the *man*."

"What do you mean? Where *are* you?" Looking around, he was certain he'd see Vanessa lurking somewhere just out of sight, tricking him, playing stupid mind games to throw him off and make him feel even more bewildered.

"Look at your hand, Crebold—your palm. Look at the lines there."

Unhurriedly he finished peeing, adjusted himself back into his pants, and zipped up. He walked over to one of the sinks and washed his hands. He wasn't about to let anyone rattle him. Only when he was done thoroughly washing and drying his hands did he turn them both over for a look.

Study your palms and you'll see perhaps four or five prominent lines crisscrossing it, intersected by many smaller ones.

In contrast, Crebold's right palm now had what appeared to be hundreds of lines on it, deep and shallow, long and short, straight and wavy. . . . There were so many that it looked like an aerial view of a railroad yard in the biggest city on Earth. You couldn't begin to count all the lines on his hand now because if put under a magnifying glass you would see lines on top of lines on top of lines like a palimpsest, going in every possible direction.

"Look at your other hand."

He did and it was the same—lines everywhere.

"That's us. You have all of us in you now, Crebold—all of the people in this restaurant tonight. The lines are the proof. You're going to be carrying all of us back."

"Back where? Why me?" he asked while still staring at his hands. Turning them over and back, he kept making fists and opening them again, rubbing them together and looking to see if the rubbing made any difference. . . .

"Because you hate everything here, Crebold, so you have no reason to want to stay. Almost all the rest of *us* have lots here we love and we don't want to give it up. But we're not in control. They're taking whatever they need from us."

He kept noticing ever-new details, like the mad riot of lines was not only on the palms but everywhere on his hands—across the backs, sides, all the way up and down each finger. They looked like the hands of the oldest human being who had ever lived. They looked like they belonged to someone centuries old.

And then in an instant all of them vanished.

In an instant the myriad lines on both of Crebold's hands—every single one of them—disappeared before his eyes. They shrank, shrank, shrank until from one moment to the next all were gone, leaving both of his now-trembling hands completely smooth and unblemished. They did not even have the palmar creases found on all newborn human babies.

Seeing them disappear was even more disturbing to Crebold than the moment he'd first seen the lines on his hands.

He called out, "Vanessa!" but she didn't answer. He called her name again, much louder this time. His voice echoed off the white walls of the empty men's room. Slapping his leg and grimacing from both frustration and doubt, he looked around hoping to see something, *anything* to give him a clue as to just what the hell was happening here.

He walked over to one of the stalls and pushed open the door a little too hard: nothing inside but the toilet. Moving to another: nothing there either. He stood in the middle of the floor with fists clenched trying to figure out what to do next. He checked both hands again but they were bare, empty, unlined.

Crebold was now so frustrated and angry that if he had been a fairy tale character like Rumpelstiltskin, he probably would have burned up in a furious fizzle of smoke or torn himself in half. But he was a mechanic, albeit a thoroughly confused one now, and he was going to figure this mystery out no matter what. He was an asshole—he knew it better than anyone—but he was a *determined* asshole, which made a big difference in his mind.

After one last look around he pushed open the door and walked out of the bathroom.

Right into the next shock.

The restaurant was completely empty. The large room, which only minutes before had been humming with activity and scores of people laughing, talking, drinking, eating, flirting, grousing . . . was now silent and vacant. Almost as alarming, all the tables were covered with signs of messy moments-ago life: half-eaten food and drinks, women's purses lying scattered, cell phones . . . It looked as if everyone in the place had vanished so quickly they hadn't even had time to pocket their phones, gather their purses, or take the napkins off their laps and put them on the tables before leaving.

Crebold could feel a real palpable buzzing life lingering very percepti-bly all around him—like the soul of someone who's died just moments be-fore. In the random scatter of objects left, the way many chairs sat crookedly or pushed away from the tables as if the people sitting in them had been facing each other in conversation. Half-empty wine bottles and glasses, partly eaten sandwiches, a telephone number scrawled in vivid purple ink on a torn slip of paper held down by a full bottle of Pellegrino mineral water. Crebold could feel life's heart still beating strongly everywhere in the vast empty room.

What happened here? Where were all the people who had filled the place only minutes before when he'd left to go to the bathroom?

Crebold walked around touching things, sitting in different chairs, look-ing at the room from different angles. At one point he even put his hands over his eyes and a moment later dropped them again like a child playing peekaboo with an adult. Only now he hoped when he took his hands away, the restaurant would once again be full of people and the situation back to normal.

He was a mechanic—why couldn't he understand what had happened?

Sitting down at one of the tables, he reached for an almost full bottle of red wine and poured it into a glass right up to the rim. Taking a big mouthful he gulped it down and quickly had another. Wine was all right. Crebold had to admit he liked the stuff. What Riley had said before about his hating everything on Earth wasn't true. There *were* things he liked. There were some things he liked very much on Earth but he'd just never told anyone about them. Why should he? Whose business was it that he liked wine or anything else?

One of the cell phones on the table rang. It vibrated too, so with every ring it moved a little across the table. Crebold's first reaction was to reflexively pull back, away from the now-alive and suddenly sinister pink object. He knew it wasn't an accident or coincidence; the phone was ringing for him. Whoever was on the other end of the line knew exactly where he was and what had just gone on here.

After letting it ring three times he took a shaky deep breath, let it out in a loud *whoosh*, and picked up the phone. Pressing the connect button, he put the phone to his ear and said, "Crebold."

The voice on the other end was calm and anonymous. "All of them are safely inside you now. That's why the lines on your hands have disappeared—the process is complete. How do you feel?"

"Confused." Crebold did not ask who he was speaking to.

"That's understandable. Do you have any questions?"

"Yes—why was it necessary for me to be parnaxed?"

"Because they're gathering data. They needed to see how you and Kaspar would react toward each other after his years as a human. You failed the test and proved you're not to be trusted."

Crebold couldn't help wincing at the thought of what he was about to say. "Is he . . . is he *in* me along with the others?"

"No, Kaspar is dying; he just doesn't know it yet. He'll finish his life here. They'll strip him of certain memories he has now to make him more comfortable and then leave him alone."

"He's *dying*?" Surprising himself, Crebold was dismayed to hear Kaspar was dying and they weren't going to stop it. "But don't they need him? He's one of the few allowed to keep his memory when he was retired. Don't they *need* his information—all he's learned here?"

"No."

The single word and blunt tone in which it was spoken fell like a hammer blow on Crebold's ear and assumptions.

He was going to say something else when suddenly he cocked his head to one side and looked, as if listening to a distant sound he couldn't recognize. A sudden clear vision of the magazine store owner Whit Ayres had come to him for some unknown reason. At first he didn't recognize the man because he'd never seen him before—but in an instant he did. Crebold said out loud what he already knew was the truth. "Ayres was a mechanic too, wasn't he?"

The voice on the telephone said indifferently, "Yes. Everyone in this room was a retired mechanic. All of you previously worked together in the same group. Even idiotic Barry Rubin who revealed things he shouldn't have and had to be eliminated. They used Vanessa to take care of him. She did well, although she had no idea who was behind it."

Crebold pointed toward the bar and asked why Riley Rivers had said before some of the people in the room were *not* mechanics.

"Because she's not back up to full understanding yet, which is true about many of those who were here."

Crebold raised his head and looked toward the ceiling as his thoughts gradually lined up and began to make an overall sense. "Vanessa was set up to kill Rubin although she thought it was her own doing. Something about him had gone bad or wrong and he revealed stuff he shouldn't have. Like a healthy cell in the body that kills another because the second one has become infected and threatens the others."

"Right again. Sometimes mechanics do go bad when they retire. Then they must be destroyed, like infected cells."

Crebold put the telephone on the table and reached for his wineglass. He drained what was left and touched the glass to his forehead as if to cool the overheated engine inside it. His mind was working at a ferociously fast speed processing, separating, and divvying up the ideas, truths, and revelations that bombarded it now.

He'd once been in an air traffic control tower at Kennedy airport in New York City, watching what appeared to be hundreds of green blips representing planes approaching and leaving local airspace on the controllers' crowded screens. At the time, despite being a mechanic, he thought he'd go mad if he had to monitor and manage this constantly changing pandemonium all day long. Yet that's exactly what it felt like inside his skull right now.

New information kept coming in. He took his head in his hands at one point and muttered, "Wait! Just *stop* a second and let me *process* some of this." But it did not stop and for a time he was overcome. Crebold saw moments of joy and satisfaction, fear and failure, deaths and births . . . the countless experiences of countless human lives all roiled together inside his mind. It felt like being swept up in a mountainous tidal wave that engulfed him in its frenzy, power, and roar.

There was no way to judge how long this went on. It might have been a minute or millennia. But it passed and finally like the person who miraculously survives the monstrous might of a tsunami and is tossed up on shore naked, exhausted, and dazed, Crebold slowly opened his eyes and once again saw the empty room. Amazed and agog at what he'd just experienced, he understood what was happening now. He slapped both shaking hands flat down on the table, as if to steady himself from the aftershocks of what he'd just experienced.

Although he grasped so much, there were still questions. He knew he did not need the telephone but picked it up anyway to continue the conversation with . . . himself.

When he did, the phone voice, which he recognized now as his own, said, "There are more than a hundred trillion cells in a human being. Combine those hundred trillion together and they make a single person."

Crebold said, "They're taking retired mechanics, combining all of our experiences, all the years of life, all the worlds we've known, all the problems we've faced, and mashing them all together to create one—*what*—golem? God or *what*ever is necessary to fight Chaos?"

The other voice said serenely, "I don't know what they will do. I don't think it's possible for the likes of us *to* know."

Crebold took the telephone away from his ear and tapped it against his chest while thinking things over. He wondered if Chaos had done the same thing—split itself into an infinite number of "cells" and sent them out across the universe. But being Chaos, its cells would *disrupt* life in endlessly different and wicked ways everywhere. And at some point—maybe even now—it would gather those cells with all their new knowledge and experience to form a newer, better, smarter . . . being? Power? God of Chaos?

The voice said something but Crebold missed it. Putting the pink phone back against his ear he asked, "What?"

"You *can't* understand how they work so don't try; it's a waste of time. Just do your job, Crebold. All the people who were in this room are inside you now. Even Rubin has useful information despite his mistakes.

"All their knowledge *combined* is the only reason why you understand as much as you do about what's been going on here; you never would have figured any of this out alone. So forget what the big boys are doing or why—it's beyond our understanding."

Crebold knew this same thing was happening in many places now and he hated the idea: scores of ex-mechanics being gathered together like iron filings pulled to a magnet. Then somewhere someplace unimaginable they'd be mixed together into one entity. He couldn't abide it. He knew it was true but could not accept how *demeaning* it was.

"After all we've experienced, each of us will only end up a single cell in this big final body? Every retired mechanic, all our different lives, personalities, and experiences . . . all these completely singular, unique existences kneaded together like *bread dough* and fed to some *superwarrior* who'll use it to fight Chaos. Is this right? That idea *disgusts* me. It makes me hate the system and what I spent my whole life doing."

The voice on the phone waited a few beats before saying gently, "Remember your analogy of the ant colony—everything is sacrificed for the community; like ants, the individual doesn't matter for us."

"*Screw* the community—we matter. I matter. The individual *does* matter." Crebold jabbed himself again and again in the chest with his thumb. The tiny sound was the only one in the cavernous empty room.

Kaspar Benn sat contentedly on the top step of his front porch, flanked on either side by D Train and Kos. There was nowhere else he wanted to be and with no better company. He'd had a lovely visit with Vanessa where the two ate themselves silly while talking and laughing their way through a splendid late fall afternoon until it was time for her to go sing at the bar. The fact they hadn't slept together didn't matter. They hadn't for a very long time. There seemed to be an unspoken tacit agreement between them now that the physical part of their relationship was finished, which was just as well. Vanessa was a lazy unimaginative lover, despite her boasting and big talk about being crazy for sex. But even without it he really did enjoy her company as long as it came in small doses. Especially when it came to food, because Vanessa was a superb cook who enjoyed eating as much as he did. Kaspar willingly sat through her monologues and self-absorbed rants if they were at a table covered with delicious food and drink and a limited amount of time to spend together.

While savoring the memory of the different cheeses and wines they'd consumed with such gusto earlier, he noticed someone walking down the sidewalk toward his house. It was dark out so Kaspar couldn't see the man's face clearly until he stopped and stood at the front gate. When he did recognize the guy, Kaspar was amazed.

"*Crebold!* Good lord, what are *you* doing here?"

His old nemesis shuffled up the stone path to the house, eyes moving apprehensively back and forth between the two dogs, arms stretched and tensed at his sides, ready for anything.

Although they watched the stranger approach with keen interest, neither dog budged from their places next to Kaspar.

"Don't worry about these boys—they're friendly. Both of them are big pussy cats." Kaspar hadn't seen Crebold since before retiring. He was genuinely surprised to see *him* here both because mechanics *never* revealed themselves to "civilians," plus the two had such bad blood between them going back, well, a very long time.

Kaspar climbed down the stairs to greet his visitor. He extended a hand and the two men shook. After several seconds Crebold tried to take his hand away but Kaspar held on longer, the whole time smiling and nodding. His smile grew bigger and bigger until it was almost disconcerting.

"I *never* thought it would be you, Crebold. Will wonders never cease? Can I get you a drink, or how about something to eat?"

"A glass of wine would be nice if you have it, thank you." Crebold stopped at the bottom step, leaned against the banister, and slid both hands into his pockets. It was getting chilly out there. He looked exhausted and sad.

Kaspar went into the house and returned shortly with an expensive bottle of Prager Grüner Veltliner he'd brought back from a business trip to Austria. It took him a while to open the bottle, pour without spilling a drop, and hand a glass over to his longtime exasperating colleague whom he'd once hoped never to see again—until now. The men clinked glasses in a toast that silently said, "Well, here we are together again; let's try and make the best of it."

"Don't you want to sit down? You look very tired."

Crebold eyed the dogs and shook his head. "I'll stand. I need your help, Kaspar. I know you never expected to hear me say that, but it's true now. I'll probably get hammered for having come back here, but I don't care—it's the only thing I could think of to do. You were always the best at this. I never wanted to admit it, but it's true."

For the next half hour Crebold told Kaspar Benn everything, including the news Kaspar was dying. Crebold had flipped himself back to the night months before when both Jane and Dean visited Kaspar. But when both people left, Kaspar's memory of meeting them was erased because he would not regain any of his mechanic's powers for months.

So when Crebold arrived to ask for help, Kaspar was just sitting on his front porch with the two dogs enjoying the sights and smells of an autumn evening in Vermont while remembering the fine gluttonous afternoon with Vanessa.

When Crebold finished talking, the two men shared a companionable silence drinking the good wine. Kaspar topped off Crebold's glass twice when he noticed it was almost empty. At one point D Train got up and walked slowly down the steep porch steps to investigate something intriguing-looking in the yard. Crebold stiffened when D passed. Kos watched but did not move. Kaspar began scratching Kos's ear. The dog tipped his head slightly toward the man to offer more area to scratch.

"Are they anything?" Crebold pointed his glass at Kos.

"You mean are they anything *more than* plain old animals? Nope: just two good furry fellows. This guy lives a few doors down but spends a lot of time with us. He and D Train are best buddies. I've grown very fond of dogs since I've been here; they're wonderful friends."

Crebold made a sour face and sloppily slurped his wine.

Kaspar smiled, remembering the other's great dislike of all animals. "You never asked why they let me keep my memory, Crebold."

The tired man put his glass down on a step and wiped a corner of his mouth with the back of a hand. "I wasn't there when they made the decision. I assumed you wouldn't *tell* me. We were never good friends or anything."

Kaspar wiggled his eyebrows a few times. "That's true. But I'm going to tell you now because you need to know: They let me keep my memory because of *this* moment, old comrade; because of this very meeting we're having right here on my porch. They knew it would happen sometime or other."

Just north of drunk now, Crebold put up a hand to stop Kaspar. "Wait a minute! Hold it! How did you recognize me before?" He gestured toward the sidewalk. "I just realized it—how could you possibly recognize me when I first walked up the path a few minutes ago, Kaspar? You knew me in an instant but you're a *civilian* now."

It was true—to the world Crebold looked like any Bob you'd pass on the street and forget a moment later. He had absolutely no distinguishing features, including the clothes he wore, which were all dreary shades of beige and gray.

Kaspar said, "It's one of the reasons why they let me keep my memory— so I'd recognize any working mechanics who appeared in my retirement life.

"You're wrong about what they want from us, Crebold, completely wrong.

"We're seeds. When mechanics are retired they're planted like seeds across the universe into different civilizations." Kaspar slowly moved an arm in a 180-degree arc in front of his body as if to indicate how widespread the practice went. "These seeds grow like plants—hybrid plants— that combine a mechanic's knowledge and experience with whatever culture they've been planted in.

"These singular plants bear whole new species of fruit. Periodically it's harvested, but never the whole plant. That would be like pulling up all the trees in an orchard only to get the apples. They *want* us hybrids to keep growing, developing, and bearing new fruit."

Crebold's eyes were burning from fatigue. Wiping his mouth again, he tried to grasp all this and add it to everything else he'd recently learned, but the alcohol he'd had to drink fogged his brain. "You lost me between the seeds and the apple orchard. Talk about *us*; just tell me about right now." Making a fist he brought it down hard for emphasis on the porch banister.

Kaspar nodded. "Okay, I'll talk about Earth. When retirees come here and mix with human society, new hybrids that have never existed before are created. Just like cross-pollinating plants. It's not even necessary for us to physically mate with humans—we only need to live among them. After a while together a kind of organic synapse takes place. This same kind of synapse happens wherever retired mechanics are mixed with sentient beings anywhere in the universe.

"When the fruit from these hybrids is ripe, it's gathered from everywhere and distilled into the food that's needed to feed the ones who battle Chaos."

Crebold choked out, "We're *fruit?*" He looked at Kaspar in disbelief.

"*Part* of what we are is, yes; part of what we create while living here is, yes."

Crebold's mouth was dry and his tongue felt heavy as lead. "How do you know these things, Kaspar?"

"Before I was retired they told me to be on the lookout here for working mechanics. Whenever they appeared in my life I would be able to recognize them even though I was human. And I did, Crebold—it happened once before last summer and when I saw you just now.

"Their instructions were, whenever it happened the first thing I was to do was shake hands with any mechanic I recognized because eventually one would have that fruit with them. When it was given to me everything I needed to know would be made clear. And it has; what you gave me just now explained everything." Kaspar smiled and nodded reassuringly.

"It *did?*" Staring at the ground now because he felt he could concentrate better by looking at nothing, Crebold shook his head. "What did I give you? How could I—I don't know *shit!*"

Kaspar said, "That's true—*you* don't, but you held the lives and knowledge of others inside you and many of them know a lot, believe me—*a lot.*"

Crebold was flummoxed. "Well, what about the crazy dream you shared with your friends? I thought it caused all this trouble in the first place. They told me that's why they were sending me here. Did they lie? What was *that* all about?" Crebold remembered *this* Kaspar hadn't had the dream yet; it would happen to him several months from tonight. "Wait— were they inside me too just now—your three friends? Do you know?"

"Yes, they were." Kaspar spoke with the confident air of a man who knows the answers. "When the dream happens in the future it will be part of what's called *the joining.* Before the fruit is harvested anywhere, there's a joining together of all retirees' minds for a short time so their information can be gathered in one . . . *place,* like putting all the apples from a harvest in one basket.

"But that joining has to take place gradually and with the greatest care because every retiree is different—some understand what's happening immediately while others fight it. A shared dream is one way of bringing a bunch of minds up to a basically equal level."

Crebold didn't want to ask the next question because he was afraid of the answer, but knew he must. "What will happen to us after this *fruit* is harvested?"

Kaspar drank some wine and softly said, "Nothing. What happens to a tree after its apples have been picked? Nothing—when spring comes it starts growing more apples. Every retiree will return to their second existence without a single memory of what's happened and their days will putter along as normally as they have in the past.

"Nothing is taken from us anyway—they just make a copy of it. Eventually we'll die as mortals after having had, with any luck, very happy retirements."

"What do you mean nothing happens to us?" Crebold was so thrown by Kaspar's answer that he literally lost his balance for a moment and had to grab hold of something to steady himself. Luckily the porch banister was near. Seconds before Kaspar had spoken, Crebold had a horrible vision of being thrown into a cannibal's big pot and boiled alive to extract his "fruit."

Kaspar scratched Kos's head. "How do you feel now, right this minute?"

Crebold did *not* like the sound of the question; it reeked of *uh-oh*. "I feel fine, why?" He swallowed hard—was the other man going to pounce or set the dogs on him?

"Because it's already happened." Kaspar clapped his hands together twice, the sound very loud in the otherwise silent night. He joined them together as if in prayer and held them out toward Crebold. "Everything is inside *me* now; I took it from you when we shook hands before. Do you feel any different?"

"N-n-no."

"See? Your job is done; you can go and enjoy your retirement now. The minute you leave here tonight, both of us will forget this meeting and we'll just be plain old human beings living out the rest of our lives in peace." Kaspar looked for a reaction on the other's face. "You don't believe me, do you, Crebold?"

"No."

"Take my hands and I'll show you. Come on—nothing bad will happen, I promise."

Crebold looked as deep as he could into Kaspar Benn's eyes for a lie or a trick but saw none. In a whispery voice he said, "What the hell," and took them.

The contact lasted three seconds and then it was Kaspar who pulled his hands away.

Crebold's heart took forever to slow and beat normally again, even longer for his eyes to become focused. For a few sublime seconds both men grew almost exactly the same secret smile when looking at each other, silently sharing the awe and wonder of what was now contained within Kaspar.

"*Son of a bitch!*"

"You said it pal, son of a bitch."

Crebold patted his chest over his heart as if it were a child, trying to calm its irregular beat. "But what are *you* going to do with it? What do you *do* with all that stuff inside you?"

Kaspar shrugged. "Nothing. I live my happy life here until I die. *Then* they'll take it from me. Luckily I won't know that because after you leave here tonight, I go back to being jolly old Kaspar Benn, pants salesman without a single memory of this or anything else to do with mechanics or Chaos or the cosmos . . . I'll be wiped completely clean. So will you and all the others.

"It's great because I like this life very much; no, I *love* it. And you know what? That's more than enough for me; I am a happy man. I hope you find something to love too in this life, Crebold."

D Train returned from his walkabout in the yard and stopped next to the visitor. Looking up at the stranger, D asked with gentle golden eyes for a little love.

Cautiously Crebold reached down and touched the dog's thick warm neck. D Train immediately raised his head up into the hand. Crebold patted it gently with a flat stiff palm. "Kaspar, can I stay here for a little while?

Just drink some more wine with you for a few more minutes before I have to go?"

"Absolutely." Kaspar went into the house to get another bottle. Crebold kept petting the dog, his hand relaxing the more he did it. D Train leaned with full trust against the man's leg. The two of them waited together in the beautiful fall night for Kaspar to return.